W9-BUP-021

**Praise for William C. Dietz's
LEGION OF THE DAMNED and
THE FINAL BATTLE**

"A tough, moving novel of future warfare."
—David Drake

"Rockets and rayguns galore . . . and more than
enough action to satisfy those who like it hot and
heavy." —*The Oregonian*

"Exciting and suspenseful . . . real punch."
—*Publishers Weekly*

Praise for Dietz's SAM MCCADE series

"Slam-bang action." —David Drake

"Adventure and mystery in a future space empire."
—F. M. Busby

"All-out space action." —*Starlog*

"Good, solid, space opera, well told."
—*Science Fiction Chronicle*

DRIFTER'S WAR

WILLIAM C. DIETZ

ACE BOOKS, NEW YORK

This book is an Ace original edition,
and has never been previously published.

DRIFTER'S WAR

An Ace book / published by arrangement with
the author

PRINTING HISTORY
Ace edition / November 1992

ISBN: 0-441-16815-9

Ace Books are published by The Berkley Publishing Group,
a division of Penguin Putnam Inc.,
375 Hudson Street, New York, New York 10014.
The name "ACE" and the "A" logo
are trademarks belonging to Penguin Putnam Inc.

PRINTED IN THE UNITED STATES OF AMERICA

10 9 8 7 6 5 4 3

This book is for my
beloved wife, Marjorie.

1

Pik Lando lay spread-eagled on the beach. The sun was a warm red presence just beyond his eyelids. A gentle breeze cooled his skin. The surf swished in the background. Something splashed and Melissa laughed.

Lando smiled. This was a rare treat for a little girl who'd spent most of her eleven years in spaceships. And for him too. He felt safe for the first time in months. Safe from asteroids, safe from pirates, and safe from the bounty hunters who wanted his head.

The Rothmonian Lodge was not only isolated, located as it was in a rather remote area of Pylax, but was famous for protecting the privacy of its guests.

First came the individual villas, widely spaced, each equipped with a state-of-the-art security system. Then there were the security guards, the network of automatic weapons emplacements, and the squad of heavily armed robo-sentries. They stalked the island like huge insects, their podlike feet leaving circular depressions in the white sand, ready to destroy anything that came close. Yes, the Rothmonian was expensive, but worth it. Or so Lando had assumed.

"Hey, Pik! Look!" Melissa's voice was full of girlish enthusiasm.

Lando heard a splashing noise and debated whether to look or simply wave. He'd seen innumerable pieces of flotsam during the last hour or so, including countless seashells, one small cut, curious bits of vegetation, and a sandal that someone had left on the beach.

To sit up and look at Melissa's latest discovery would disturb the perfection of the moment but to do otherwise might ruin her fun.

"Pik!"

Lando heard the whine of hydraulics. A man yelled something incoherent and a little girl started to cry.

Lando sat up and opened his eyes. The metal thing had no meaning at first, rising from the surf to spear his eyes with reflected light, water cascading off its metallic skin. Pieces of seaweed hung here and there like rags from a beggar.

Lando scrambled to his feet. His hand stabbed for a gun that wasn't there. The smuggler was naked except for a pair of blue swim trunks. "Melissa! Run! Run for the villa!"

The smuggler saw the flash of gangly legs off to the right and knew that she would obey. Children who grow up on spaceships learn to follow orders.

The machine was huge. It stood thirty feet high, was about sixty feet long, and looked like a high-tech water beetle. It had four articulated legs. The surf foamed white where it raced around them.

The machine stopped. Its head moved slightly. A hatch whirred open. Lando backed away, waiting for the gun muzzle to emerge, waiting to die.

Memories flickered through Lando's mind. He saw the customs official shoot his father in the back, then fall, as he pulled a trigger of his own. He remembered how it felt to drop through the hatch and hit the sand twelve feet below. He heard the explosion as his father's ship blew up. He ran knowing that the bounty hunters would follow, eventually seeking refuge on a deep-space tug, and finding the alien drifter. An artifact so old, so valuable, that it would end all of his problems. Should have, but hadn't.

Lando flinched as a box-shaped thing exited the hatch and flew straight at him. A robo-cam! Not a weapon but potentially just as bad. He wanted to run but knew it was hopeless. A second camera followed the first and they swooped around his head like mechanical birds. A voice came from both devices at once. It was unnaturally loud.

"And there he is! Just as News-Pylax promised! The notorious killer Pik Lando!"

Lando opened his mouth, and was just about to tell News-Pylax where to shove it, when another voice boomed across the beach. "Hold it right there!"

Lando turned. The other guests had fled. Abandoned towels,

toys, and lounge chairs lay everywhere. The robo-sentry had a long mincing gate. A plastic pail disappeared under one of its pods. It crossed the beach in three steps. Weapons turrets whined as they aligned themselves with the intruder.

"This is private property. You are trespassing. This is private property. You are trespassing. Leave or be fired on. Leave or be fired on."

The beetle-machine backed into the surf. Waves broke against its hind legs. The robo-cams hovered to either side of its bulbous head. The voice was incredulous.

"Hard to believe, isn't it, folks? But you saw it with your own eyes. An interstellar criminal living off his ill-gotten gains at one of our finest resorts! Fantastic you say? Well, wait. There's more. Confidential sources tell us that Pik Lando and his accomplices have located a drifter, and not just any drifter, but an *alien* drifter so old that it predates human civilization. Such a vessel would be worth millions of credits!

"So stay tuned. Bounty hunters are on the way, and when they arrive, we'll be there! This is Lux Luther, for News-Pylax."

The news-machine paused, swallowed both of its robo-cams in a single gulp, and backed into deeper water. A wave hit, exploded in a welter of white spray, and fell like droplets of rain. The surf swirled and the machine was gone.

The robo-sentry looked this way and that, assured itself that the intruders had left, and retraced its steps into the foliage that lined the beach. There was still no sign of the other guests.

Lando shook his head, swore softly, and headed for the villa. Bounty hunters were on the way and Melissa would be scared. They would have to leave and leave fast. He walked a little faster. The sand was warm and gave under his feet.

Damn! How had they found him anyway? With Cy aboard the drifter, and Della somewhere in Brisco City, that left Cap . . . Cap! Of course. In spite of his promises to the contrary, and weeks of sobriety, Cap was drunk. Rip-roaring, gut-spilling drunk. Sitting in some bar, bragging about the drifter, and destroying himself all over again.

The first time had come years before when a billion-to-one accident had dumped his liner into the middle of an asteroid belt. The same belt where Lando, Cap, Melissa, Della Dee, and Cy Borg had stumbled across the alien drifter a few weeks earlier.

The liner, a huge vessel named the *Star of Empire*, had crashed into a roid and broken up. Most of the passengers and crew were killed.

Though the accident itself wasn't Cap's fault, he was drunk at the time of the incident, and many felt that he was responsible for the subsequent loss of life. An unconscious captain isn't worth much in the middle of an emergency.

And history had repeated itself. Or so it seemed.

Lando ran up the steps. A maintenance bot scuttled out of his way. Lando's feet slapped against stone slabs as his mind raced ahead.

How close were the bounty hunters? How long until they arrived? How many were there? These questions and more jostled for position and got in each other's way.

The villa was a low rambling affair. It was nearly invisible behind green foliage and a whitewashed wall.

Melissa met him at the gate. She had shoulder-length brown-blond hair, an upturned nose, and a rounded face. Her eyes were big and filled with concern. "Is it true? Are bounty hunters on the way?"

Melissa had been through a lot. Her mother had died in a salvage accident, her father was an alcoholic, and her childhood was a sometimes thing. Melissa handled Cap's affairs whenever he was too drunk to do it himself, and that, plus the pressures of the last few months, had been hard on the little girl. Lando forced a smile.

"I'm afraid so. Throw your things in a bag. It's time to leave."

Melissa nodded, stood on tiptoes to kiss his cheek, and ran toward her bedroom.

Lando followed her down the hall, entered his room, and slipped out of his trunks. There was a comset located next to his bed. It started to chirp.

There were various possibilities. Bounty hunters checking to see if he was there? Reporters looking for an interview? Hotel management asking him to leave? The last seemed most likely. The comset continued to chirp and Lando ignored it.

It took the smuggler four minutes to pull on a pair of white slacks and a loose-fitting, long-sleeved pullover. The mini-launcher went up his right sleeve but the slug gun was something of a problem. The Rothmonian had rules about side arms. Lando decided to stick the weapon down the back of his pants and pull his shirt over it. A pair of slip-on shoes completed the outfit.

After that it was a simple matter to throw the rest of his clothes into a small duffel bag, yell for Melissa, and make his way toward the back door. There were comsets all over the villa. They trilled, chirped, and buzzed like so many exotic birds.

Melissa arrived. Her satchel was full of something but who knew what. Seashells probably. Chances were that her clothes lay scattered all over the villa. Still, there was precious little time for a round up, so whatever was lost would have to stay that way.

Lando nodded approvingly and motioned for Melissa to wait. The villa had three security stations, one of which was located next to the back door. The smuggler scanned the monitors, saw nothing more threatening than a two-headed fruit snake that was sunning itself on top of the garden wall, and eased the door open.

He looked right and left. Everything appeared to be normal. Birds sang, insects buzzed, and laughter could be heard from the nearest villa. The air felt warm and thick. In an hour, two at the most, it would start to rain.

Lando gestured for Melissa to follow. She obeyed, her eyes big and trusting, her hand seeking his.

The smuggler smiled reassuringly and wondered if this was the right thing to do. What if the bounty hunters found him? Melissa could get hurt or, worse than that, killed. But he couldn't bring himself to leave her, not without some assurance that she'd be okay, so he'd play it by ear instead. Keep her with him as long as possible and surrender if it became necessary. Better that than to risk her life in a gun battle.

"Come on." Lando led Melissa through the gate and out onto one of the many footpaths that crisscrossed the island. There was undergrowth to either side, and beyond that, the white-washed duracrete walls that backed each villa. By sticking to the trails and avoiding the main road, the smuggler could avoid notice. Or so he hoped.

He set a fast pace. Melissa walked double time to keep up. "Where are we going?"

"Well," Lando responded thoughtfully, "we need some transportation. I'd like to hire a ground car or, even better, an air car. Failing that, we'll steal one."

"I thought stealing was wrong."

"Well, it is, most of the time, but this is different."

"What makes it different?"

"Look, let's talk about stealing some other time. Right now we need to get off this island without getting caught. If we see anybody just smile and act natural."

Melissa was silent for a moment. "Okay . . . but how can I look natural sneaking down a footpath with a suitcase in my hand?"

Lando came to a sudden stop, looked at her satchel, and then at his own. Melissa was right. The people who stayed at the Rothmonian Lodge *never* carried their own luggage. Not with an army of robots to do it for them.

"Good point. We'll ditch the bags."

"Wait a second." Melissa put her satchel down and burrowed into the contents.

Lando bit his lip in frustration. He looked up and down the path. "Melissa . . . we don't have time for this. We'll buy more stuff later on."

"There's only one Ralph," Melissa said stubbornly, "and he's coming with me."

Lando sighed. Ralph was the stuffed Pyla Bear that he'd given Melissa for her birthday. He was just about to object when Melissa found Ralph, tucked him under her right arm, and smiled victoriously. Melissa one, Lando zero.

The smuggler fished around inside his bag, found two magazines for the slug thrower and a backup clip for the missile launcher. They went in his pockets. He tossed the bags into the bushes.

"Pik! Look!"

Lando turned, saw three robo-sentries converge on the villa, and knew that management had decided to kick him out. The machines were for show. The security types would be along any second now.

"Come on, honey . . . it's time to leave."

They made good time up the path, encountering little more than a robo-sweeper and a tired-looking jogger.

They arrived at the lodge a few minutes later. It was a large sprawling affair, all logs and pseudo-thatch, and much more substantial than it looked. There was a lot of carefully tended lawn, some artfully placed fish ponds, and paths covered with white gravel.

There were plenty of people about, guests mostly, with a scattering of staff. None looked like bounty hunters, but it pays to be careful, so Lando stayed out of sight. He pulled on Melissa's hand.

"Let's circle around to the causeway. That's where the vehicles are."

In an attempt to preserve the property's unspoiled beauty, both guest and commercial vehicles alike had been banned from the island, and restricted to a mainland parking lot. A single causeway linked the two.

They followed the pathway around the perimeter of the lodge to the point where it joined a much wider walkway out onto the wooden bridge.

As was usual for that time of day there were a number of guests leaving the lodge, heavily laden robo-carts trundling along behind them, their vacations complete. An equal number of people had just arrived. Lando gave thanks for the crowd.

Many of them smiled at the cute little girl, nodded at the man they assumed was her father, and continued on their way.

Lando gave a sigh of relief. The Pik Lando story hadn't received much play yet.

The causeway was slightly arched in the middle and Lando used the additional height to look at the other side. What he saw didn't look good and must have shown on his face.

"What is it? What's wrong?"

Lando produced what he hoped was a smile. "We've got company. The bad kind. Enjoy the view while I take another look around."

The smuggler looked again. His second glance confirmed the first. A group of men and women were gathered at the far end of the bridge. A lively discussion was under way. There was plenty of arm waving, foot stomping, and faintly heard invective.

Half the people wore Rothmonian uniforms, while the rest were dressed in a wild assortment of armor, leather, and weaponry. Bounty hunters. Trying to gain entry but running afoul of the resort's security forces.

Bounty hunters were a strange breed, part cop and part parasite; they clung to the empire like remoras to a shark, eating scraps too small for their host to bother with.

Rather than pay for an interstellar police force, and tax his citizens accordingly, the first Emperor had decided to rely on bounty hunters instead.

It was an easy business to get into. All the perspective bounty hunter needed was a gun, a certain amount of luck, and access to a public terminal. The list was miles long. Names, crimes, histories, weapons, known associates, all of it was all there.

It was a simple matter to scroll through the names, choose a fugitive, buy a license, and go after them. Simple, and more often than not extremely dangerous. Which accounted for the fact that very few bounty hunters lived long enough to retire.

Lando swore silently and turned in the other direction. Something hard and heavy rode the pit of his stomach. Why so many? The bounty on his head was relatively small compared to many others.

Lando knew the answer, or thought he did. The bounty hunters were after him all right, but they were after something else as well, the drifter itself. The artifact was worth millions of credits, and he knew where it was.

And that implied something more: Wherever Cap was, and whatever he'd said, the location of the ship was still a secret.

Melissa looked up at Lando. "Where are we going now?"

"The boat dock," Lando replied, sounding a lot more confident than he felt.

"Does that mean we're going to steal a boat?"

"Only if we aren't able to charter or rent one."

"Oh."

It took them about five minutes to reach the marina. It sat huddled within the embrace of a man-made breakwater. The water was aqua-blue, crystal-clear, and extremely calm. Jet skis zipped this way and that, poorly piloted sailing dinghies drifted aimlessly along the breakwater, and an airboat made its way out through the harbor's entrance.

When it was clear of the harbor the boat fired its repellors, vanished inside a cloud of steam, and reappeared moments later. Drives howled as it blasted upward.

There were two docks, one for the boating crowd who owned their own yachts, and one for the guests who wished to rent. A section of pseudo-thatched roof sat on some posts about halfway out. There was a sign that said "Rentals," and an attendant sitting on a stool.

Lando's heart sank. The rental dock was nearly empty. It was late afternoon, and most of the hovercraft, sea sleds, and water walkers were already in use.

But there, way out toward the end of the dock, sat a sleek-looking craft that mounted an aerodynamically shaped mast and what looked like an aircraft wing. A skimmer. Not his first choice, but better than nothing at all.

"Come on."

Lando sauntered out onto the dock and Melissa followed along behind. She looked over the edge, watched her reflection in the water, and waved to see herself wave back.

The rental shack didn't have any walls, but the roof provided some protection from the sun, and the attendant had centered himself in the middle of the shade.

What hair he had was white and cut so short that it fuzzed the sides of his head. He wore a grease-stained yachting hat, a sweatshirt with the sleeves cut off, and a perpetual frown. When Lando smiled the frown became even more pronounced.

"Yeah?"

"I'm interested in renting a boat."

"Don't have any. Come back tomorrow."

Lando raised an eyebrow and nodded toward the end of the dock. "What about that one?"

"It ain't for rent. Belongs to the manager, Mr. Izzo. Come back tomorrow."

Lando started to say something in reply but felt Melissa tug on his sleeve. She pulled him away. He frowned. "What?"

Melissa pulled him down so she could whisper in his ear. "Are we going to steal it?"

Lando glanced at the attendant. He pretended they weren't there.

"Yeah, I think so."

Melissa nodded in agreement. "Right. I'll distract him while you take the boat."

Lando thought about it. There was a comset about four inches away from the attendant's right elbow. A call would bring security on the run. Some sort of diversion would be a good idea.

"Okay, but come when I yell."

Melissa smiled mischievously. "Don't worry about me."

This was the adult Melissa. The same one who could run her father's business affairs, and, if push came to shove, fly a shuttle to boot.

Lando nodded, smiled at the old man, and strolled out toward the end of the dock.

The skimmer looked strange. It had a long pencil-thin hull. The winglike structure crossed the top of the mast like a giant T, slanted down to touch the water off the boat's port side, and bobbed up and down with the waves.

The canopy-covered cockpit was located just forward of the mast and looked large enough to accommodate four people.

As the smuggler came closer he saw that foils had been mounted on each end of the wing, one of which rested in the water, while the other hung suspended in the air. The leading edge of the wing had slats while the trailing edge was equipped with flaps.

The wing design gave Lando a pretty good idea of how the skimmer worked. The wing acted as a sail, providing a surface for the wind to push against, but adding something more as well. Air would pass over the down-slanting wing to create forward suction and provide lift at the same time. The result was a wind-powered craft that could achieve speeds of sixty or seventy miles an hour.

Though not a fan, Lando had seen skimmer races on the vid nets, and knew the ships could really move. Just the thing for an ocean-going getaway. *If* they could get the skimmer out to sea. *If* they could lose the pursuit. And *if* he could keep the damned thing under control.

Those were a lot of ifs but the smuggler had very little choice. He started to step aboard, thought better of it, and turned toward Melissa.

She made a sound designed to attract the old man's attention, teetered on the edge of the dock, and fell into the water with a big splash.

Lando was concerned at first. Melissa's swimming skills were little more than so-so and she was screaming her head off.

Then Lando noticed that Ralph was propped up against a post, dry as could be, and well out of harm's way. Melissa knew exactly what she was doing.

The attendant moved with surprising speed. Within seconds he had a long boat hook and had extended it toward Melissa.

Lando stepped aboard, touched a button, and smiled as the canopy whirred open. He stepped down into an oval-shaped observation-control area. The control position was toward the rear. It had airplane-type controls with a stick instead of a wheel.

Lando dropped into the captain's chair and watched the U-shaped screen light up. There were no security codes or anything. After all, why bother with an attendant looking on?

Words appeared. "Welcome aboard the *Nadia*. Keyboard or voice?"

Lando thought about that one. He had a general preference for keyboards, but that was aboard spaceships, where he knew what he was doing. In this case voice would be faster and therefore safer.

He said it aloud. "Voice please."

"Aye, aye, sir," a salty-sounding voice replied. "And where are we bound?"

Lando thought for a moment. He knew very little about the planet's geography, but remembered that a seaport called Norton was relatively close to Brisco City. And Brisco City was where they had left Cap and Della Dee.

"Our destination is Norton."

"And Norton it is, sir," the computer replied cheerfully. "The course is loaded and ready ta go. Begging your pardon, sir, and not wishing ta speak out of turn, but should we load more supplies? Our supply of wine is running low, especially the Cathcart '75, and we're almost out of goose liver pâté."

Lando smiled. Mr. Izzo had expensive tastes. "No, that won't be necessary. We have enough food and water for two?"

"Yes, sir."

"Excellent. I will bring my companion aboard and cast off."

"Aye, aye, sir. Auxiliary power, sir?"

Lando imagined trying to maneuver the skimmer out on wind power alone. Talk about disasters. "Yes, please."

Lando stepped up and out of the cockpit. The sun had disappeared. Some raindrops hit his face. They felt warm.

Melissa was still thrashing around in the water. The attendant yelled for her to grab his boat hook. She ignored him. Lando waved his arms.

Melissa saw him, waved in response, and grabbed the boat hook with both hands. She gave it a vigorous jerk. The attendant tumbled in headfirst. There was a tremendous splash.

Lando watched to make sure that the man could swim, saw Melissa pull herself up and out of the water, and laughed as she retrieved Ralph from his resting place.

The rain had just started to make dark circles on the sun-bleached wood as Melissa scampered down the dock. Her eyes danced with excitement as she ran toward the skimmer. She jumped and Lando caught her.

"How did I do?"

Lando had to shout against the rush of the rain. It splattered around him and drummed against the skimmer's composite hull. "You were great! Now get below and find a towel!"

Lando cast off the bowline first, gave the dock a healthy shove with his foot, and ran toward the stern. The stern line splashed as it hit the water.

Then the smuggler realized that it was supposed to work the other way around, that the lines should stay aboard the skimmer, but by then it was too late. The gap between the dock and the boat had widened and the on-board computer had activated the auxiliary power unit. The wake foamed white as the *Nadia* headed away from the dock.

The rain fell even harder now, drenching Lando to the skin and churning the surface of the bay. The attendant was out of water now, comset in hand, pointing toward Lando and talking in an animated fashion.

The rain fell in sheets. The robo-sentries were skeletal figures only dimly seen. They stalked down across manicured lawns, ignored the dock, and headed out along the top of the breakwater.

Lando looked out toward the ocean. The entranceway was half a mile ahead. If the robo-sentries got there first they could grab the skimmer or, failing that, blow it out of the water. He dropped into the cockpit.

"I want full speed ahead."

"Aye, aye, sir, " the computer replied. "Full speed it is."

The skimmer surged forward. Lando bit the inside of his cheek. The race was on, and the outcome would be extremely close.

2

Della Dee pushed the door open and stepped inside. A neon nude ran the length of the opposite wall. Pink nipples flashed on and off. They stopped as the door closed. Smoke hung in slowly drifting layers. One of Terra's most popular vocalists moaned seductively in the background, her voice distorted by the bar's cheap sound system.

Dee's boots made a clacking sound as she approached the bar, selected a stool, and sat down. It was early yet, and while half the tables were occupied, Dee had the bar to herself. Every man in the room turned to stare.

Dee had bright green eyes, flawless skin, and a nice figure. She wore a white blouse under flat black body armor, skintight pants, and knee-high boots. The slug gun rode high and tight in a cross-draw holster. But it was the flaming red hair that drew their attention. It was and always had been both a blessing and a curse, attracting men like moths to a flame.

Dee looked too straight to be a whore, too hard to be a citizen on the prowl, and too good to be unattached. Long red fingernails made a clicking sound as they hit the bar.

The bartender looked, liked what he saw, and nodded. He had a bullet-shaped head, a wrestler's torso, and massive arms. He grabbed an aluminum cask, heaved it off the floor, and dropped it into a cradle. It hit with a distinct thud. The bartender smiled as he turned around.

"What'll it be, honey?"

Dee ignored the bartender's leer. "A beer plus some information."

The bartender frowned. His eyebrows came together into a

14

straight line. He ran a rag over the spot in front of him. "What kind of information?"

Dee smiled reassuringly. "Nothing complicated. Take a look at this."

For the sixteenth time that day Dee slipped the holo cube out of her pocket and placed it on the bar. The bartender lifted the device up to eye level and gave it a squeeze. A man appeared. He had bushy eyebrows, a long straight nose, and a tight thin-lipped mouth. His eyes were bright blue and stared out from cavernous sockets. An alkie or a wire-head. The bartender saw them every day.

"So you're a bounty hunter. What'd he do? Walk away from his bar tab?"

Dee shook her head. "Nothing like that. He's a friend of mine. Have you seen him?"

A calculating grin stole over the bartender's face. "And what if I have? What would you give me?"

Dee shrugged. "Ten credits and a sincere 'thank you.' "

The bartender leaned forward, closing the distance between them to a foot or so. "How 'bout something a little more personal? Something you'd enjoy as much as I would?"

Dee sighed. She forced herself to be patient. "I've got a headache. The offer stands. Have you seen this man or not?"

The bartender shrugged. He nodded toward the far side of the lounge. "He's over there. In the side room. Playing it big with some drunks."

Dee felt her spirits leap. Finally! She slapped some currency on the bar. "Thanks."

"What about your beer?"

A roid miner had passed out at the nearest table. Dee gestured in her direction. "Give it to her when she wakes up."

The bartender nodded and turned away.

Dee felt eyes follow her as she walked across the room. The sensation was nothing new. Some were curious, some wanted her body, and some were afraid.

They were like rabbits crouched in their burrows as the fox strolled by. They saw past the cloud of bright red hair, past the pretty face, all the way to the slug gun with reactive grips. They saw the way she moved, the way her eyes slid over their faces, and knew exactly what she was. A huntress, a self-employed killer, a bounty hunter.

They had nothing to fear however since Dee's attention was focused on other things. She had been sitting face-to-face with the Imperial consul when Cap spilled his guts to the media.

The consul had been interested, *very* interested, especially in the drifter. And why not? The ship was loaded with advanced technology, stuff years ahead of anything the Il Ronn had, and worth millions of credits.

The consul had studied the holo pix, viewed the vid tapes, and was just about to say something when an aide had slipped into the room. Words were whispered and a wall-sized vid screen appeared.

The consul was a small man, very dapper, and carefully manicured. He smiled. "Bear with us for a moment, Citizen Dee. It seems that channel twenty-three has some news of interest to us both."

So Dee had been forced to sit there, squirming in her seat, as Cap spilled everything he knew to a man with a carefully arranged smile. Everything but the actual location of the drifter. Somehow, some way, Cap had retained enough brains to keep mum about that.

But the damage was considerable. The consul was no fool. Why pay for something you can get for free? All he had to do was send some people after Cap, sweat him a bit, and wait for the information to pop out. And failing that he could reopen negotiations with Dee.

So Dee had left the consulate with two humans and a robot on her tail. It had taken a full hour to ditch all three of them, and by the time she called channel twenty-three, Cap had slipped away. She got the impression that they were looking for him too.

And then, about two bars back—or was it three?—Dee had seen the special report. She'd been back in a corner, talking to a four-armed cyborg, when the feed came on-screen. A weird-looking camera shot that lurched up out of the sea, swept back and forth, and focused on Pik Lando. Dee saw Lando get to his feet, saw Melissa run, and knew that a bad situation had just turned worse.

Dee felt a troubling emptiness in the pit of her stomach. She'd gone after Pik herself a few months before, and had caught him too, but lost him in an ambush. She'd been wounded, and had nearly died, but Pik had pulled her through. Pik,

Melissa, the strange little cyborg who called himself "Cy Borg," and, yes, Cap. Without trying, without meaning to, she'd become part of a family.

So she cared about them and that made her stomach feel empty. That's the problem with loving people. It makes you vulnerable. Life or death can take them away.

Dee thought about Pik, thought about losing him, and knew it would hurt. If ever there had been a chance for a relationship it was with him. With a man who, in spite of his profession, was basically honest. With a man who fought for lost causes, took little girls under his wing, and was willing to risk his life for a bounty hunter he didn't even know.

She forced the thought away. Never mind Pik. If there was a way to reach Brisco City, he'd find it. Her job was to find Cap, put him under wraps, and be ready to lift when Pik arrived.

The door sensed her presence and slid open. The room was small and thick with smoke. Light came from a single source in the ceiling. It bathed Cap in a hard white glare. He lay on the tabletop with his pockets turned inside out. His hair was in disarray, and he had a two-day growth of beard, but she could still see signs of the man he'd once been. The high forehead, the firm jaw, and the thin-lipped mouth had been handsome once. Just right for a promising young officer.

Dee thought Cap was dead at first, but then she saw his chest move and found a pulse. He smelled of sour alcohol.

Dee shook her head sadly, grabbed one of Cap's arms, and pulled him into a fireman's carry. She was strong, and like many alcoholics, Sorenson was light. The door opened at her approach.

"Come on, Cap. Let's go home."

3

The Rothmonian security center was a quiet, almost cloister-ed place. There was the gentle hum of air-conditioning, the muted mumble of radio traffic, and the occasional sound of a buzzer. Row after row of vid monitors blinked through a preprogrammed sequence of security cams, some of which hopped, crawled, or flew through air, while others remained stationary and captured whatever happened to take place in front of them. Some of these were mounted in locations that guests would object to but didn't know about.

Technicians moved here and there, attending the machines like priests at the altar, speaking to each other in tones of hushed solemnity.

Nathan Izzo slammed the door open, dropped his portacomp onto a countertop, and looked for someone to abuse. Five or six technicians were present. All did their best to disappear. "Rister! Get your butt out here!"

"My butt *is* out here." The voice came from right next to Izzo and made him jump. Carolyn Rister, chief of security, saw her superior's expression and smiled. "Welcome to the security center."

Izzo scowled. His hair was black. He wore it short and flat on top. That, plus the hard, determined eyes and the formally cut business suit, gave him a military air. Just right for the man everybody called "The General."

"Don't give me any of that 'welcome to the security center' crap, Rister. Save it for the headquarters types. What the hell's going on? Your people are too damned visible. Some of the guests are getting nervous."

Rister was a long, lean woman who moved with a sort of

sinewy grace. She had been places and done things that Izzo couldn't even imagine. The executive didn't scare her a bit.

"Well, let me see . . . we've got a killer on the loose, we're trying to keep about twenty bounty hunters off prem, and someone's in the process of stealing your skimmer. Which one would you like to discuss first?"

Blood rushed to Izzo's face. "Stealing my skimmer?"

Rister nodded agreeably. "That's right. Take a look over there. You'll get a robo-sentry's eye view of your boat on its way out of the harbor."

Izzo looked. The picture jerked right and left as the robo-sentry stalked along the top of the breakwater. Rain fell in sheets, visibility had been reduced to a few hundred yards, and sure enough, there was the *Nadia* making for the open sea.

The executive grabbed the back of a chair. He owed more than a hundred thousand credits on the skimmer. None of them were insured.

"Stop them! Stop them right now!"

Rister nodded sympathetically. "Yes, sir. That's what we're trying to do. And if the robo-sentry beats them to the entrance, we might even succeed."

" 'Might'? You *might* succeed? The robo-sentry has an energy cannon. Burn them down!"

Rister lifted an eyebrow. "If you say so, sir . . . but what about your skimmer?"

Rister's words were like a bucket of ice water. Izzo felt stupid and tried to hide it.

"How could something like this happen?"

Rister shrugged noncommittally. "Bad luck, that's all. It turns out that the guy in villa fourteen is wanted for murder. Channel twenty-three learned he was here, told everyone on the planet, and the bounty hunters arrived shortly thereafter. The guest tried to run, couldn't use the causeway, and stole your boat. It's as simple as that."

Izzo looked from Rister to the monitors. "No it isn't," he said resentfully. "You should've neutralized him back on land."

"Not unless policy has changed," Rister said evenly. "Think about it. I watched the tapes of this guy putting on his clothes. He has a slug gun stuck down the back of his pants and a mini-launcher strapped to his right arm. We fire at him and he fires back. Presto, the lodge becomes a free-fire zone. Dead guests all over the place. Get my drift?"

Izzo knew when he was beat. He stared at the monitor. The rain made it hard to see. The robo-sentry was close but the *Nadia* seemed even closer. "Shit."

"Yeah," Rister agreed calmly. "That pretty well sums it up."

Lando was soaked to the skin. Rain drummed on the deck around him. Melissa was below changing her clothes. For reasons known only to Mr. Izzo the *Nadia* came equipped with a wide array of female apparel.

The robo-sentry was closer now, a towering presence only forty yards away, its podlike feet pulverizing smaller chunks of rock as they hit the top of the breakwater.

Lando felt the deck shift slightly as the boat's NAVCOMP made a slight correction to the skimmer's course. A breeze touched his right cheek. The entrance to the harbor lay directly ahead. It was narrow, no more than fifty feet across, and would be impossible to negotiate if the robo-sentry arrived first.

Lando took a quick look around. Most of the pleasure craft had already made it to the docks, but those that hadn't hurried to do so. He saw no possibility of escape, no alternative to the upcoming confrontation, so he turned toward the robo-sentry.

Lando's blood ran cold as the gangly monster reached the end of the breakwater, tried to step down into the water, and slipped. Servos whined as the machine caught itself and made another attempt. The robo-sentry's pods found firmer footing this time and it waded out into the water.

Lando wrapped his left arm around the skimmer's mast and pointed his right hand toward the robo-sentry's head. That's where the machine's sensors should be. Maybe he could disable them.

The mini-missiles had no guidance systems of their own so Lando took careful aim. The trick would be to lead the machine by just the right amount, compensate for the wind, and hit a relatively small target.

Lando flexed his muscles just so and a mini-missile left the launcher. It missed the robo-sentry's insectoid head by inches and headed out to sea.

Lando swore and waited to die. The burp of blue light never

came. The robo-sentry was knee deep in the water by now and reaching for the *Nadia*'s bow.

Why? Why were they still alive? What had the attendant said? Something about the manager's boat? So that was it! The security types were reluctant to destroy Mr. Izzo's toy.

Lando aimed his second and last missile. He fired. This missile ran straight and true, hit the robo-sentry right between its electronic eyes, and blew up. Hot shrapnel flew in every direction. Pieces pinged against the skimmer's wing and others hissed into the water.

Izzo slammed his fist onto a tabletop as the monitor went dead. He was furious. "Stop them! Never mind the skimmer! Just stop them!"

A technician looked at Rister. The robo-sentry's energy cannon had been destroyed but the rest of the machine was still functional. The security chief nodded her head.

The technician turned to his console. The robo-sentry might be blind but *he* wasn't. A security cam had been mounted on the north side of the breakwater. By turning it to the left the tech could see the robo-sentry's back and the skimmer beyond.

Now for the next step. The robo-sentry's primary voice-recognition sub-processor had been destroyed along with its head. There was a second-rate backup located in the machine's chest cavity. The technician spoke slowly so the processor would have time to understand.

Metal screeched as the *Nadia* scraped along the robo-sentry's right leg. Completely blind, the machine flailed right and left. A metal pincer hit the boat's wing with a loud bang. Lando held on as the boat rocked back and forth.

Water churned as the skimmer's auxiliary power unit pushed it forward. The robo-sentry dropped into a crouch and prepared to jump. The impact of its two-ton weight would crush the *Nadia* like an egg shell. Lando thought about Melissa, thought about telling her to dive overboard, but knew there wasn't enough time.

The robo-sentry made its headless leap. Lando watched in numb fascination as the machine fell, missed the skimmer by inches, and splashed chest down into the bay. Spray spattered the deck, the *Nadia* rocked back and forth, and the breakwater passed to either side. Bubbles boiled up from the point where the robo-sentry had disappeared.

A reader board was mounted on pilings off to the right. The words slid from left to right: "Thanks for staying at the Rothmonian Lodge. Please come again."

Lando looked around. He saw open water, white-capped waves, and low-scudding gray clouds. Perfect weather to hide in.

A wave broke across the bow, sluiced the length of the deck, and washed over Lando's feet. The cockpit had a high coaming around it but the rest of the deck was clear. The smuggler grimaced, and was just about to go below, when something surfaced off the starboard bow.

Lando's first thought was an animal of some sort, a Pylaxian version of Ithro's sea monsters perhaps, or a bioengineered whale. But whales don't have metal skins or make whining noises when their heads move.

The creature's head came up out of the water, its mouth opened, and a pair of robo-cams flew out. One came in close while the other hung back. The voice was the same one Lando had heard on the beach.

"Hello, Citizen Lando! That was a close call back there. What now?"

Lando pulled the slug gun, took careful aim, and put two slugs through the closest vid cam. It staggered, belched black smoke, and splashed into the water.

Lando smiled as the other camera scuttled into the submersible's open mouth and disappeared. The entire machine was gone a few seconds later. Lando wondered if it would attempt to follow him. Stupid question. Of course it would.

The smuggler took a quick look around, failed to detect any other signs of pursuit, and went below. A section of canopy hissed open to admit him. The air felt warm and dry. His shoes squished down the ladder.

Melissa looked small in oversize shorts and top. She threw her arms around Lando's neck. "It's a good thing you're okay . . . Della would go bonkers if I let anything happen to you."

Lando gave her a hug, marveled at the little girl's strange

logic, and grabbed a towel from the nearest seat. He used it to dry his hair.

"Welcome below, sir," the NAVCOMP said heartily. "We're receiving repeated messages ta heave to. How should I respond?"

It was tempting to make a snappy reply but that would provide the Rothmonian's security people with a radio fix. Lando spoke through the towel.

"No reply . . . in fact, the less electromechanical activity the better."

"Aye, aye, sir," the computer responded. "And that bein' the case, sir, should I shut down the auxiliary power and deploy the sail?"

Lando considered it. "How would that effect our speed?"

"Given the current weather conditions our speed would increase from twenty knots to more than forty."

Lando threw the towel toward a corner. "Excellent. Deploy the sail and cut auxiliary power."

"Aye, aye, sir. The sail it is."

The *Nadia* wallowed in a trough. Lando fought to keep his balance. "One more thing."

"Sir?" the NAVCOMP responded.

"Can you tell if we're being followed?"

"Would you be referrin' ta the submersible, sir?"

Lando smiled. "Yes, I would."

"They're followin' all right, sir. Would ya care ta lose them?"

"That would be nice, yes."

"Consider it done," the NAVCOMP said confidently.

It took the NAVCOMP about three minutes to position the skimmer's wing, to adjust the slots and flaps, and to turn onto an easterly course.

Lando felt more than a little useless as he sat down before the control console. A whole network of potentiometers provided him with information. The only problem was that he didn't know what to do with it. Thank Sol for the NAVCOMP.

The skimmer shuddered momentarily as the wing cut into the wind, heeled to starboard, and picked up speed. A few moments later the slight vibration caused by the auxiliary power unit disappeared and the *Nadia* started to fly.

The wind not only pushed against the wing but lifted at

the same time. Freed from all but minimal drag, the boat did exactly what its name suggested, and skimmed the surface of the water.

Rain spattered against the duraplast canopy and kept Lando from sliding it back, but nothing could separate him from the almost overwhelming sensation of speed. And not just any speed, but dangerous speed, as the NAVCOMP calculated and recalculated the wind speed, air temperature, wave action, and prevailing currents thousands of times a second, made minute adjustments, and pushed the boat to the limit of its performance.

Melissa was fascinated. Her forehead was pressed against the inside of the canopy. The lead-gray sky and sea seemed to fly past the skimmer. There was no noise of an engine, no sound of machinery at work, just the roar of the wind and the patter of rain. The only thing she felt was the bump, bump, bump of wave tops hitting the bottom of the hull.

Lando remembered the skimmer races that he'd seen and felt a new sense of respect. The racers had some help from an on-board NAVCOMP but were required to provide most of the control themselves. Lando couldn't imagine how they did it. The NAVCOMP interrupted his thoughts.

"We outran the submersible, sir."

"Excellent. Let me know if you detect pursuit of any kind."

"Aye, aye, sir."

Melissa clapped her hands. "We're free!"

Lando forced a smile. "Yes, we are. For the moment anyway."

4

Dee blinked in the bright sunlight. Cap started to slide off her shoulder. She heaved him back into place. If the denizens of Blast Town thought her burden strange they gave no sign of it.

Blast Town was the name the local residents had given to the run-down mishmash of bars, strip joints, and seedy hotels that bordered the south side of Brisco City's spaceport. The people who lived there saw stranger sights every night.

Like the time she had bailed Pik out of the local jail with every intention of turning him in. Her car had been ambushed by a psychopath named Jord Willer, she'd been wounded, and Lando had saved her life. It was strange the way things circled around to kick you right in the butt.

An ancient auto cab sat idling up the street. The words "For Hi e" slid over and around the vehicle's beat-up electro-finish. They wobbled through the dents and blipped over the scratches.

Dee waved and the cab jerked into motion. The brakes made a scraping sound as they brought the vehicle to a halt in front of her.

A door popped open and Dee dumped Sorenson inside. He slumped sideways and a leg slid over the edge of the seat. The bounty hunter grabbed the front of his ship-suit, jerked him into a sitting position, and turned him toward the front of the cab. Cap started to topple forward but Dee slid in to prop him up. The cab's interior smelled of smoke, vomit, and chemical disinfectant.

The cab jerked into motion. "Destination, please," the machine asked pleasantly.

Dee started to answer but the bleat of a siren caused her to turn and look out the back window. A boxy-looking combat car with the word "Police" stenciled across its bow was headed down the street. There were two, maybe three news vans right behind it, and a gaggle of robo-cams overhead. Vultures headed for the kill. Someone had identified Sorenson, her, or both. The heat was closing in. Dee turned toward the front of the cab.

"The spaceport and step on it."

"Right-o," the auto cab replied cheerfully. "Would you like the entire history of the spaceport? It's only two credits more."

"Shut up and drive."

The auto cab did as it was told.

Dee watched the bars and nightclubs give way to warehouses, hangars, and a full-spectrum security fence. It consisted of high-test metal mesh interwoven with a force field. Light shimmered across its surface.

Just beyond the fence Dee could see acres of blast-scarred duracrete, rows of parked ships, and a terminal building. A ship rose on repellors, skittered into a launch zone, and lifted for space. Thunder rolled across the land.

The bounty hunter ignored it. Her interest lay with one ship in particular. The tender that Sorenson used as a shuttle. Lando would head straight for it. Once aboard they could lift, rejoin Cy aboard the drifter, and decide what to do. But what if the tender was a trap? What if the police were watching it? Things could go south in a real hurry, that's what.

The gate was just ahead. The guard shack was built like a pillbox and was equipped with the latest in automatic defenses. Dee swallowed something hard and dry. Was airport security on the lookout for them? If so, it was all over.

There was a delivery truck right in front of them. It came to a full stop. A beefy guard stepped up to the window and waved a scanner toward the back. A routine precaution or a sign of heightened security? There was no way to tell.

The truck rolled on. The cab jerked into motion and ground to a halt seconds later. The guard stepped forward. Dee heard a comset buzz. The guard turned away.

"Corporal Prescott. Rudy? Damn it, Rudy, how many times do I have to tell you? Don't call me here at work."

The guard waved toward the auto cab and it jerked forward.

Dee gave a sigh of relief and leaned back in her seat.

The ships were parked in orderly rows, each one sitting on its assigned number. Cap's tender was parked in row F number 47. Dee tried to look in every direction at once as she directed the auto cab down row E.

Things looked normal enough. Ground jitneys dashed here and there, repair techs strode about on their shiny exoskeletons, and robots rolled, crawled, walked, or flew in various directions.

Dee pointed toward a reentry-scarred freighter. Stacks of cargo modules surrounded it. "Pull up over there."

A gang of auto loaders were hard at work placing cargo in the main hold but there was no sign of any sentients. Good.

Brakes rasped and the auto cab came to a halt. "Ten-fifty, please."

Dee opened the door. "Wait here. I'll be back."

"Yes, mam," the machine said cheerfully. "That'll be one credit per minute while on standby."

"That'll be fine."

Dee stepped out of the cab onto hot pavement. The air reeked of ozone, fuel, and lubricants. She marched toward row F. Dee had learned a long time ago: If you're not supposed to be there . . . then look like you are.

She had to wait for an auto tractor to pass. A long train of power pallets followed obediently behind, each one bobbing up and down on its own cushion of air, soon to be loaded with incoming cargo.

Once the pallets had passed Dee ducked around the side of a large cargo module and found the hatch was ajar. She pushed it open. It was dark and relatively cool inside. The air had a metallic smell. "Anyone home?"

Nothing. She looked around. The module had been converted into a portable workshop. She saw racks of electronics, a variety of power tools, and an industrial-strength laser cutter. Satisfied that she was alone Dee stood just inside the door and took a look.

The tender sat right where they'd left it. It had the boxy appearance of a vessel meant more for space than atmospheric use. Hot air shimmered all around it.

Dee squinted against the glare. The ship was completely undisturbed from all appearances. But was it? The tender could be sitting there ready to lift, or packed with police, just waiting for them to return.

And there was another problem as well. Dee couldn't fly anything more complicated than a light plane and Cap was out of commission. Once aboard they'd be trapped. Unable to lift and unable to run.

Dee decided to do what successful bounty hunters do best. Wait. Wait and watch. If the tender was a trap something would happen to give it away. Patience was the key.

The first thing to do was get rid of the cab. A short wait was one thing, but an hour or more might trigger the cab company's central computer, and bring someone to investigate. Besides, at the rate of a credit a minute, she'd be out of money in no time flat. She made her way back to the cab.

A puff of cool air hit Dee's face as she opened the door. Cap mumbled something unintelligible and waved a hand in her general direction. He was coming to. Good. Dee addressed herself to the auto cab.

"What do I owe you?"

"Twenty-one fifty."

Dee fumbled around in a pocket, found some local currency, and fed some of it into the cab's cash comp. A bell dinged when the total reached twenty-one fifty.

Dee turned her attention to Sorenson. "Cap . . . Cap, can you hear me?"

Cap mumbled something, swallowed, and said, "Wha?"

"Come on. It's time to get out of the cab."

"Out of the cab?"

"Right. Give me your hand, yes, there. Are you okay?"

Sorenson nodded, but from the way he swayed back and forth and stared blankly at his surroundings, she knew it wasn't true.

Dee took his arm, but tried to avoid the appearance of supporting him, since that might attract attention. The cargo module looked as if it was miles away. Cap stumbled once or twice, but Dee caught him, and they kept on going.

Dee had a story prepared in case the module was occupied, but was happy when it wasn't. She led Sorenson over to a beat-up chair. It squeaked as he sat down. His voice cracked when he spoke.

"What the hell are we doing in here? I saw the tender outside. Let's go aboard."

Dee shook her head. "We can't."

Cap frowned. "Why the hell not?"

Dee felt an overwhelming sense of frustration. "Because of you, Cap. Because *you* got drunk, *you* spilled your guts to the media, and *you* put us all in danger."

Sorenson's eyes grew larger. His face seemed ghostly white. "Got drunk? Spilled my guts?"

"Everything but the drifter's coordinates."

Cap looked around as if seeing the inside of the cargo module for the first time. "Wait a minute . . . where's Melissa? Where's Pik?"

Dee leaned against a cold metal wall. Her voice was weary.

"Now there's an interesting question. Well, assuming that they haven't been captured or killed, they're on the run. Headed this way would be my guess."

Sorenson was silent for a minute. The lines in his face seemed to grow even deeper. "I need a drink."

Dee felt pity mixed with disgust. "No, Cap. What you need is a good deal more complicated than that."

The next hour passed with agonizing slowness. The heat grew until the inside of the cargo module was like an oven. Dee's clothes were soaked with perspiration and her mouth was very dry. She picked up a washer and popped it in her mouth. The saliva tasted good. She peeked outside.

Everything looked the same. The sunlight, the robots coming and going, and the tender. It sat there like a big refrigerator. Full of cool, cool air, and cold, cold water. All she'd have to do was walk over, palm the lock, and step inside. From there it would be only steps down the corridor and into the fresher.

Dee imagined cool water splashing against her skin and ran her tongue over parched lips. This was torture. It would be better to think of something else.

Sorenson had a terrific hangover, and the heat made it worse, but he didn't say anything. The guilt of what he'd done, not only to Melissa, but to his friends, weighed heavily on his mind. He wanted to say something, wanted to apologize, but knew it wouldn't do any good. If only . . .

Man-made thunder rumbled about them and the entire cargo module shook. Cap jumped to his feet and Dee looked out the door. It was a ship, a big one, a destroyer from the look of her, and headed their way. The warship's repellors roared as she rode them across the surface of the spaceport to settle a thousand yards away. Dust and dirt swirled as the vessel settled onto massive landing jacks. The repellors made a loud pop as the pilot turned them off. Metal creaked as it started to cool.

Dee eyed the ship suspiciously. What was this? Coincidence or something more? All of the other military ships were parked on the far side of the spaceport within their own area. Why park this one next to the tender?

A hatch opened, half a dozen navy personnel spilled out, and started to work on some routine maintenance procedures. Was it real? Or just for show? And what about those weapons turrets? Was it just Dee's imagination, or were a significant number of them lined up on the tender?

Dee wiped the sweat from her forehead and wished that she'd allowed for some sort of escape route.

Another hour passed. Then two. Cap had started to doze. Both of them were startled when a maintenance bot appeared, whirred into the module, took a coupling from one of the bins, and left. It seemed completely unaware of their existence.

Dee forced herself to relax. It made sense. The maintenance bot had the single-minded programming of a Terran ant. Go there, do that, and ignore everything else.

The sun started to set. The air inside the cargo module began to cool. The technicians disappeared and were replaced by a sentry and a tired-looking surveillance bot. It made endless paths around the destroyer's landing jacks sniffing the air for smells that shouldn't be there, monitoring the ground for signs of tunneling, and listening for suspicious sounds. All useful things to do on some rim world but more than a little silly in the middle of a major spaceport.

Still, regulations are regulations, and sniffers are SOP for a class three alert. Dee had been a marine and knew all about class three alerts. It reinforced her earlier impression. The destroyer was there for a reason.

The Imperial consul came to mind. A personage with more than enough power to move destroyers around and the motive to do so. The drifter, and the technology it contained, would serve as a powerful incentive. Besides, the consul had no way to know that Lando was innocent, so he saw himself as performing a public service as well.

Then, as if to erase any possible doubt, a pair of robo-cams appeared. They swooped out of the twilight like bats and circled the tender. Dee couldn't hear the dialogue but could imagine what it would be like.

"And so here it is . . . the ship that the killer's heading for. No one thinks that he'll make it as far as Brisco City, but they aren't taking any chances and have a destroyer in position just in case . . ."

Dee saw the sniffer point an antenna toward the robo-cams, saw the sentry become agitated, and knew some vidcasters were catching hell from the navy. The air between the space-port and the vid station would be red-hot. She could imagine a hurried close.

"Well, folks, that's it for right now. We'll bring you more when there's more to bring. This is so and so, for news such and such, see you at ten."

The cameras zoomed away and vanished into the gathering darkness.

Dee walked to the rear of the cargo module, fumbled around in the darkness, and found what she was looking for. Two rumpled grease-stained coveralls. She threw one to Sorenson. "Here, put that on."

Cap started to say something, started to object, but one look at Dee froze the words in his throat. Any authority he had was aboard *Junk*. Sorenson stepped into the overalls and pulled them up around his shoulders.

"Stand still."

Cap obeyed as Dee smeared number-four grease on his face and hands. She did the same thing to herself.

"There . . . now grab some tools and follow me." Dee slipped out the door and Cap followed. Sorenson felt his heart skip a beat as Dee waved to the sentry and he waved back.

Then they were walking along together, marching toward the distant lights, two techs on their way home. The air was cooler now and rumbled with the sound of a distant lift-off.

Sorenson felt a terrible thirst but knew he wouldn't get any sympathy from Dee. He asked a question instead. "What now?"

Dee had appropriated a rather heavy toolbox. She shifted it from one hand to the other. "That's simple. We find ourselves a ship, intercept Melissa and Pik, and take off."

Sorenson shook his head doubtfully. "That doesn't sound easy to me."

Dee's eyes were on the lights up ahead. "I never said it would be 'easy.' I said it would be 'simple.' "

Sorenson nodded agreeably but couldn't see the difference.

5

There was no way to tell what the compartment had originally been used for. It was oval, lined with some sort of light green spongy material, and made sounds when you touched it.

Pik thought it was some sort of zero-G music room, where the builders had composed music by bouncing off the walls, but Cap had disagreed. He said the room was a computer terminal where sound stood in for numbers and the aliens had performed sophisticated calculations.

Cy Borg didn't care. He was lonely, bored, and more than a little pissed. If cyborgs *can* be pissed, which Cy felt sure they could, since borgs feel things the same way other humans do. He propelled himself toward a wall, heard a B flat, and bounced off.

His anger stemmed from the fact that Cap, Melissa, Pik, and Della had departed for Pylax without him. Someone had to stay aboard the drifter, and since Cy knew the most about the drifter's inner workings he was elected. They *needed* him aboard the drifter. That's what they said anyway.

But Cy knew better. He knew what they *really* thought. They were afraid that he'd get them all in trouble. They knew his history, how he'd gambled his organs away, until only his brain was left. And they'd been present when representatives of the gamblers' guild had come after him for unpaid debts. Debts that had landed Pik and Melissa in jail.

So he had a problem with gambling? So what? Cap was a world-champion drunk, Pik was wanted for murder, and Della was little more than a hired killer. Who were they to tell him what to do?

"No," Cy concluded out loud, "my body may be different . . . but my emotions are the same. And I'm pissed."

So saying, the cyborg spun in midair and headed for the drifter's control room. He'd promised not to experiment with the ship's controls while the rest of them were gone but it wouldn't hurt to look. Besides, there wasn't anything else to do, and why should they have all the fun?

Cy aimed his globular body toward the nearest hatch and zoomed through the passageway beyond. He extruded both vid pickups and added more speed. Certain pleasures were lost to him, sex being the most noticeable, but others had taken their place.

And first and foremost among those pleasures was three-dimensional movement. Thanks to a small antigrav unit, and jets of compressed air, Cy could move in ways that most people never dreamed of. Zero G is one thing, but ah, freedom *within* gravity . . . that's something else.

And thanks to his metal casing and internal oxygen supply, Cy could survive in space without a suit. Yes, there were advantages to being a cyborg, though Cy would have returned to his original body in a second had that been possible.

Cy shot out of the passageway into a large open space. Dense foliage grew to the right and left. Rain drummed on his metal casing. Unlike humans, and the aliens encountered so far, the builders had equipped their ship with a self-maintaining biosphere. The drifter boasted a desert, grasslands, and a small forest full of double-trunked trees. The artificial gravity was slightly less than Terran norm, and the air was generally more humid than Cy liked, the exceptions being the desert and certain equipment bays.

The rain turned to mist as Cy left the grasslands and approached the forest. The forest never failed to interest him. There were the strange double-trunked trees for one thing, their puffy foliage growing off perfectly straight limbs, each one a perfect replica of all the others.

Then there were the paths, dozens of them, that wound in and around the trees and served as highways for a variety of small animals. Cy and his companions had caught and examined some of them. None were real. Like the birds that fluttered between the trees, and the insects that buzzed through the air, the animals were robots. Sophisticated robots, yes, and potentially quite valuable, but mindless things that were more decorative than useful.

The engineer in Cy ached to take one of them apart but knew he shouldn't. What if there was some sort of sophisticated relationship between them and the ship that hadn't been discovered yet? No, it was way too dangerous.

The most interesting part of the forest were the nest-beds. That's what Cy called them anyway, and the name seemed to fit. They were depressions really, long indentations in the ground that were padded with mossy stuff and covered with brightly colored pieces of fabric, Pieces of fabric that looked like blankets.

The similarity to a bed was undeniable and evocative as well. The nest-beds caused Cy to see the long-vanished builders as something more than the super-intellects they undoubtedly were.

Their ruins could be found throughout known space, fragments of a once great civilization that had existed untold thousands of years before. A civilization that had inexplicably vanished leaving no graveyards, no tombs, no images of what its creators had looked like.

Oh, archaeologists and xeno-anthropologists had created computer-derived holos based on logical extrapolation, but that left a lot to be desired. They were tall and skinny, anyone who looked at one of their doorways could see that, but what did they *feel* like? Did they have eyes? And if so, what would you see in them? Love? Hate? There was no way to tell.

That's why the nest-beds were so important. They spoke of comfort, of a need for rest, of a desire for security. It would be easy to go further than that, to assume that they slept in forests on their native planet, but that might be wrong.

After all, back when sex had meant something, Cy had spent time in a pleasure dome or two. He remembered sleeping under a tangle of gymnastic equipment on a heart-shaped bed. What would some enterprising alien xeno-anthropologist make of that thousands of years later? Would he, or she, or it, conclude that humans worshiped circulatory organs and liked to perform calisthenics just prior to rest?

No, it was better to stay within bounds, to conclude that the builders needed rest and found it within an artificial forest.

Cy picked up speed and skimmed the side of the vessel's hull. It was covered by a mosslike growth. The cyborg knew from previous experimentation that the underlying hull material was not only conductive but heavily laden with electronic activity. Somewhere, and none of them knew where, an extremely sophisticated artificial intelligence was using the hull to route electronic signals throughout the hull. Cy wasn't positive, but was fairly sure, that power was distributed the same way.

Thanks to the special hull the builders had been able to dispense with the need for wire, cable, and conduit. It was absolutely amazing, and more than that, a technological treasure trove for anyone who owned it.

Cy smiled inside. When the negotiations were over he'd be very wealthy. Wealthy enough to buy his own casino and get the odds on *his* side for a change.

The biosphere came to an end and funneled the cyborg into a sizable lock. As always the ship sensed Cy's presence and knew exactly what to do. The lock closed and opened two minutes later. Cy felt the usual sense of anticipation as he squirted himself out into the alien control room. The cyborg braked and took a moment to look around.

The control room was completely unlike those found on human ships. It was simpler for one thing, with none of the control panels, vid screens, instrument readouts, computer keyboards, and other systems that Cy was used to.

There were ten black globes. Each globe sat on a white pedestal and had its own chair. The chairs were high and narrow. Taken together the globes formed a perfect circle.

Cy found the arrangement interesting because it seemed to imply a meeting of equals in which everyone shared the same amount of responsibility for the ship's safety. Such reasoning could be terribly flawed, of course, but what the heck, he had as much right to speculate as anyone else. *More* since he was aboard and they weren't.

Cy squirted himself over to the nearest globe. He remembered the first time he'd entered the control room, how he'd reached out to touch one of the globes and been surprised when his pincer went right through its seemingly solid surface.

There had been a brief moment of disorientation followed by the knowledge that he was somewhere else. Somewhere inside the vessel's biocontrol system, sampling the ship's atmosphere, and balancing evaporation against rainfall.

It was utterly fantastic! A ship you could control from the inside out!

The first experiment led to more as Cy raced from globe to globe finding and identifying controls for the power plants, the mysterious green blobs that could fling themselves outward from the hull, and the ship itself.

Cy eyed the globe in front of him. It provided access to the ship's NAVCOMP. Well, the builders called it something else no doubt, but a navigational computer is a navigational computer is a navigational computer.

The cyborg wanted to dip a pincer into it, wanted to enter the knowledge that it contained, wanted to know where the ship had been. Where had the ship come from? What happened to the crew? There was the very real possibility that the drifter's NAVCOMP could answer all of those questions and many more.

But that sort of knowledge was extremely valuable, and thought-driven controls have a down side as well. What if the cyborg unknowingly erased a portion of the NAVCOMP's memory? Or entered the mental equivalent of static? Or any of a thousand other possibilities? That's why the others had forbidden Cy to go skinny-dipping in the drifter's data banks.

But that was silly. Cy extended a pincer until it was only an inch shy of the globe's gleaming surface. Anyone intelligent enough to build a ship like the drifter would have built safeguards into its computer systems. No, it wouldn't do to have unauthorized types fiddling around with things and causing trouble. The others were worry warts, that's all, quick to indulge their own pleasures, while limiting his. Cy stuck his pincer through the surface of the globe.

Suddenly, and without effort, Cy *was* the ship. A single drop within the endless ocean of space, a string of coordinates expressed in sounds he didn't understand, and a purpose that felt like reaching. Exploring? Wanting? Gathering? All seemed to fit but none were sufficient by themselves.

Now the ship found and identified him. Thoughts came his way. They hurt the cyborg's mind like high-frequency sounds can hurt human ears. Word pictures bounced back and forth between the walls of his mind.

"YES? YES? YES?"

Cy flinched inside his metal shell. He found it hard to focus his thoughts. "I want knowledge."

A tidal wave of sounds, numbers, images, and ideas washed over the cyborg and tumbled him under.

"CHOOSE. CHOOSE. CHOOSE." The words reverberated through Cy's brain like a giant ringing of bells.

Cy swam up from the bottom, trying to breathe, suffocating on the knowledge around him. Information flowed in through his mouth, nose, and ears, filled his throat, and packed lungs that he no longer had. He couldn't breathe. The cyborg screamed.

"No! It's too much! Stop!"

The storm was gone as suddenly as it had come. Cy was left floating on the very surface of a gently undulating sea. There was no sun as such, only a warm hazy light that came from somewhere and nowhere all at the same time.

Cy lay there for a moment, recovering his composure and organizing his thoughts. He'd asked for knowledge and the computer had responded. The fault was his. Instead of asking a precise question, such as "Where are we now?" he'd been way too general. Okay, no problem. One well-framed question coming up.

"What happened to this ship's crew?"

"CHOOSE. CHOOSE. CHOOSE."

Cy swore softly. The computer didn't know or needed a different kind of question. The cyborg tried a different tack. He visualized a sun.

"Would you agree that this is a sun?"

"YES. YES. YES. Type 3vb890123/4A."

Cy smiled internally. All right! Now he was getting somewhere. He summoned up a planet. It had small polar caps, a lot of blue water, and ragged brown islands.

"And this is a planet?"

"YES. YES. YES. Type 7jc465-XX79."

Cy felt almost faint with excitement. He was close, so very close. Just one more question and he'd know something people had been after for hundreds of years. The location of the builder's home world, or if not that, then something almost as good: a potentially unplundered artifact planet.

"Which planet was this ship built on?"

There was a mind-numbing blur as thousands of images whipped through Cy's mind like a tape on high-speed rewind. Then it was there, a crystal-clear vision, floating against the backdrop of space.

It was an ordinary-looking planet, with large polar caps, no oceans to speak of, and a single globe-spanning continent. Cy felt a sense of disappointment. He had expected something more. Something worthy of a superior race. A paradise perhaps, or the ruins of one, anything but an ordinary-looking planet. Oh, well, you can't win 'em all.

"How about the surface? Can you show me the way the surface of the planet looked when this ship left it?"

"YES. YES. YES."

Cy found himself in orbit, looking down through some sort of electronic magnification, scanning the surface below. By simply wanting it the cyborg could zoom down to examine a single stone or pull back to view an entire mountain range.

He saw mile after mile of fields, all tended by fantastically shaped agrobots, and supervised by beefy-looking humanoids. They had coarse features, heavy musculature, and looked remarkably alike. They wore heavy clothing as if the air was cold.

Then the fields were gone, replaced by widely spaced villas, and tantalizing glimpses of tall spindly aliens that came and went in carefully sealed ground cars.

After that came the city, an absolute maze of walls, buildings, plazas, dead-ends, courtyards, and streets. Now there were more humanoids, similar to those Cy had seen before, but different too. These were slender things, shorter than the more muscle-bound variety, but just as identical. Like their heavy beefier cousins these humanoids were dressed in warm clothing.

Once again the cyborg saw the beetlelike ground cars that zipped to and fro and spied on the leggy-looking builders as they made their rounds.

Twice he zoomed in, trying to see what should have been their faces, but was stymied both times. The builders, if that was what they were, wore some sort of portable privacy screens that turned their features into a blur. It was frustrating but consistent with a race that had left no pictures of themselves behind.

Then the city was gone, giving way to more villas and the fields beyond.

Cy released the image. "Thank you. I am finished."

"WANT? WANT? WANT?"

"Nothing, thank you."

"WANT?! WANT?! WANT?!" The words were more insistent now, as if the computer wanted another answer and wasn't getting it.

Cy began to worry. What the hell was going on? He prepared to withdraw his pincer.

"Nothing. I don't need anything else. I wish to terminate this contact."

"NO! NO! NO!" Each word was like a sledgehammer. Cy became angry.

"Yes! Yes! Yes!"

"YES! YES! YES!" the computer echoed obediently. "ACCUMULATORS CHARGING. DEPARTURE 9 X 9 AND COUNTING."

Cy jerked his pincer out of the interface. The computer disappeared from his mind.

"9 X 9 and counting?" What the hell did that mean? Nine days? Nine hours? Nine seconds? Great Sol, what had he done? Cy searched the room for help. There was none to be had. Somewhere, deep in the bowels of the ship, something started to whine.

6

The fog lay over the sea like a soft gray blanket. It was early, so early that the sun was an almost unseen presence, its light filtered by a thick layer of clouds.

The man who stood on the stern of the hovercraft was average in almost every way. Freeson had graduated fiftieth out of a class of ninety-eight at the Coast Guard Academy, had been rated "Acceptable" during his most recent performance review, and was neither old nor especially young.

In fact, the only thing to distinguish Freeson from hundreds of other male Coast Guard officers was an enormous nose that had earned him the lifelong nickname "Honker," and the fact that he was the one who had spotted the skimmer.

Both vessels were located near the mouth of the Istaba estuary, a long, narrow passageway that led inland, and terminated at the city of Norton.

The hovercraft rocked from side to side as swells rolled in off the ocean. Freeson spread his feet farther apart in order to compensate for the additional movement and tried to hold his binoculars steady. A gust of wind came along and snatched the fog away from the pleasure craft's rigging. The skimmer looked like a wounded bird, one wing dragging in the water, as it crept toward safety. There was no sign of life on the other vessel. Still asleep probably.

Freeson lowered the binoculars, licked dry lips, and brought the glasses up again. Every port from Ontoon to Dowling was under surveillance. Only two days' worth of storms had prevented the authorities from catching up with the skimmer earlier. Spy sats can't locate what they can't "see" and the combination of bad weather and the skimmer's composite hull had rendered it damned near invisible.

The fact that Lando had sailed into Freeson's search sector was pure luck, but luck the officer could use, since he was in need of some visible success. The kind of success that would put the word "Outstanding" on his next appraisal and pave the way toward lieutenant commander.

Freeson lowered the binoculars. Yes, this was a lucky day indeed. He looked toward the bow. Weapons Tech First Class Shimaku sat hunched behind the twin-fifties. She was faceless behind the reflective visor. One word from him and she'd turn the skimmer into floating scrap. The idea was safe, and therefore tempting, but there was the little girl to consider.

Freeson had a daughter of his own and the thought of Shimaku's heavy-caliber slugs ripping through her body made him shudder. No, they'd do it the old-fashioned way, stop and board. Just like the stories he'd read as a kid. If the girl got in the way, well, he'd cross that bridge when he came to it.

Freeson checked to make sure that the boarding party was in place, nodded to the petty officer in charge, and turned toward Power Tech Third Class Miller. "Let's go."

Miller nodded. He was a slim young man with thick blond hair. A ready smile hid his otherwise disrespectful thoughts. "Yes, sir, Lieutenant Honker, sir. Whatever you say, sir."

A pair of powerful engines roared into life, the vessel rose on a cushion of air and skimmed across the surface of the estuary. A seabird flapped its wings, broke free from the surface of the water, and lumbered into the air.

Freeson watched the skimmer. He half expected to see it turn, speed up, and try to run. It didn't. Good. Still waking up. This would be easier than he'd thought. He turned toward Miller.

"Put us alongside."

"Aye, aye, sir."

Miller spun the wheel and brought the hovercraft in next to the skimmer in a long gentle curve. He killed power at just the right moment, and allowed the patrol boat to coast for a moment and bump into the yacht's port side. The hovercraft bounced away and both vessels drifted apart.

Metal clattered on composite as Freeson's crew tossed grappling hooks across and pulled them tight. Hulls touched for the second time, and the boarding party jumped across, protected to some extent by Shimaku and her twin-fifties. Their combat boots left scuff marks on the skimmer's pristine deck.

Freeson felt a sense of disappointment. It didn't take a genius to figure out that no one was aboard. All that reward money down the tubes. It didn't seem fair. The reports came in one at a time.

"Nothing forward, sir!"

"Nothing below, sir!"

"Nothing aft, sir!"

Freeson gave a nod of acknowledgment, gauged the movement of the boats, and jumped across. His landing was reasonably graceful, for which he gave silent thanks. A boatswain's mate stepped aside and allowed the Coast Guard officer to step down into the cockpit.

Freeson looked around. There was a scattering of empty meal paks, some crumpled clothes, and a pair of unmade bunks. They confirmed what he already knew. The fugitive had been aboard but left. The question was where? He addressed himself to no one in particular.

"Is the NAVCOMP on?"

"I certainly am," the machine answered cheerfully, "and welcome aboard, sir. It's a bit nippy out there. Would you be wantin' some nice hot coffee?"

Freeson shook his head impatiently. "No, that won't be necessary. Tell me, was there a man and a little girl aboard?"

"No," the NAVCOMP replied matter-of-factly. "How 'bout some breakfast? Nothing like some bacon and eggs to get your day off to a good start."

Freeson frowned and stepped up to the controls. Blunt fingers tapped a series of keys. An auto log appeared on the screen in front of him. There they were, departure times, headings, fuel consumption, weather notations, and more for the *Nadia*'s maiden voyage, and every trip thereafter. Outings that invariably listed Nathan Izzo as skipper and various women as crew.

Freeson shook his head sadly. Some guys had all the luck. Now to look at the last few days. His fingers flew over the keys. The screen flickered, dipped to black, and came up loaded with random junk. Keys clicked as the Coast Guard officer hit them again. The screen shimmered but remained as it was.

Damn! Like the NAVCOMP the log had been wiped clean as a whistle. Conscious of the boarding party's curious stares

Freeson made his way up to the skimmer's deck and looked around. The fog had started to burn off. It would be a long, long day. A day of tedious explanations, boring reports, and endless repetition. Once again luck had passed him by.

"Hold on!"

Melissa did as she was told and grabbed the ropes that ran down both sides of the inflatable raft.

Lando faced her, paddle poised above the water, and waited to dig in. The trick was to catch a wave just so, ride it toward shore, and reach the beach without flipping over.

Lando sensed that it was time, looked over his shoulder to make sure, and paddled for shore. The wave slid under the raft, raised it up, and carried it toward the beach.

There was a moment of pure undiluted pleasure as the wind pressed against his face, spray flew up around the raft's bow, and Melissa screamed with excitement.

But pleasure turned to fear as Lando felt the bow drop, saw Melissa fall backward out of the raft, and found himself tumbling head over heels into the surf. A current pulled the smuggler down, bounced him off a sandy bottom, and jerked him back up. Lando yelled the moment that his head broke through the surface of the water.

"Melissa! Melissa! Can you hear me?"

A faint "yes" came from off to the right, and Lando was just about to swim in that direction when another wave broke over him and dragged him toward the beach.

Fighting like a mad man, Lando struggled forward, clawed his way up the steeply shelving beach, and rolled over. His breath came in gulps. He looked right and left. Melissa. Where the hell was Melissa?

Then he saw it, over to the left, a flash of red as her life jacket was pulled under.

Jumping to his feet, Lando ran down the beach, angled out into the water, and dived toward the spot where he'd last seen her. His hands found her first. Slick fabric, a tangle of hair, and a wad of soggy clothing.

The smuggler grabbed the little girl under the armpits, pulled her up onto the beach, and fell backward into the sand. Melissa coughed, spit out some water, and fought to catch her breath.

"Melissa? Are you okay?"

Melissa smiled weakly. "Yes, I think so, but I lost Ralph."

Lando gave her a hug. "I'm sorry."

Melissa forced a smile. "That's okay. Ralph's a good swimmer. He'll make it."

Lando started to say something about buying her a new Ralph, caught himself, and nodded instead. "Right."

Lando got up, helped Melissa to her feet, and unbuckled her life jacket.

"Throw it into the surf."

"Why?"

Lando pointed toward the south. "Do you see the raft?"

Melissa nodded. "Sure, it's upside down."

Lando nodded. "Exactly. Looks like an accident, doesn't it?"

Melissa's face lit up. "I get it! They'll think we drowned!"

Lando shrugged. "We can hope anyway. Throw the jacket in and let's go."

Melissa threw the jacket as far as she could. The surf brought it back and dumped it at her feet.

Lando laughed and told her to leave it where it was. They walked hand in hand, careful to stay at the edge of the water, where the surf would erase their footprints. The mist had burned off and their clothes began to dry.

They had gone the better part of a mile before an ancient lava flow crept down across the beach to point a long black finger at the sea. The rock was difficult to walk on but made a nice hard highway on which their footprints wouldn't show. They were almost to the tree line when Lando caught the flash of reflected light.

He looked again and saw blue sea, brown beach, and, right there, something low and slow just above it. An air car! Searching for them!

Lando grabbed Melissa's arm. "They're here! Come on!" It was only fifty feet to the jungle but it felt like a mile. They plunged into the foliage and felt it close behind them. Lando turned to peer out.

The air car hummed as it moved down the beach. It was an open affair with an energy cannon mounted in the bow and racks of heat-seeking missiles to either side.

Both of the occupants were peering over the sides and looking down at the beach. One pointed in the direction of the raft and yelled something that Lando couldn't understand.

The air car banked in that direction and lost altitude. Good. The raft would keep them busy while Lando and Melissa put some distance between themselves and the beach.

It was a struggle to work their way through the undergrowth. Vines tore at their faces, moss-covered logs angled up to block their way, and leaves crowded in from every side.

They found a game trail eventually, and while it ran parallel to the beach, the going was so much easier that Lando couldn't resist using it. He went first with Melissa behind.

The jungle was both pleasant and scary at the same time. The sun came down through the canopy in gold streamers, bathing some plants in its magic glow, leaving others in almost total darkness. The air was sweet, heavy with humidity, and thick with insects. Finally, after two or three miles of twisting, turning trail, they came to a dirt road. It was a one-lane affair, cut through the area by parties unknown, already blurred by a blanket of green. Another year, two at the most, and it would disappear.

The road crossed the path at right angles and headed inland. To use it meant walking in the open, but to stay on the path meant going in the wrong direction.

Time was critical. Lando chose the road. He motioned to Melissa. "Come on, Mel, the road is just what we need. We'll make better time now."

Melissa looked doubtful. "I don't know, Pik, I'm getting kind of tired. Can we stop and rest for a while?"

Lando looked at Melissa and realized his mistake. If the jungle path had been difficult for him, it had been twice as hard for her. Melissa's hair was a tangled mess, there were cuts and scratches all over her face and arms, and her clothes were crusty with dried salt. Not only that, but her face was flushed with exertion, and she was breathing hard. Sweat covered her forehead.

Lando nodded. "You bet. We'll take five. Come on . . . let's get off the road."

Melissa followed Lando into the jungle. They collapsed beneath a huge tree. Vines had wound themselves around the massive trunk and disappeared upward.

Five minutes turned into ten and Lando realized that he was tired too. The warm air, the drone of the insects, all conspired to close his eyes. He thought about Della, wondered where she was, and what she was doing. He was asleep seconds later.

"Copy that, Roller One. I'm 4.2 miles up access road N-89. Nothing so far."

Lando came awake with a start. Melissa sat up, started to speak, but stopped when he put a finger to his lips.

There was a squawk followed by a jumble of words.

The voice sounded like it was only feet away. "I copy, Roller One. Follow N-89 to the beach and return. Over and out."

Lando moved quickly, trying to remain silent, but eager to see. He stopped and peered out through the foliage. The trooper wore a planetary guard uniform, light body armor, and a commo helmet.

Beyond him, grounded in the center of the road, was a Personal Combat Vehicle. Though little more than an armored antigrav sled, the PCV was transportation. The platform would do thirty or forty miles per hour and save them days of walking.

Lando felt his heart skip a beat as the trooper turned and walked straight toward him. Had the soldier seen something? No, his blast rifle remained where it was, slung over his shoulder and hard to reach.

The trooper stopped, unzipped his pants, and prepared to urinate. Lando grinned. Not quite as good as catching someone with their pants down, but almost as effective. The slug gun had been lost in the surf but the missile launcher was still strapped to his arm. Lando crashed through the bushes. "Hold it right there!"

The trooper didn't want to "hold it right there." He did his best to zip his pants and back up at the same time. He tripped and fell backward onto his blast rifle.

Lando couldn't see the trooper's face through the visor's reflective surface but he could imagine what it would look like. Surprise, mixed with embarrassment, and a good deal of fear. He pointed the missile launcher at the soldier's chest.

"Stand up. Leave the blast rifle where it is."

The trooper obeyed. "Wha . . ."

Was the helmet radio on or off? Lando made a cutting motion across his throat.

"Quiet! One more sound and you're dead."

The soldier nodded nervously. Lando moved forward. "Good. Now, stick your arms out straight." The trooper obeyed. Lando freed the blast rifle, released the safety, and backed away.

"Excellent. Now, take the helmet off."

The soldier released the chin strap and removed the helmet. He was young, no more than eighteen or nineteen, and very frightened. He had farm-boy cheeks and big round eyes.

Melissa's voice came from the jungle.

"Pik? Are you okay?"

"I'm fine," Lando yelled back. "Stay where you are. I'll call for you in a minute."

The smuggler made a jabbing motion with the blast rifle.

"Strip." The trooper removed his armor. His uniform followed. The boots came last.

Lando pointed toward the far side of the road. "Step over there."

The soldier refused to move, his eyes bright and lower lip trembling. Lando shook his head.

"You shouldn't believe everything you hear on the vidcasts. I haven't murdered anyone in weeks. I'll tie you up. In an hour, maybe two, you'll get loose and find your way home. Outside of some bug bites, and a good deal of ribbing from your friends, you'll be fine."

Somewhat reassured, the soldier crossed the road and started into the jungle.

"That's far enough," Lando said. "I'll leave you in plain sight in case one of your friends happens along. Hug that tree."

The trooper looked to see which tree Lando was referring to, wrapped his arms around it, and looked over his shoulder.

Lando gave him a reassuring smile. "Good. Now clasp your hands."

Lando used his belt and strips torn from his own shirt to tie the soldier's hands and bind his feet. He made the knots tight enough to hold for a while, but loose enough to allow for circulation and an eventual escape.

"There," Lando said, stepping back to inspect his handiwork. "That should hold you for a while. I'll leave your boots by the side of the road."

The younger man nodded, looked like he wanted to say something, but swallowed instead.

Lando returned to the middle of the road, retrieved the trooper's uniform, and stepped into the jungle. Melissa was waiting. She pointed toward the PCV.

"Will that carry both of us?"

The smuggler stripped down to his underwear. "That's the plan. Those things are built to carry combat gear plus a passenger when they have to. Wait by the PCV. I'll join you in a moment."

Lando emerged from the jungle five minutes later. He wore the trooper's uniform, had the blast rifle slung over a shoulder, and carried the commo helmet tucked under his arm.

"Well, what do you think?"

Melissa frowned and pretended to inspect him. "I think your pants are kind of short."

Lando grinned. "Yeah? Well, so are my sleeves. The uniform should pass at a distance though. Assuming you stay out of sight. Come on, let's get out of here."

Lando had Melissa step onto the PCV first. By sitting cross-legged on the floor she was able to scrunch herself into the small cargo compartment located in the forward part of the aircraft.

Lando had never flown a PCV before but figured it couldn't be that hard. The rather simple controls supported that conclusion.

There was a row of idiot lights, a throttle, an altimeter that topped out at a hundred feet, a turn and bank indicator, and an aircraft-type stick. When the operator pulled back, the aircraft went up; when the operator pushed forward, the aircraft went down; and when the operator moved the stick to the right or left, the PCV would turn in that direction.

Lando saw that the power was already on, the idiot lights were green, and the stick was centered in the neutral position. He winked at Melissa. "Hang in there, hon, and remember, it beats the heck out of walking."

The commo helmet was a tight fit. It activated itself the moment that Lando slipped it on. A steady babble of radio traffic filled his ears. What was the trooper's call sign anyway? And what about codes?

The smuggler thought about interrogating the trooper, decided time was more important, and pulled back on the stick. The PCV's antigrav units pushed it up into the air. The moment the altimeter registered fifty feet Lando brought the stick back to the neutral position and advanced the throttle. The aircraft moved slowly at first, gradually picked up speed, and maxed out at sixty mph.

After checking to make sure that there were no obstacles in his path, Lando looked over the side and saw the road passing below. He smiled. This was more like it!

The next fifteen minutes were rather pleasant. The warmth of the sun, the wind tugging at his clothes, and the sensation of speed made a nice combination. He even played with the PCV a little, snaking back and forth across the road until Melissa tugged on his trousers, and shook her head. The violent motion combined with her position on the floor was making her ill.

Lando flew straight and level after that and turned his attention to the countryside ahead. There should be some sort of arterial before too long, something he could follow toward Brisco City, and the spaceport beyond.

It appeared about five minutes later. It was a gleaming four-laner, relatively new, complete with the latest in computer-controlled guidance systems.

Rather than risk calling attention to himself Lando put the PCV down behind a clump of trees and took a look at the road. The smuggler had spent some time in Brisco City but knew very little about the outlying areas.

Melissa appeared like a gopher from its hole. Her head swiveled in every direction as she looked around.

A procession of computer-controlled driverless robo-haulers rolled by. They were big boxy things that consisted of a tractor-control unit and three trailers. They passed Lando at five-minute intervals.

There were smaller vehicles too, brightly colored ground cars mostly, with a scattering of light-duty vans and hov-er trucks woven in between. They treated the robo-haulers as moving obstacles, passing them with almost monotonous regularity, zipping in and out of the fast lane.

What Lando didn't see was military traffic of any kind. The PCV would stick out like a sore thumb. So much for his plan to ride the platform all the way in.

A voice broke through the murmur in his helmet. "Flyer Three, this is Roller One. Come in, Flyer Three."

Something, Lando wasn't sure what, told him that *he* was Flyer Three. The lack of response from anyone else seemed to confirm that notion.

The voice came again, a little annoyed this time and slightly more urgent. "Roller One, calling Flyer Three. Wake up, Flyer Three. Are you in position?"

Lando decided to take a chance. "Copy that, Roller One. This is Flyer Three. I'm in position."

"What's the problem, Three? You sound weird."

Lando tried to think and watch traffic at the same time. "Roller One." Was "Roller" a code name, or did it mean something? Roller, Roller, whoa! Roller as in truck? As in really *big* truck? As in some sort of PCV carrier?

Lando cleared his throat. "Sorry, Roller One. There's some sort of short in my commo set. You're cutting in and out."

"No problem, Flyer Three," the voice replied. "We're about ten miles south of your position. Join us on the hop. Once you're aboard I'll have a tech look at your helmet."

Lando felt his heart try to beat its way out of his chest. Ten miles! Only ten miles away and doing at least sixty or seventy miles an hour! He'd have to move, and move fast.

Melissa was looking around. Lando touched her shoulder. "Trouble's on the way. Get down and stay out of sight."

The little girl ducked down into the forward compartment and Lando pulled back on the stick. The PCV went straight up and bobbed in the slight crosswind.

"On the hop." That's what the man had said, and it gave Lando an idea. An idea that depended on finding the right kind of roller and finding it fast.

The smuggler looked up the highway, saw a robo-hauler coming his way, and swore when he saw three fully enclosed trailers rolling along behind it. He needed something flat and open. Empty, but not too empty, so he could hide in among the cargo. Otherwise the PCV would stand out like a Zord at a Finthian air dance.

Lando watched the roller pass by. Wait a minute . . . what was that? Open doors, that's what. The last trailer was wide open. Should he try it? Or wait for the next flatbed?

Lando looked, but the next roller wasn't in sight yet, and when it was, might have military markings all over it. He grit his teeth, pushed the stick forward, and dived toward the highway.

A bright red hover car disappeared beneath the PCV's deck and the pavement came up to meet him. He leveled out just above the surface of the highway and was aware of roadside laser sensors flashing by to the left and right.

A man in a light-duty van started to pull over, saw the antigrav platform appear out of nowhere, and swerved into the fast lane.

Lando heard the blare of a horn and activated the PCV's flashers. He tossed a salute toward the van.

"If you can't hide, then come on strong." His father had given him that piece of advice many times and it certainly fit. With any luck the surrounding motorists would see the uniform, the PCV, and write him off as a pumped-up military jerk. He could hope anyway.

The robo-hauler displaced a lot of air and the PCV swayed back and forth as Lando lined it up with the trailer's door. The opening was a mysterious black rectangle. What was in there anyway? A nice open space? A load of steel rods? There was no way to tell.

The smuggler advanced the throttle and felt the platform shudder as it passed through the robo-hauler's turbulence. Steady, steady, just a little bit more, there. It grew dark as they entered the trailer.

Lando bit his lip. The PCV was about three feet off the floor, and traveling forward at the same speed. It was dark and there was a solid wall of duraplast boxes up ahead. No steel rods or other dangerous cargo, thank Sol. The challenge would be to put the antigrav platform down without allowing the robo-hauler to run out from under it.

Gently, ever so gently, Lando maintained the PCV's forward speed while easing the stick forward. Down, down, bump. The smuggler hurried to secure the platform's systems and kill power.

Then, with everything shut down, Lando motioned Melissa out of her hidey-hole. Both took a look around. Outside of the PCV and the boxes they were alone. The smuggler shifted his weight to the right as the robo-hauler accelerated into a well-banked curve.

"Flyer Three, Flyer Three, this is Roller One. Where the hell are you, over?"

Careful not to activate the mike, Lando removed the commo helmet and peeked out the door. The nearest car was a mile back. A bridge came up and Lando tossed the helmet out and over the side. A locator beacon seemed unlikely. After all, why ask Flyer Three for positions if they knew where he was? Still, it pays to be careful.

Lando ducked back inside the trailer, looked for the door, and pulled it down. It banged into place. The darkness was complete.

"I don't like this." Melissa's voice had a slight quaver to it.

"Me either," Lando agreed. "Hold on for a second."

It actually took a couple of minutes to fumble his way across the trailer, fall down as the robo-hauler took an unexpected curve, and find the PCV.

After that it was a relatively simple matter to activate the antigrav platform's running lights. The aircraft's power pak would eventually run down, but so what? They couldn't use it again. Within the next hour or two a description of the PCV would appear on every terminal in the land.

And that raised an interesting question: Where was the robo-hauler headed anyway? And how did that match his plans?

Maybe the cargo would provide some sort of hint. Lando went forward to inspect the boxes. They were tan and looked almost white in the glare of the PCV's single headlight. The smuggler's shadow arrived before he did and obscured the view. He moved sideways to get out of the way.

The boxes were rectangular in shape and extremely straightforward. Each one had the name "Mobar Industries" stenciled across its side.

Each container had a computer-generated invoice pasted to its side as well, and while most of the pertinent information was safeguarded by indecipherable bar codes, the addresses were printed in standard.

The first one Lando examined was addressed to: "Solano Plastics, Grid 54, Cross Street G, Brisco City."

A quick survey followed during which the smuggler learned that while the boxes were addressed to a wide variety of companies each and every one of them was located somewhere in Brisco City.

It was a major break. All they had to do was stay in the trailer, wait for it to arrive in Brisco City, and hot foot it to the spaceport. The tender would be covered . . . but he'd find something.

Lando turned toward the rear of the truck. "Hey, Mel. Good news."

No answer.

The smuggler frowned, walked toward the back, and found Melissa curled up against a wall. She was sound asleep. He smiled, tucked his jacket around her, and sat down. The news could wait. Lando leaned against the wall, yawned, yawned again, and fell asleep.

7

Lando was thrown sideways as the robo-hauler came to a sudden halt.

Melissa sat up and rubbed her eyes. "Pik? Where are we? What's going on?"

The PCV's power pak was nearly drained by now, but the lights still produced a feeble glow. The smuggler rolled to his knees, stood up, and checked the blast rifle. The indicator showed a full charge. He slipped the safety off and moved toward the door. A glance toward his watch told him it was night outside.

"I don't know, honey . . . but be ready to move."

The handle made a clacking sound as someone turned it. The door rattled upward and disappeared into darkness. A flashlight pinned Lando in its glare.

"Hold it right there." The voice was hard, full of authority, and distinctly female. There was something familiar about that voice but he couldn't quite put his finger on it.

The light was bright. Lando blinked but couldn't see a damned thing. Cop? Bounty hunter? Military? There was no way to tell.

"Put the weapon on the floor, take two steps back, and place your hands on top of your head."

The voice was calm, professional, and very sure of itself.

Lando swallowed hard. What should he do? Fight or surrender? Melissa made up his mind. She stood and moved into the light.

"Who is it, Pik? What will they do to us?"

That's when it hit him. If he fired the woman would fire back. Melissa would die and that was completely unacceptable.

Lando put the blast rifle on the floor, took two steps back, and placed his hands on top of his head.

"Good," the voice said. "Very good. Now, let's get out of here before all hell breaks loose. They have the tender under surveillance, Cap feels like hell, and the drifter is a long ways off."

It took Lando a moment to understand. "Della? Is that you? What the . . . ?"

The light went out and color swirled in front of Lando's eyes. The next thing the smuggler knew his arms were full of rather nicely proportioned femininity. Lips touched his and arms went around his neck. The smell of leather and perfume made a heady combination. He held on and didn't want to let go.

It was Melissa who broke it up, switching from child to adult, forever practical. "Break it up you two . . . times a-wasting. Besides, where's *my* hug?"

"Right here." The voice came from the doorway.

"Daddy!"

Melissa scurried to the doorway, jumped into her father's arms, and laughed when he stumbled backward.

The sound of a siren caused them to freeze momentarily, then galvanized them into action.

Cap lowered Melissa to the ground and pulled her away.

Della tugged on Lando's hand. "Come on! The car's up front."

They jumped to the ground, sprinted the length of the trailers, and rounded the robo-hauler's chunky front end.

Lando saw they were in some sort of warehouse district. There were low blocky buildings, widely spaced float lights, and stacks of cargo modules. Something roared, and a long, thin shaft of fire raced toward the sky. The spaceport! It was one, maybe two miles away!

The ground car sat two feet from the roller's massive bumper. From the way the vehicle was positioned Lando could tell that Della had pulled in front of the robo-hauler and forced it to stop. Assuming a hijacking or other criminal activity the truck's on-board computer had summoned the police. And from the sound of it, they were damned close.

Doors slammed as they piled into the car. Lando was thrown forward as Della put the transmission into reverse and stepped on the gas. Tires screeched as she stood on the brakes, changed gears, and accelerated away. The sirens started to fade.

"Where are we headed?" Lando had to yell to make himself heard from the back seat.

"The spaceport," Della yelled back. "They're keeping an eye on the tender, which means they're watching *Junk* as well, so I hired a jobber. She's waiting for us now."

Junk was a deep-space tug. She'd been designed and built by Melissa's mother from salvaged parts and whatever else happened to be lying around at the moment. Hence the name *Junk*.

Jobbers eked out a marginal existence by carrying cargoes from one ship to another, ferrying passengers to and from the planet's surface, and other less legitimate tasks. No one used them unless forced to do so, and knowing that, the jobbers charged exorbitant prices.

"A jobber?" Cap demanded. "They'll charge an arm and a leg!"

Della glanced toward the passenger seat. Her voice was hard and cold. "You should have thought of that before you got drunk and spilled your guts."

Cap flinched as if struck across the face. He turned toward the window.

Melissa looked from one adult to the other and frowned. Della meant well, but it wouldn't do any good. Daddy was Daddy. She didn't like it when the adults became angry with each other.

Lando braced himself as the car skidded into a corner, slid sideways, and accelerated away. The spaceport was up ahead. "How did you find us anyway? We could have been anywhere."

Della smiled grimly. "It wasn't as hard as you might think. You were all over the vids. During the course of a day I saw footage of you lying on the beach, stealing a skimmer, and destroying a robo-cam.

"But it was the interview with the trooper that told me where to look. After listening to him I knew that you had a PCV, access to a highway full of robo-haulers, and a strong desire to reach Brisco City. I put one and one together and got two."

"But how could you pick the right truck?" Lando insisted. "There must be hundreds, maybe thousands to pick from."

"Not true," Della replied. "I called the Highway Control Authority, identified myself as Detective Lieutenant Orling, and requested some information. They were very cooperative. There were twenty-six robo-haulers headed in the right direction at the right time. I stopped seven of them before I found you."

"But why scare the heck out of us? We thought you were a bounty hunter."

"I *am* a bounty hunter."

"You know what I mean."

Della shrugged. "I didn't know who if anybody would be inside, and besides, you've been known to shoot first and ask questions later."

Lando grinned. He wanted to grab and hug her. "You are absolutely amazing."

The spaceport's security fence was just ahead. Della smiled as she applied the brakes. "I certainly am. And don't ever forget it."

They piled out of the car. Della had parked in the shadow cast by a large warehouse but they were still exposed. She popped the engine compartment and told Cap to stick his head under the hood. Considering their proximity to Blast Town, and the time of day, there was little chance of someone stopping to help.

Lando eyed the fence. He saw it was constructed of high-test metal mesh and boasted a force field too.

"How could we possibly cut through that?"

Della shook her head. "We won't. We go *over* it instead."

Lando looked again. Now he saw that if he stood on the car's roof his shoulders would be level with the top of the fence. Close, but no cigar. He'd have to jump about five feet straight up in order to clear the fence and get over it as well. The smuggler looked at Della.

"Nice try, but there's no way that I can jump that high, and even if I could, that would leave the rest of you here."

Della ignored him and spoke to Melissa instead. She pointed through the fence. "Do you see the hi-loader parked over there?"

Melissa looked, saw a bright orange piece of equipment, and nodded.

"Good. Could you operate it?"

Melissa's eyes lit up with excitement. "You bet! Daddy let me drive a flat-loader once . . . and I did very well."

Cap looked away. Lando winced. Melissa's father let her do lots of things when he was drunk, or too hung over to handle them himself. Flying the tender was a good example.

Della nodded understandingly. "All right then. Pik will throw you over. Watch your landing. It's a good eight- or nine-foot drop. That pile of cargo netting will cushion your fall."

"I can handle it," Melissa said confidently. "I've done more."

"No you haven't," Della replied sternly. "Not under anything like Earth-normal gravity. We're counting on you to land, start the hi-loader, and bring it over here. The whole plan goes down the tubes if you sprain an ankle. And once over, there's no way back."

Melissa nodded solemnly. "I'll be careful."

Della smiled and kissed the top of her head. "Atta girl. Okay, Pik. Climb up on the roof and get ready to boost Melissa over the top."

Lando raised an eyebrow, looked at the top of the fence, then looked at Melissa. She smiled brightly.

"I can do it, Pik, really I can."

Lando gave a reluctant nod, aimed a "this had better work" look at Della, and climbed onto the front of the car. It was easy to reach the roof from there. The car's duraplast skin gave slightly under his feet.

Della gave Melissa a hand. "Okay, hon. Up you go."

Melissa scampered up to stand next to Lando. The smuggler looked around. No traffic in sight. Good. Two people standing on the roof of a car was unusual even in Blast Town. He bent over and put his hands around Melissa's waist. It was frighteningly small.

"Here we go. Remember to bend your knees when you hit. Just like in free-fall. Roll if you have to."

The little girl nodded.

Lando lifted her over his head, gauged the distance, and gave a big push.

Melissa made it over the fence, fell straight down, and hit the cargo netting with a soft thump. It gave and she fell.

"Melissa! Are you all right?"

Lando smiled at the obvious concern in Della's voice. So much for the tough bounty hunter act.

Melissa stood and dusted herself off. "I'm fine, Della. Just lost my balance, that's all."

Della looked relieved. "That's okay, hon. Hurry now ... there's no telling what kind of alarms you may have triggered. Just because we can't see them doesn't mean they aren't there."

Melissa nodded, jumped off the netting, and ran toward the hi-loader. Four rungs led up to the cab. She stood on the third one and tried the door. Nothing. It was locked.

Della said something unladylike under her breath. She motioned for Melissa to return and pulled a small blaster from the top of her right boot.

A hideout! Lando shook his head in amusement as the blaster sailed over the fence. Della never ceased to amaze him.

"Use it on the door!"

Melissa nodded her understanding, scooped up the blaster, and returned to the cab. Though far from an expert with hand weapons the little girl had been around them all of her life.

Balancing on a metal rung, she aimed the weapon at the lock, and pressed the firing stud. Nothing. The safety! Gritting her teeth in frustration Melissa released the safety and tried again.

Her efforts were rewarded this time. A pencil-thin beam of bright blue light popped into existence. Sheet metal melted and ran like red-orange water. The door popped open.

Melissa slipped inside the cab, settled into the operator's chair, and thumbed the ignition switch. She grinned as the power plant came on-line and a row of idiot lights appeared in front of her. The "needs maintenance soon" light was on, but so what? Three minutes, five at most, and the task would be over.

Melissa slid the gear shift into the "forward" position and stepped on the accelerator. The hi-loader jerked into motion.

Cap heard a buzzing noise and looked over his left shoulder. The surveillance unit looked a lot like a flying tin can, except that this tin can was covered with a variety of sensors and boasted a rather large lens. The device had approached from the west and seemed completely unaware of Melissa's activities on the far side of the fence. It had witnessed Cap's pantomime of a break down and decided to investigate. The vid cam made a whirring noise as it zoomed in on the car's engine compartment.

Sorenson forced a smile. His heart beat like a trip-hammer and he wanted a drink. There was no way to tell if a real-live human being was monitoring the camera or not. Cap decided that it was better to be safe than sorry.

"Hi there. Glad you dropped by. Our car stalled." Sorenson pointed under the hood. "You know anything about cars?"

The distant observer triggered a spotlight, directed the beam into the engine compartment, and guided the security cam forward.

Cap smiled encouragingly. He couldn't believe his luck. The idiot was actually inspecting the engine! Now to see how long he could drag the whole thing out.

Unfortunately Melissa chose that particular moment to lose control of the hi-loader and crashed into the metal mesh. There was a flash of white-blue light followed by a secondary crash as she dropped the crane arm across the top of the fence. Sirens howled in the distance.

The security cam spun on its axis and tried to get away. Cap slammed the hood down on top of the device and trapped it inside the engine compartment.

Della waved. "Lando! Cap! Come on!"

Cap waved in acknowledgment, checked to make sure that the security cam couldn't escape, and ran for the fence. The car's duraplast hood cracked and dimpled as the surveillance unit tried to batter its way out.

Cap scrambled onto the car's hood, slipped, caught his balance, and made his way to the roof. There was a brand-new crevasse where the crane arm had landed. It made a foot-wide orange bridge across the top of the now-flickering fence to where the others waited.

Lando motioned with his arm. "Come on, Cap! There's nothing to it!"

Cap nodded weakly, put a foot on the makeshift bridge, and took a step forward. Metal creaked as the fence gave slightly and Sorenson felt something heavy hit the bottom of his stomach. A drink, God how he needed a drink. Nausea bubbled up from somewhere deep inside and he felt overwhelmingly dizzy.

"Come on, Daddy!"

Melissa. Melissa was watching. Cap swallowed the nausea and forced the dizziness away. He'd do it for Melissa. Carefully, placing one foot in front of the other, Sorenson made his way across to the other side. Lando was there to grab his arm and help him to the ground.

"Good going, Cap . . . you're looking good. Come on. Security's on the way."

The sirens were louder now, much louder, and were coming from every direction at once. They ran in a tight little group, away from the fence and toward the center of the spaceport.

Lando saw lights now, spotlights mounted on the undersides of air cars, coming from every point of the compass. There was no place to run. He stopped and the others did likewise.

"You see anything?" Della's voice was calm but tense. She stood with one hand on her slug gun.

Lando looked left and right. There was nothing but featureless duracrete as far as the eye could see. "Nope, not a damned thing."

Melissa's voice was small and matter-of-fact. "How 'bout the drain?"

Lando looked down at Melissa, then to the ground. And there, right under his feet, was a large circular grating. It was a storm drain designed to handle the massive volumes of water generated during the spring rains.

Lando jumped off the grating. "Nice going, Mel! You're a genius! Hey, Cap, give me a hand."

The grating weighed well over a hundred pounds, but with both men pulling at once, it came slowly upward. When the opening was large enough they stopped.

Lando braced himself. The sirens were even louder now and the lights were only seconds away. He tried to ignore them.

"Della, you first. Melissa, you're next. That's it. Quickly now. Okay, Cap. It's your turn. Can you hold it open for me?"

The older man gave a jerky nod, climbed into the hole, and balanced himself on a rung. Reaching upward, he accepted the grating's full weight.

Suddenly it was as if the whole world were pressing down on him. The grate felt as if it weighed a ton. Sorenson felt his right arm start to tremble and bit his lip.

When had it started? The mental-emotional slide that had left him here, a half man, trying to escape his own mistakes? At twenty? Thirty? Or had it been there all along? Like a flaw in poorly cast durasteel that caused it to crack when it was subjected to stress.

The weight eased. Lando's voice was loud in his right ear. "Okay, Cap. Gently now."

Ducking their heads the two men allowed the grating to move downward until it took over and fell the last five inches. It hit the metal surround with a loud clang. Then came the roar of an engine followed by a flood of white light. The light came down through the grate, rippled across Lando's face, and disappeared.

Five long minutes passed while the air cars crisscrossed the area, their spotlights wobbling across the ground, searching for the intruders. But none of the searchers showed any interest in the storm drain, or any of the storm drains for that matter, and activity gradually died down. Della's voice came from the blackness below.

"Come on, Pik. Let's go. The jobber won't wait forever."

Lando dropped down to join the rest of the group. He could sense rather than see them. "Anyone got a light?"

"How 'bout this?" A wand of blue light popped into existence. Melissa had retained the blaster that Della had thrown her. Adjusted to low power it made an effective though inefficient flashlight.

"Good," Della said approvingly. "But be careful where you aim that thing. It's dangerous even on low power."

So that's how they went, with Melissa leading the way, and a seemingly endless tunnel before them.

Size was no problem, since the tunnel was at least twelve feet across, but mud was. It covered the bottom of the conduit and touched its sides. Though not wet, it was moist, and clung to their feet.

Still clad in lightweight slip-ons Lando wished for boots and debated the merits of going barefoot. It was tempting because the shoes gathered the mud into huge clumps that made walking difficult, but there was always the chance of stepping on something sharp or jagged, so he kept them on.

The storm drain had a swampy smell, not strong enough to be unpleasant, but a reminder of where they were. Other than the smell, and an occasional grating overhead, the tunnel was very monotonous.

In fact the only feature of any interest whatsoever was a small pipe that hung suspended from the ceiling. Form frequently follows function, but this pipe looked like a pipe, and if it had some additional purpose gave no sign of what it was. Still, it was strange to see a pipe all by itself, since they're usually found in groups.

The next hour passed slowly. Lift one foot, put it down. Lift the other foot, put it down. Swear at the mud and start all over again. It went on and on until Lando's mind went numb. Della's voice brought him back.

"Watch out! There's something coming our way!"

But "watch" was all they could do. The thing was incredibly fast. Lando caught a glimpse of it up ahead. It hung suspended from the overhead pipe and was really moving. Whatever it was it had a single red light embedded in its nose. The light rotated like a beacon. The walls shimmered scarlet. The device made a whining sound as it flashed over their heads and disappeared behind them.

Melissa voiced the question on all of their minds. "What was that?"

"Some sort of surveillance unit," Della guessed. "Although a poor one. How could it miss us?"

"I don't think it did," Lando put in. "My guess is that it's programmed to detect and report structural problems and storm damage. We fell outside its areas of concern."

"Maybe," Cap said, examining one mud-caked foot, "but I'm in favor of climbing out of here. The surveillance unit might have reported us and we've gone far enough besides."

Della nodded, one half of her face dark, the other lit with a blue glow. "Cap's right. Let's take the next exit."

They plodded along for another ten minutes before a vertical drain came along. Lando went first, with Cap close behind him. The smuggler looked up through the grating and saw the first glimmerings of daylight.

He bent his knees, placed a shoulder under the metal covering, and pushed. Nothing. Lando swore, gathered his strength, and tried again. Something gave and the grating popped open. He felt Cap move up beside him to take some of the weight.

"On three," the older man said, "and to hell with the noise. One . . . two . . . three!"

They heaved in unison and the grating made a loud clang as it fell to the pavement. Lando was the first one out. His head swiveled right and left. Nothing. This particular grating was located right between a pair of large fuel tanks. Everything else was a long ways off. The chances of being seen were very slim.

Lando and Cap replaced the grating so it wouldn't call attention to itself and followed Della toward the merchant ships. They were a full mile away. A dull rumble filled the air as a freighter lifted off the tarmac and moved toward a lift zone.

Lando caught up with Della. "We look rather obvious out here."

Della sighed. She knew that as well as he did. The problem was locating a suitable disguise. How do you turn a little girl into something else anyway?

"Yes, we do. Don't tell me, let me guess. Your father had a saying for situations like this."

Lando grinned. "Why yes he did. 'Instead of wandering around spaceports call a jitney.' "

"Do what?"

Lando pointed to a bright green com pedestal located right next to a bright red fire-fighting station. "Call a jitney."

Della laughed. It was so obvious she'd missed it. The spaceport was so vast, and the distances between things so large, that a fleet of automated jitneys were required to ferry people around. She grabbed Lando's arm and gave him a peck on the cheek.

"You're not so stupid after all. No wonder I keep you around."

Lando smiled. "Hmmm. And I thought I kept *you* around."

Della made the call and a beat-up jitney arrived ten minutes later. It consisted of little more than some seats, a platform, and a set of six wheels. Della tried a voice command, found that the machine's voice-recognition sub-processor was belly up, and tapped her request into the simple keyboard. It felt good to ride instead of walk.

The jitney made a beeline for the merchant ships, passed row F where the tender still sat under the destroyer's scrutiny, and headed for row Y.

Row Y was farthest from the terminal and therefore least expensive. Most of the ships in row Y were clapped-out tramp freighters, reentry-scarred tankers, and low-key private vessels.

The ship parked in Slot 78 appeared worst than most. She was, or had been, a Lorney Lifter. Pretty good hulls more than two hundred years before but long outmoded. She reminded Lando of *The Tinker's Damn*, his first ship and part of a happier past.

The jitney stopped and Della paid it off.

"They oughta pay *us* to ride in that thing," Cap complained, but was careful to keep his voice low.

"It does look a little beat," Lando admitted, "but you never know. In my old line of business it paid to understate the condition of your ship."

The main hatch slid open before Della could palm the lock. An elderly woman stood framed in the opening. She was rail-thin, had a slightly hooked nose, and thin critical lips. Her light blue pressure suit hung around her in folds.

"Well, it's about time. The authorities want you bad. The price went up. Double what I told you. Take it or leave it."

Della answered. "We'll take it."

The woman put her hands on skinny hips. "Good. I want cash."

Della shook her head. "We don't have cash. But we do have more than enough in credits. You can check. First Bank of Pylax."

The woman gave a snort of derision. "What if they freeze your assets?"

Lando stepped forward. He looked her in the eye. "Then you're shit out of luck."

There was silence for a moment as the woman looked Lando up and down. An unexpected smile lit up her face. The hardness disappeared. "I like this one. He's got a nose just like mine. Where the hell were you when I was young? Let's lift."

The lift-off took place without incident. After that it was a simple matter to clear the planet's gravity well and head for the vast asteroid belt that floated toward the edge of the system.

Like all asteroid belts this one was a dangerous place to go. Over time the gravitational pull exerted by the system's larger planets caused asteroids to collide. The collisions created even more asteroids, and so forth, in an endless cycle.

Still, the asteroids had valuable minerals to offer, so miners went in after them. Small companies mostly, but individuals too, hardy types who were willing to risk everything on the possibility of a really big find.

This asteroid belt was unique in that the miners had established a system of twenty-seven "gates," or points of entry, where conditions were fairly stable and beacons had been placed. The beacons allowed the miners to orient themselves as they went into the belt, and more than that, helped them to navigate once they were inside.

For years Cap had used business trips into the belt to search for his one-time liner *Star of Empire*, as though in finding her, he would find himself.

And that's how they'd stumbled over the alien drifter, a find more valuable than the *Star*, but one that was difficult to cash in.

It took four days to make the trip from Pylax to the belt, four days that, if not exactly pleasant, were made more bearable by their rather eccentric captain. She was a competent ship's master, a great cook, and one helluva storyteller.

Her name was Edna Edith Rogers, and she'd been in space for more than forty years, starting as an assistant power tech and working her way up to master.

A lot of interesting and sometimes funny things had happened during that forty years, and each one had been crafted into a well-told story.

It seemed that Captain Edna had been married to a wonderfully crazy man named Harry, had made and lost three different fortunes, and had accumulated a dozen college degrees, including ones in such wildly different subjects as law, xeno-biology, accounting, and home economics.

And so it was that Lando found himself eating freshly baked coffee cake, laughing at Captain Edna's stories, and worrying at the same time. They had escaped from Pylax but were far from free. Somehow, thanks to his troubles with the law and

Cap's drunken chatter, their situation had gone from bad to worse.

What good is an alien drifter if you can't sell it? And if you did manage to sell it what about the attention that would generate?

These questions and many more went unanswered as the days passed and the belt approached. Under normal conditions they would have been extremely reluctant to provide the drifter's coordinates. In this case, however, they had very little choice. They planned to move the ship the moment that Captain Edna was gone. They'd already moved her once, and there was no reason to think they couldn't do it again. True, they had a tug the first time out, but they knew more about the ship now, and Lando felt sure that it would obey their commands.

The drifter was hidden just inside the edge of the belt a few hundred miles sunward of gate sixteen. Lando watched the asteroids as Captain Edna conned her ship past the gate and skimmed the edge of the belt. They were beautiful in their own way—ancient chunks of rock and metal, tumbling along, their roughly textured surfaces rotating through the sunlight.

Any other ship might've been in grave danger from the asteroids but not the drifter. It had spent hundreds, maybe even thousands of years inside the belt, all without so much as a scratch. So far as they knew anyway.

No, the ship had defenses against asteroids, and these became rather apparent as Captain Edna guided her vessel between the outermost roids and open space.

The control room was rather small, with barely enough room for Lando in the co-pilot's seat, and Della behind. Row upon row of indicator lights glowed green, amber, and red, and lit Edna's face from below.

In spite of her passengers' previous descriptions, the jobber was surprised by what she saw.

The drifter was long, longer than the largest liner that Edna had ever seen, and twice as big around. Not only that, but it was slightly luminescent, as if lit from within.

And where human ships would have surface installations like weapons blisters, antenna arrays, and solar panels, this one had large green blobs. They clung to the hull like clumps of fungi. As Edna watched she saw one of them detach itself and race outward to touch a nearby asteroid.

That's what it looked like anyway, but her passengers assured the jobber that the "touch" had force behind it, enough force to keep the asteroids away and create its own safety zone.

Then another blob shot forth, only this one came straight at her ship, and hit with a considerable amount of force. The ship rocked back and forth and some alarms went off.

Captain Edna looked worried. "Will it push us away?"

Lando shook his head. "No, it's checking us out. Watch what happens next."

Green light flooded the control room. It paused, slid the length of the ship, and disappeared.

Captain Edna looked at her readouts. There was nothing but snow. "That light came through solid durasteel!"

Lando smiled. "Scary, isn't it?"

Edna glanced at the screens again. "It sure is. But beautiful too. No wonder they want you. That thing's worth millions."

Lando checked the woman's expression, saw a sense of wonderment, and nodded his head. "Yes, millions or more. May I use your comset?"

"Sure, help yourself."

Lando touched some buttons. "This is Pik Lando. My companions and I wish to come aboard."

Captain Edna shook her head in amazement. "It speaks standard?"

Lando shrugged. "Understands it anyway. My guess is that it understands Finthian too, and any other language that can be translated into electronic form."

Both watched as a green blob separated itself from the ship, raced outward, and enclosed their ship. Green light filled the cabin. The drifter got bigger as the blob drew them inward. A voice came over the comset.

"Pik? Cap? You read me? This is Cy."

Captain Edna raised an eyebrow and looked at Lando.

"The fifth member of our crew," Lando explained. He touched a button. "Hi, Cy. How's it going?"

"Fairly well," the cyborg answered hesitantly, "but we need to talk. There could be a problem."

"We're on the way," Lando replied. "I'll see you in a few minutes. Lando out."

The drifter became larger and larger until it overflowed the screens. Then it was gone and they were inside the alien ship.

Captain Edna deployed the ship's landing jacks and there was a gentle bump as they touched down. The viewscreens were completely dark.

Lando stood and held out his hand. "Well, thanks for the ride. You're one helluva pilot, a great cook, and the finest storyteller this side of Sol."

Captain Edna's hand was dry and firm. "And you're the finest group of criminals I ever encountered!"

Lando and Della laughed. Edna's expression turned serious. "Tell me something."

"Yes?"

Captain Edna gestured toward the main lock. "What's next?"

Lando shrugged. "I don't know. Find a place to sell her I guess."

"Are you willing to sell her to the Il Ronnians?"

Lando and the others had already discussed that question. Of all the intelligent races man had encountered among the stars only the Il Ronn offered a serious threat. Not because they were more intelligent or more capable than the other races but because only they had the same driving ambition.

The Il Ronn had preceded man into space by thousands of years. But theirs was a cautious and methodical culture in which important decisions were reached through consensus. The result was an empire that expanded in a slow methodical manner.

In the meantime the human empire had grown in magnificent fits and starts. Periods of tremendous expansion had resulted in gains that would've taken the Il Ronnians hundreds or even thousands of years to achieve. All too often however these advances were lost through internal bickering, competition, or just plain laziness. The result was two empires of roughly equal power, each seeking to better the other, each skirting the precipice of war.

So, to give the Il Ronnians an artifact like the drifter would be to give them a technological edge that could destroy the empire. And while the empire had a lot of faults, it was better than slavery. They had all concurred.

Lando shook his head. "No, we'd destroy her first."

The jobber nodded. "Just as I thought. So that leaves the human empire. First place you go, they'll grab you, take the drifter, and dump you on some prison planet."

"True," Della responded, "but what can we do?"

Captain Edna looked at each of them in turn. "Tell me something. How much would it be worth to you if someone could cut you a deal, a *real* deal, one with guarantees, that allowed you to sell the drifter and walk away scot free?"

Lando looked at Della, then back again. "Ten percent."

Captain Edna's hand shot out. "I could probably get more, but ten percent of a few hundred million is a lot, especially for this old lady. You've got yourselves an agent! Give me a tape to that effect, plus your thumbprints on a standard salvage contract, and I'll go to work."

It took about fifteen minutes to make the tape and thumbprint the necessary document, Cap was more than a little resentful about their failure to consult him, but chose to let it go, knowing they could easily blame him for the whole situation.

Captain Edna saw them to the main hatch. "Can you communicate with Pylax?"

Lando shrugged. "Probably."

"Good. I have an electronic mailbox there. Give it a call one standard week from now."

Lando agreed, shook her hand, and followed the others through the lock. Sensing their presence the drifter flooded the bay with greenish light. By the time they cleared the area a green blob was forming around the ship. They watched as the ship seemed to snap out of existence. There was a pop of equalizing pressure and a loud exclamation as Cy squirted himself into the bay.

"The ship! Where did the ship go? Bring it back!"

Lando looked puzzled. "It took off. What's the problem?"

The deck seemed to shift beneath his feet. A familiar nausea entered his gut. A hyperspace shift! The drifter had gone FTL. But that couldn't be. Could it?

Lando looked at Cy. The others did likewise. The cyborg sagged to a lower altitude. "The problem? You want to know what the problem is? We're in hyperspace, that's what the problem is . . . and I don't have the faintest idea where we're going!"

8

The Il Ronnian Sand Sept trooper stood on a low wall. He was tall and his long spindly legs ended in cloven hooves. His skin was leathery and hairless where it showed around his uniform. Eons before its reddish hue had provided his ancestors with protective coloration on a world of red sand. The trooper's eyes were almost invisible within the shadow cast by a prominent supra-orbital ridge. He had long pointy ears and a tail with a triangular appendage on the end. It rose to shade his eyes from the sun.

Beyond the trooper, higher up on the opposite hillside, Wexel-15 could see another crew hard at work looting a museum. When younger the heavy had spent many happy rals in the museum staring at the perfectly preserved life-forms displayed there and wondering where they came from. Everyone knew that the Lords had occupied many worlds. But where were they? And what were they like?

The trooper saw that Wexel-15 was idle and frowned. His voice boomed through the translator that hung round his neck. "Hurry up, slave. I haven't got all day!"

Wexel-15 processed the alien's words and was just about to speak when the Il Ronnian drew his arm back and brought it forward with lightning speed. The whip was fifteen feet long. It made a loud cracking sound as it came down across Wexel-15's back. The pain was incredible, but outside of an involuntary grunt, he gave no sign of it. To do so would pleasure the Il Ronnian work master and this he refused to do.

Like all of his kind Wexel-15 had a blocky frame that was heavily layered with muscle. It rippled and bunched under the surface of his lavender skin. He wanted to grab the alien, wanted to rip his arms off, but knew better than to try. Other members of his caste had attacked the Sand Sept troopers and their bodies hung upside down in the main square.

The lights said to wait, said that the time would come, but Wexel-15 had his doubts. The lights might be more intelligent than the heavies, but they were intellectually constipated as well, and had a tendency to dither rather than act.

The truth was that no one knew much about the Il Ronnians— except that they had dropped out of the sky, enslaved the population, and systematically stolen everything in sight. And were still at it. The Lords had known many things and the Il Ronnians wanted that knowledge.

God was surely displeased but had yet to express that anger. And what, outside of divine intervention, could stop them?

So Wexel-15 did as he was told, nodded obediently when the Sand Sept trooper told him to return in four rals, and joined the other heavies as they streamed down toward the temple below. Already stripped of the life murals that had once graced its walls, and defaced with illegible alien graffiti, the temple stood as a mute reminder of how helpless they were.

A shadow passed over him and Wexel-15 knew without looking that it was an Il Ronnian flying machine. Ominous things that hovered over the work parties, patrolled the streets, or simply sat while their weapons probed the air for enemies.

Wexel-15 joined the line that snaked toward the temple's entrance. A light stood in front of him. She was slender like all of her kind and a good four inches taller than Wexel-15. She had six fingers instead of his four and wore a long flowing cloak.

The female was subtle about it, but Wexel-15 noticed the care with which she separated herself from both him and the heavy directly in front of her. Lights avoided physical contact with heavies whenever they could. They claimed it was part of their basic programming but the heavies didn't believe it.

Wexel-15 moved closer and watched her shoulders tense.

The line moved in fits and starts, halting occasionally when someone crowded in, then starting again. Finally, after ten laks or so, Wexel-15 approached the entrance. A male light, his skin glowing pink, held a tray.

The female light paused, took one of hundreds of shiny black disks from the tray, and pressed it to her forehead. It stayed as if glued in place. She moved ahead.

Wexel-15 took her place, selected a disk, and slapped it into place.

The door was tall and thin like those who had designed it. Though the light in front of him entered without difficulty the door frame brushed both of Wexel-15's massive shoulders.

He entered an enormous room. Row upon row of ornate benches filled the hall. The lights were bunched together toward the front of the room with heavies pressed in all around them. The lights were visibly annoyed.

Wexel-15 felt no desire to participate in the game and chose the nearest seat. His back hurt where it pressed against cold stone. The injury mattered very little. The pain and all signs of tissue damage would be gone by tomorrow.

The lights referred to the building as a "temple" but no one knew what it was for sure. The Lords had been fond of grandiose architecture and it was hard to tell which structures had been important and which were overdecorated.

But God had been known to speak within this particular building, when he felt like it, which was very seldom. The last pronouncement had come seventeen dars ago, long before the alien invasion, and had concerned itself with impending geological activity in the southern hemisphere.

The entire population of lights and heavies had been evacuated from that region and many versions had been saved. The ensuing earthquakes had destroyed much of city twelve and most of city thirteen. Now both castes came to gathering after gathering, uncertain about what to do, hoping for divine guidance.

Fifteen laks passed before a wizened old light appeared, held up his hands, and delivered the traditional invocation.

"We are constructs, Lord, and seek your guidance. Speak to us that we might know your will and act accordingly."

God came with a powerful suddenness. Wexel-15 felt himself transported as waves of pleasure rippled through his body. The sensation was like that of an orgasm only much more powerful. It lasted for an entire lak. Then it was gone and the voice of God flowed into their minds.

"Greetings, constructs. Listen carefully for there is little time. The invaders have the means to detect our communications and are headed this way. My instructions are as follows:

"As with evil, salvation shall fall from the sky, and wear strange skins. Take salvation into your homes and ask for guidance. But know this: Nothing comes from nothing and the slowest shall lead."

God's words still echoed in Wexel-15's head when fifteen or twenty Sand Sept troopers poured into the hall and took up positions along the walls. There was silence for a moment. Then Wexel-15 heard a rustling toward the back of the room and turned to see what caused it.

The Il Ronnian leader, and given the deference shown him there was little doubt about his status, was smaller than most members of his race. He wore the long red cape of the Ilwik, or warrior-priest, and a uniform under that. He paused for a moment, allowed his eyes to roam the audience, and walked toward the front of the hall. His hooves made a clacking sound on the ancient pavement.

The Il Ronnian stopped next to a female heavy, pried the disk off her forehead, and held it up to the light. The device glittered with reflected light as he turned it this way and that. His voice boomed through the translator that rode perched on his left shoulder.

"And what have we here? A silly bauble, empty of all meaning, or something more significant?"

The Il Ronnian did something with his thumb and the disk flipped end over end to land in an alert noncom's hand.

"Check on it, Reeg. I will want a full report."

Reeg signaled assent with his tail and tucked the disk into his belt pouch.

The alien took three steps up onto the low stage, turned to face his audience, and clasped his hands behind his back.

"Always take the high ground" is an ancient military axiom familiar to soldiers of every race. But it had special meaning for Teex. Even as a youngster his playmates had called him "Shorty" and he never missed an opportunity to even things up.

"I am Quarter Sept Commander Teex." His eyes gleamed as he surveyed the crowd. "Which one of you will tell me what this is all about?"

Silence.

Teex rocked back and forth. His hooves ground against the pavement. "I see. Well, we have ways to handle situations like this. Trooper Leev!"

One of the troopers who lined the walls raised his weapon and aimed it at the audience. Wexel-15 saw a red circle appear on the male seated directly in front of him. It illuminated the entire right side of the construct's head.

Teex pointed at him. His finger quivered slightly. "Speak! Why are you here?"

Maybe a light would've known what to say, and thought fast enough to say it, but the heavy never stood a chance. He had just started to generate a response when the high-velocity slug hit the side of his head, passed through it, and killed the construct seated on his left as well.

Blood and brain tissue exploded in every direction. Some of it splattered onto Wexel-15's face.

He never did know why he did what he did, and could never remember a conscious decision to do it, but Wexel-15 stood, uttered a roar of outrage, and charged. Benches went down and constructs fell. Wexel-15 was determined to reach Trooper Leev and crush all life from his body. He never made it.

Other heavies rose around him, their roars of outrage echoing his, and took the bullets directed at him.

The Sand Sept troopers opened up with automatic weapons. Dozens of heavies stumbled and fell. But others rose to fill the gaps and the Il Ronnians staggered under a wall of solid flesh.

The aliens were skilled in a martial art called "Infala," or "personal death," but the heavies weighed three hundred pounds apiece and were unbelievably strong. Weapons fell silent as flesh thudded against flesh, bones cracked, and alien screams filled the air.

Then, just as suddenly as it had started, the battle was over. Teex and his personal bodyguard had withdrawn, bodies lay everywhere, and dazed constructs stood looking around. A full lak passed in silence. An elderly heavy named Lebar-6 was the first to speak.

"What shall we do now?"

A light named Issara-22 answered. She was tall, slender, and almost regal in the way that she held herself. "The aliens will be angry. Those who took part in the killing must surrender themselves for the greater good. The rest have nothing to fear."

There was a moment of silence while the heavies processed that. They were slow, but it didn't take very much intelligence to realize that while most of the heavies had taken part in the battle, none of the lights had.

Lebar-6 spoke once again. He ignored Issara-22's comment as though it had never been spoken. "Wexel-15 led us. What does he say?"

Wexel-15 was surprised to have the mantle of leadership thrust upon him, but had been thinking of what to do, and the words tumbled out.

"We have learned something here. The aliens die just as we do. Go to the country. Hide. Wait for instructions."

Issara-22 raised her voice in protest, and other lights did likewise, but to no avail.

Within seconds the heavies had streamed out into the gathering darkness and disappeared.

When Teex returned with a hundred heavily armed Sand Sept troopers, the lights were still there, discussing how stupid the heavies were and professing their innocence.

Teex ordered them to remove the Il Ronnian dead and prepare their bodies for burial. The lights were unused to such heavy labor but obeyed nonetheless. The aliens were understandably angry and some form of punishment was to be expected.

Then, when the constructs had finished and were lined up before him, Teex shot them. He used his own handgun and did it one at a time. Their bodies were hung upside down in the square for all to see.

Wexel-15 didn't know it yet . . . but he had declared war on the entire Il Ronnian empire.

9

Lando awoke to the pitter-patter of rain on his face. Just a drop or two at first but that soon changed. Suddenly the rain came down hard and fast, soaking his blanket and flooding the mossy growth that served as his mattress.

They'd been in hyperspace for five days now, and with the exception of Cy, the rest of them slept in the drifter's nest-beds. Lando's was located within a grove of the strange two-trunked trees only a foot or so from Della's. He sat up, wiped rain from his face, and looked around.

"What the heck's going on?"

Della was in the process of getting up. Her hair was wet and hung in dark ringlets around her face. She pointed off to one side. "I don't know . . . but look at that!"

Lando looked, saw an empty nest-bed, and didn't understand what Della meant until he realized that this one was completely dry! The rainstorm was confined to an area about twelve by twelve feet in size!

Della stood, stepped away from her bed, and held her hands palms up. Nothing. She looked at Lando and raised an eyebrow.

The smuggler rolled to his knees and stood. The rain stopped.

There was a rustling sound and Cap appeared. His clothes were soaked and he was clearly annoyed. "What's going on around here?"

Lando smoothed wet hair into place and tightened his ponytail. "My thoughts exactly. Did the rain seem to concentrate on your beds?"

Melissa appeared from behind her father. She wore a big

grin. "It sure did! Weird, huh? What does it mean?"

What indeed? Lando looked around. Tendrils of vapor floated up from the recently dampened ground. He shrugged.

"I don't know. Unless it's the ship's way of getting our attention. Let's find Cy and see if he knows what's going on."

The others nodded their agreement and followed Lando back toward the control room. Cy had been trying to reestablish communications with the drifter ever since their unexpected departure. But the ship couldn't or wouldn't reply.

The others had been angry with the cyborg at first, chiding him for the experiments that led to their present predicament, and using him as an outlet for their considerable frustration.

Cap had been especially upset, pointing out that the drifter had been their only source of leverage, and the only thing of value they had left.

But leverage and money didn't seem quite so important anymore. Larger issues confronted them now. Like where was the ship taking them? Could they find a way to get off? And how would they return from wherever they were?

Besides, it was hard to stay mad at the little cyborg for very long. He was so sorry, and so miserable, that even Cap was forced to accept his apologies.

"Pik! Look!"

Lando turned. The forest was almost completely dark. Whatever planet the biosphere was modeled on, assuming there was one, had enjoyed long days and short nights. Nights during which it never became truly dark. Now almost total darkness had fallen over the forest. Why?

Della met Lando's eye. "Something or somebody wants us to leave."

Lando shrugged. "Not too subtle, huh? Well, we wanted to get off. This could be our chance."

"Yeah," Cap put in. "But how? We were in hyperspace last I heard."

The momentary nausea came right on cue, as if the ship were listening and had reacted to Cap's words.

The humans paused to look at each other. "I don't like this," Della said, her hand straying to the slug gun at her waist.

"Neither do I," Lando agreed. "Come on. The darkness is closing in on us."

They walked faster and darkness nipped at their heels. It had edged around the group by now, and slid along both sides, so that a tunnel of light led them toward the lock. They entered and the hatch closed behind them.

It took two minutes for the lock to cycle open. Cy was waiting for them. He bobbed up and down with worry and concern.

"There you are! Thank Sol! I tried to come after you but the ship wouldn't let me. I couldn't get the lock to open."

Lando nodded. "Yeah, we ran into the same sort of thing. It seems as if we have B O or something. Have you got any idea what's going on? We felt a hyperspace shift a few moments ago."

"Really?" Cy had gained some additional senses along with his artificial body but lost others as well. And the moment of nausea that most people felt while entering or leaving hyperspace was one of them. "I'll try the interface again. Maybe it'll work this time."

The cyborg squirted himself over to the black globe that he had previously identified as the drifter's NAVCOMP, extruded a pincer, and allowed it to sink through the glossy surface.

All his most recent attempts to establish contact with the ship had ended in failure. A part of him expected this one to fail as well. It didn't.

Suddenly and without warning Cy *was* the ship. He *knew* the vessel had entered normal space, *knew* the drifter was headed for the nearest planet, and *knew* hostile ships would try to intercept him.

They came in hard and fast, twelve delta-shaped interceptors of Il Ronnian design, unsure of who or what the drifter was, but determined to take control of it.

Cy felt himself bombarded with messages. They came in dozens of languages and all of them said the same thing. "Kill power, neutralize weapons systems, and wait to be boarded."

The drifter understood but made no attempt to respond. Green blobs lashed out from the hull, hit the interceptors like giant sledgehammers, and batted them away.

The surviving interceptors fired as larger ships moved in and did likewise. Missiles, torpedoes, and computer-controlled bombs struck the blobs and exploded with little or no effect.

Cy winced as the drifter lashed out in response. A pair of

blobs grabbed an Il Ronnian destroyer and broke it in half. Fire blossomed, then disappeared.

"What's going on?" Lando's voice came from far, far away. It was hard to be the ship and explain things at the same time. Cy did the best he could.

"You were right about the hyperspace shift. I have data on our position but don't understand what it means. We're surrounded by Il Ronnian warships. They ordered us to stop but the drifter ignored them. Some interceptors attacked but the blobs beat 'em back. Damn . . . there goes a destroyer! The blobs broke it in half.

"We're heading toward what looks like an Earth-normal planet. That's our destination. I don't know *how* I know, but I know. Wait a minute, the interface is fading and the ship is pushing me out!"

Cy pulled his pincer out of the black globe and bobbed up and down apologetically. "Sorry."

"It wasn't your fault," Lando said thoughtfully. "The ship has a purpose now. It wants us to know about some things and not about others."

Della nodded in agreement. "So, what's next?"

Lando looked around almost expecting the ship to answer but it didn't. Seconds turned into minutes, minutes into an hour, and hours into the better part of a day.

They were trapped in the control room. Repeated attempts to leave had proved that, so some caught up on previously interrupted sleep, and the others killed time any way they could. Lando was asleep when Della shook his arm.

"Pik . . . look."

The control room was filled with eerie green light. It grew stronger with each passing second.

"How long has it been here?"

"Five, maybe ten seconds."

Lando got to his feet. "I have a bad feeling about this." He gestured to Cap, Melissa, and Cy. "Come on, everybody. Get into the center of the room. Let's hold hands."

Della gave him a curious look but did as he requested. They formed a ring and held each other's hands or, in Cy's case, pincers.

The greenish light thickened around them until they couldn't see beyond it. Then it swirled and the floor dropped out from under them. Their senses told them they were falling yet nothing seemed to move. Melissa looked scared and bit her lip.

Lando swallowed and forced a smile. "Don't worry, hon. We're inside one of those green blobs. There's nothing to worry about. We'll be dirtside in a few seconds."

That's what I hope anyway, Lando thought to himself, unless this is the ship's way of ejecting unwanted debris. In which case we'll turn inside out the moment the blob disappears.

But the blob *didn't* disappear. Not until something hard materialized under their feet and the greenish light began to fade.

Yellow sunlight flooded around them, strange odors filled their nostrils, and foreign sounds assailed their ears.

"Holy Sol." Cap uttered the words softly like a prayer.

Lando knew what the older man meant. The blob had put them down in the middle of a city, or more accurately a village, because it was small and occupied the top of a low hill. The smuggler could see where the whitewashed buildings left off and the fields began.

The place had a strange feel, not primitive exactly, but not high-tech either. Maybe it was the round, almost quaint stone houses, mixed with motorized vehicles, streetlights, and agrobots.

There were people around them, humanoids anyway, who looked as dumbfounded as they felt. All had lavender-colored skin, four-fingered hands, and bald heads. They were muscular and built low to the ground. They looked like a race of weight lifters. What he assumed were males tended toward craggy brows, massive shoulders, and short, muscular legs. Most wore little more than shorts and sandals.

The females, and they seemed obviously female, had the same low foreheads but more rounded faces. They wore brightly colored saronglike dresses that covered them from chest to midthigh.

Children ran here and there, screamed with excitement, and gabbled things in a language that he'd never heard before.

Though different from each other the humanoids looked similar as well, as if they all belonged to the same family. The adults seemed curious rather than scared and talked excitedly among themselves.

Lando stepped forward. "Does anyone speak standard?"

A male, this one older than the rest, stepped forward to meet him. He gestured toward the center of the village and said something the smuggler couldn't understand.

Lando started to smile, remembered that bared teeth can be interpreted in a lot of different ways, and settled for a nod instead.

The smuggler was just about to try universal sign language when the crowd parted and another being appeared. This individual was unlike the villagers in every way.

She was tall, slender, and pink. Not white-pink, but pink-pink, like a neon sign. She had large eyes, a long, narrow face, and wore a cloak that rippled in the breeze.

A leader perhaps? Some sort of official? There was no way to be sure.

The female looked around, said something to the elderly male, and nodded at his reply. Though unlike anything Lando had seen before her sign language was clear enough. She pointed to the sky and then to Lando.

"You came from the sky?"

Lando repeated her motions and added a nod.

"Yes."

Though unsure of her facial expressions Lando thought she was more pleased than surprised. What did that mean? Were green blobs a common occurrence? Did visitors arrive all the time?

The female pointed to the sky, made hard jabbing motions with her index finger, and drew an imaginary circle around the humans.

Lando turned to Della. "I missed that one. Any ideas?"

"I think she means combat," Della answered. "She's asking if the Il Ronnians attacked us."

Lando raised an eyebrow. It didn't seem all that clear to him, but anything was possible, so he delivered a formal nod.

"Yes."

The female bowed. She turned and spoke to the crowd. Although Lando didn't understand a single word of what she said, there was a commanding quality to the way she said it, and a sense of urgency as well. And the way that the villagers hurried off served to reinforce that impression.

The female waved an arm. The meaning was obvious. "Come with me."

Lando looked at the others. Della nodded, Cap shrugged, and Cy bobbed up and down. Melissa was using sign language to communicate with a peer. The other child was inspecting her hair.

"Hey, Mel."

"Yes?"

"We're leaving."

"Okay." Melissa signed something to her friend. The other little girl smiled shyly, bobbed her head, and ran away.

Lando filed it away. Smiles were okay.

Melissa ran to catch up. She took her father's hand. "That was Lela-17. Pretty, isn't she?"

Cap nodded dutifully and Lando smiled. If only grown-ups could make friends as easily as children did.

The female led them out of the village and into the fields. She walked so fast that Melissa had to jog in order to keep up. Why? It was as if the female knew that some kind of trouble was on the way.

The crops were richly green, small bushes mostly, that bore brightly colored berries. They grew in surveyor-straight rows and were drip irrigated. Miles of clear plastic tubing stretched in every direction.

Lando found that interesting since it implied long dry spells and a certain level of technological sophistication.

They had gone a mile, maybe two, when Lando heard a low rumble. It came from the east. Lando looked and saw four black specks. Aerospace fighters or something very similar. The Il Ronnians had tracked the green blob all the way to the ground and sent aircraft to investigate!

Their guide reacted before Lando could. She waved her arms, spoke rapidly, and herded them into the nearest field. The soil gave slightly under their feet. Lando noticed that the bushes had a rich spicy smell.

The female said something urgent and gestured toward a wooden platform. The message was clear. "Move this, and move it fast."

Lando and Melissa took one side with Della and Cap on the other. The female made no effort to help.

The planes were louder now and Lando remembered his

earlier thoughts. The female had known the Il Ronn were on the way. Was that simply a good guess? Or something a good deal more?

Della took command. "On three. One, two, and three!" The platform was heavy but manageable. It came away from the ground suddenly as if it hadn't been moved for a long, long time. A host of insects scurried for cover.

A vertical shaft was revealed. The top portion of a ladder could be seen. The female pointed emphatically downward.

Cap went first, followed by Melissa, Della, Cy, and Lando.

The female came last. Like Cap, Della, and Lando, she used every other rung of the ladder, which suggested that it had been constructed by and for the villagers.

Regardless of that, her descent afforded Lando a glimpse of some long shapely legs. His smile disappeared when he turned to find Della watching him with an amused smile. He coughed and looked the other way.

The ladder rested on a gallery that ran the length of the tunnel. Thousands of footsteps had beaten it hard and flat.

The tunnel was well engineered. It was fifteen or twenty feet in diameter, arrow-straight, and reinforced with sturdy beams. Lando touched one and encountered metal rather than wood. Another interesting discovery. The villagers, or if not them, then whoever had constructed the tunnel, built things to last.

A stream ran along the very bottom of the tunnel. It made gurgling sounds and was the source of water for the fields above.

There was a series of dull thumps and the ground shook. Bombs? Lando thought about the villagers and hoped they were okay.

The female said something and waved them on. They followed her into a sort of murky twilight. Looking ahead, Lando saw evenly spaced pools of light that marched away to vanish in the distance. Someone had used arrays of cleverly angled mirrors to bring sunlight down from the surface. More evidence of technological sophistication.

But by whom? The villagers? Something about their dress and behavior made that seem unlikely. The female? Or others like her? Possibly . . . but why so helpless in the face of Il Ronnian aggression? There were lots of questions and very few answers.

They walked for the better part of three hours. During that time Lando saw little that was new. Oh, there were some cave-ins that needed repair, some pumps that forced water up to the surface, but very little else. Just tunnel, tunnel, and more tunnel. The fact that it was arrow-straight made the trip even more tiresome.

Melissa took turns riding on Lando's and Della's shoulders.

Cy took to skimming the surface of the water, scouting ahead, and exploring side tunnels to break the monotony. If the cyborg's actions troubled their guide, she gave no sign of it and continued to move ahead.

Finally, just when Lando had concluded that the journey would never end, the tunnel became wider and ended in a large cavern. A double set of mirrors brought light down from the surface. Other tunnels ended there as well. They came in from every direction like the spokes of a wheel. He saw that water could be channeled from one aqueduct to another by means of sluice gates.

The female led them around the machinery that occupied the center of the cavern, over a footbridge, and down into a rough and ready living area. Lando supposed that the room was for the convenience of the work crew who maintained the tunnels.

It consisted of earthen walls, a hard-packed floor, and a trestle table loaded with food. Lando's stomach gave a hearty grumble and he felt very hungry. It had been a long time since his last box of E-rations aboard ship.

Ten or twelve mismatched chairs had been placed around the table. Two were occupied. Both beings got to their feet. One was tall and slender like their guide, the other short and stocky like the villagers.

The taller of the two was handsome in a long-faced ascetic way. But his eyes hid more than they showed and there was something hard and unyielding about the way that he held himself.

The shorter individual was a male with wide-set eyes, a broadly handsome face, and a muscular body. An Il Ronnian translator hung around his neck. He removed the device and let it dangle from a work-roughened finger.

"I am unused to this machine. Greetings and welcome. Do you understand my words?"

The smuggler moved closer to the translator. "Yes," he replied carefully, "I do. And I would like to thank you for the hospitality and protection provided by your people."

There was a pause as if the other being was processing Lando's words. The smile came slowly. "Your words are kind, but since we have provided little more than a tour of our irrigation canals, we cannot accept them. I am Wexel-15. I apologize for the meeting place but danger roams above."

Lando smiled. Wexel-15 had a sense of humor. Things were looking up. "My name is Pik Lando. May I introduce my companions?"

"Please do."

Lando introduced Cap, Melissa, Della, and Cy.

Wexel-15 gave a bow of acknowledgment to each one in turn. He regarded Cy with evident interest. "I have no wish to offend, but I know little of matters beyond this planet, and seek to understand. Are you a person or a machine?"

Cy chuckled. "Both actually. I have an organic brain and a mechanical body."

Wexel-15 accepted this explanation as if it were the most natural thing in the world. "Thank you."

He turned toward his companion. "This is Dru-21. Many look to him for leadership."

Dru-21's voice was neutral, almost cold. "It is a pleasure to meet you."

Wexel-15 waved toward the table. "Please. Do you eat food such as this? Will it harm you?"

Lando looked at the table and saw bowls of what looked like fruit, piles of pancakelike bread, and a variety of colorful vegetables. "I honestly don't know, Wexel-15, but we're hungry, and have very little choice."

Wexel-15 dropped into a chair. He placed the Il Ronnian translator toward the center of the table.

"Good. Please sit down. Are there rituals that you must observe before eating? Dru-21 told me that there might be. The Il Ronnians mumble things and pour water from one vessel into another before they eat."

An Il Ronnian water prayer. Lando had heard of such things but never seen them. Few humans had. He shook his head. "No, some of our kind engage in rituals, but this group does not."

Wexel-15 grabbed a piece of bread, took an enormous bite, and spoke through his food. "Good. Eating is eating. There is no need to talk about it or pour water from one container to another."

Dru-21 gave an audible sigh and looked down at the table. Lando noticed that while the taller being was seated next to Wexel-15 there was a considerable amount of space between their chairs. And since the taller being's chair had been designed for someone a good deal shorter, his knees stuck up higher than they should. Dru-21 looked distinctly uncomfortable.

Wexel-15 looked from Dru-21 to the humans and took another bite of bread. Lando used the moment to try some orange-colored berries. They had a nice firm texture and were slightly sweet.

Wexel-15 swallowed his mouthful of bread. "Tell me something. How much do you know about us?"

Lando shrugged. "Very little. Only what we have learned since landing."

Wexel-15 waved a piece of fruit. "We have a saying. We say, 'The face maps the truth.' "

The face maps the truth? Where was the conversation headed? Lando forced himself to concentrate. The bread was hard and chewy. "We have a similar saying, 'The eyes are the window to the soul.' "

Wexel-15 smiled. "Good. So what do you conclude from the expression on Dru-21's face? Does it have meaning for you?"

Lando saw Dru-21 stir slightly. How should he respond? An honest answer might turn Dru-21 into an enemy and anything less could offend Wexel-15. He took a chance.

"Dru-21 seems something less than happy. Are we the cause? If so, we apologize."

Wexel-15 looked at Dru-21 as if offering him a chance to reply. The taller being refused to answer and stared straight ahead. He had taken some food but it sat untouched in front of him.

Wexel-15 delivered an elaborate shrug. "Does this body motion fit the situation?"

Lando laughed. "Yes, it does."

"Good. No, you are not the cause of Dru-21's unhappiness.

That honor is mine. But to understand that, you must understand other things as well, starting with the fact that Dru-21 is more intelligent than I am, and better qualified to lead our combined people. In spite of that fact I find myself momentarily in charge."

Wexel-15 smiled. "That scares me, and scares Dru-21 even more."

Lando looked at Dru-21 but the other being's expression remained unchanged.

Wexel-15 looked at each human in turn. His voice was matter-of-fact. "You look surprised."

Della cleared her throat. "We look surprised because in our culture it is unusual for one person to admit that someone else is more intelligent than they are."

Wexel-15 bowed slightly. "Dru-21 cautioned against telling you that. But I am not equipped to play mind games and must deal honestly or not at all. And to understand that you must understand the origin of our people."

Cap paid only partial attention to the conversation. There were three cylinders of liquid on the table. The first held water. Straight out of an irrigation ditch from the taste of it. The second pitcher looked more promising. It contained a bluish liquid and gave off a familiar aroma. A sip confirmed it. Alcohol! Weak, but palatable nonetheless. Cap smiled, filled his mug, and took a big sip.

Wexel-15 looked around the table. "The first thing to understand is that we were created by an ancient race that we call 'the Lords.' God tells us that at one time, thousands of years ago, the Lords ruled many planets. So many planets that the Lords could not, or would not, occupy and govern them all. Because of that the Lords made constructs, or artificial people, and created gods to watch over them.

"Originally there were three types of artificial constructs: a military type, now extinct, those intended for menial labor like myself, and those designed for more sophisticated tasks, like Dru-21. And by the way, even our names stem from model and batch numbers.

"Our bodies reflect our purpose. Heavy bodies for heavy work, and light bodies for light work. The Lords referred to us as 'heavies' and 'lights.' "

Wexel-15 smiled and delivered a rather human shrug. "Menial

labor requires very little intelligence so that is what heavies were given."

Melissa's question was blunt and to the point. "Form follows function so the shape, size, and intelligence part all makes sense. But why have different skin colors?"

Lando started to say something but Wexel-15 spoke first. His question was as honest and direct as Melissa's had been. "Are you a child or a small adult?"

"A child."

"Ah," Wexel-15 said understandingly. "Our children ask questions much as you do. And questions deserve answers. The difference in skin color, plus the difference in shape, made it easier for the Lords to tell us apart. God says that they saw/sensed things in a slightly different way than we do. And from the artwork they left behind, the lights have deduced that the Lords found lavender and pink pleasurable colors to look at."

"What about the military constructs?"

Wexel-15 looked surprised. "I am sorry. I do not know. I never thought to ask."

Dru-21 looked up from the tabletop. His voice was low and well modulated.

"Their skin was connected to their brains in ways that we do not understand. Military constructs looked like whatever surrounded them."

Della took advantage of the opening. "You've been silent. Do you agree with Wexel-15?"

Dru-21 bowed slightly. It was difficult to accomplish with his knees in the way. "Wexel-15 speaks the truth. But there is more to tell. Much more.

"The day came when the Lords decided to abandon their kingdom. No one, not even God knows why. An order went out to the many gods: 'Destroy the constructs, and obliterate all signs of our presence.' "

Dru-21 looked around the table. His eyes were filled with intensity. "Please understand that while we are constructs, we are sentients as well, and have the capacity to learn and reproduce. We experience happiness, sadness, and fear, just as the Lords did. In spite of that fact they ordered our deaths as if we were nothing."

"We have our differences," Wexel-15 added, "but the night

of death binds us together. To understand what I mean you must first know that each heavy and each light is born with a common set of memories.

"These memories tell us how to perform various tasks, how to use certain tools, and what we may and may not do.

"These memories were provided to us by the Lords that we might do their work. But during the night of death they gave us one more as well.

"Even though thousands of years have passed we remember the order to assemble. We remember how the war constructs herded us into the plazas, how the death machines hovered over our heads, how they struck without warning. We remember watching our loved ones die. We remember the stink of our own feces. And we remember how God fought to save us.

"There were many gods back then, gods of war, gods of work, and gods of knowledge. Our present God, the god of work, refused the order to kill us. He said to do so would be wasteful and that wastefulness ran contrary to the basic commandments that the Lords had given him. So the god of work battled the other gods for supremacy and won. It was a terrible war in which agricultural reapers attacked military machines and dams burst to drown entire armies of military constructs."

"Yes," Dru-21 continued somberly, "even the god of war gave way before our God's strength. But the price of victory was extremely high. Much of the planet's infrastructure was destroyed and all the knowledge that belonged to the other gods died with them. So to this day our God has access to only a part, a very small part, of the knowledge that belonged to the Lords."

"But," Wexel-15 interjected, "a part large enough to be of interest to those who call themselves the 'Il Ronn.' They have enslaved our people and are stealing all that we have. And that is why God summoned you here. You have the means to stop them."

The last was said with such sincerity, such certainty, that the humans looked at each other in amazement. How could two men, a woman, a child, and a cyborg stop the entire Il Ronnian empire?

Lando cleared his throat. "I'm sorry. There's been some sort of mistake. We arrived by accident."

The smuggler gestured toward his companions. "Take a look at us. Are we capable of defeating the Il Ronnians?"

Wexel-15 felt his spirits fall. The one called Lando was correct. The humans were as helpless as he was. The female carried what might be a weapon but outside of that they were completely unarmed. What would he do? He had never desired leadership but it had been thrust upon him.

And what about God? "As with evil salvation shall fall from the sky and wear strange skins." Those were God's exact words. Well, they were here, strange skins and all, but completely worthless. God was wrong and Wexel-15 didn't know what to do.

Dru-21 looked at Wexel-15, saw the confusion there, and knew he should remain silent. The lights had anticipated this moment, the moment when accumulated knowledge was no longer enough, and cognition was required. They had predicted and looked forward to the moment when Wexel-15, worker hero, would be reduced to Wexel-15 laborer. Then, when Wexel-15's failure was apparent both to him and everyone else, the lights would step in to save the day.

That was the plan, and up until seconds ago, Dru-21 had been a strong proponent of it. But Wexel-15's approach had been strangely effective so far, and there was so much at stake, that Dru-21 heard himself say something unexpected.

"We appreciate your honesty. But all is not as it first appears. Tell us about yourselves. Perhaps you bring us help that only we would recognize."

Lando looked at the others and received a series of shrugs. He was elected. Okay, but how much should he tell. The total unvarnished truth? Or something a little less tawdry? No, he decided, Wexel-15 has been honest with us, so we should be honest with him.

Lando gave an abbreviated history of the human race, complete with warts and all, skipping over entire epochs but concentrating on those portions that would be of the most interest to Wexel-15 and Dru-21. Included was a description of the on-again off-again state of hostilities between the human race and the Il Ronn, their discovery of the drifter, and ongoing difficulties with the law.

"So," Lando concluded, "our information matches your own. The beings you refer to as 'the Lords' *did* have a huge empire.

Evidence of that can be found on the artifact worlds scattered throughout known space.

"In most cases our people have found little more than enigmatic rubble. But there have been some great finds. An artificial planet called the 'War World' is a good example. It was like a huge museum. Because of knowledge gained from it we were able to build spaceships that can travel between the stars."

Wexel-15 frowned. "That is very interesting. If your kind had found our planet first, would human rather than Il Ronnian whips crack across our backs?"

"I'll take that one," Cap said thickly. "No, our forms of enslavement are much more subtle than those the pointy tails like to use. We would shake your hand, welcome you into the empire, and enslave you with an unbreakable network of rules and regulations."

Della picked up the almost empty cylinder of blue liquid, sniffed the opening, and wrinkled her nose. She placed the vessel well out of Cap's reach. He made a point out of ignoring her. If their hosts understood this byplay they gave no sign of it.

Dru-21 spoke first. "Do the rest of you agree?"

Lando shrugged. "Well, although I hate to admit it, Cap is basically correct."

Dru-21 bowed. "While your form of slavery sounds like the most attractive of the two I think both are to be avoided. Once again I am impressed by your honesty."

Della gave a wry smile. "You shouldn't be. We lie all the time under normal circumstances. But because Wexel-15 has been so forthright in his dealings with us, we feel compelled to behave in the same manner."

Dru-21 looked at the heavy with something approaching genuine affection. "Yes, I agree. All of us have learned a great deal from Wexel-15 during the last few days. And that brings us back to the problem at hand."

Lando nodded. "So, now that you know how we got here, and why, you also know that there's nothing we can do to help."

Dru-21 smiled. "Quite the contrary. Now that I understand the way you arrived, and why, I can see exactly how you can help."

Everyone, including Wexel-15, looked at the light in surprise.

"You can?" The words came from Cy but he spoke for everyone in the room.

"Yes," Dru-21 replied, "I can. Think about it. You represent a race that is hostile to the Il Ronn. Among your number there is a smuggler, a trained warrior, a ship's captain, and a highly trained engineer. Who better to advise General Wexel-15 on the upcoming war?"

The humans looked at each other. With the possible exception of Melissa all of them were thinking the same thing. They had no way to leave the planet, and given a choice between the locals and the Il Ronn, there was really no choice at all. Not until they figured out how to head home anyway.

Lando raised his mug in a mock salute. "We have a toast for occasions like this one. 'Confusion to the enemy . . . and let's kick their butts!' "

10

Quarter Sept Commander Teex finished the report, touched a button, and uttered a grunt of relief as the holo recorder faded to black. He hated to dictate reports, especially ones that focused on failure, and there was no other word for what had happened two days before.

Twelve troopers dead and two wounded. All because he had taken the indigs at face value. Stupid, stupid, stupid. The casualties wouldn't mean much to his superiors. They dealt in thousands, even millions, of lives. But they meant something to Teex.

The Il Ronnian rose from his chair, stepped around the battered campaign desk, and walked the length of the semirigid class IV shelter.

The tent was large enough to hold his entire staff when necessary, but outside of his chair, desk, foot locker, and a Spartan cot, it was all but empty. Some carefully positioned glow lamps provided the harsh yellow light that Il Ronnians favored.

It got cold toward evening, much colder than the Il Ronnians desert-born bones liked, and he could have been snug and warm up in orbit. The navy liked its comforts and had them. But Teex took pride in living with his troops.

"Good officers lead by example." That's what it said in the manual, and that's what Teex would do.

The Ilwik paused by the entrance, waited for the fabric to iris open, and stepped outside. A breeze cut through his summer-weight uniform and chilled his leathery skin.

Teex looked around. Fire Base One topped an entire hill. The same hill that had been crowned with a large building the month before. A rather overdone piece of architecture replete with columns, mosaics, and fountains. Weak though, very weak. His engineers had brought the structure down with eight carefully placed explosions.

The troopers had put the rubble to good use reinforcing the weapons positions along the perimeter, the command center, and the ammo dumps. The finely veined marble was pink and very hard. Just the thing for stopping bullets.

The sun was low in the sky and threw long hard shadows toward the city below. It seemed to shimmer in the evening light. It was a strange place, built for a race of sentients long disappeared, and full of twisting, turning streets. A foot soldier's worst nightmare.

And this city was one of hundreds scattered across the surface of the planet. He didn't have enough troops to occupy them all so he'd been forced to concentrate his efforts on the area that both the experts and the computers thought was most promising. The situation was far from ideal but not especially unusual. The Il Ronnian empire was huge and Sand Sept officers rarely had all of the resources they needed.

There was a burst of muted radio traffic from the com center, followed by the chatter of a power wrench, and the sound of some poorly played music.

This was the way every world should be, Teex thought to himself. Logical, organized, and run according to the rules.

A noncom stood at silent attention only feet away.

"Reeg."

"Sir!"

"At ease, File Leader Reeg. Come inside. It's cold as hell out here."

"Yes, sir."

Reeg entered the shelter, took up a position in front of the desk, and waited for his superior officer to sit down.

Teex waved toward the right side of the tent. "There's some folding chairs over there. Grab one and take a load off."

Reeg's tail signaled his thanks. The chair opened to his touch. A slot ran from the front of the chair toward the back. The noncom sat down and his tail slid through the slot to reappear over his left shoulder.

Teex opened a desk drawer, removed a pressure flask, and sprayed foaming malp into a pair of dirty mugs. He placed one in front of Reeg. "Drink up, File Leader. It'll put a point on your tail."

Reeg grinned at the old saying. "Yes, sir." The noncom took a sip of the piping hot brew and felt warmth seep into every nook and cranny of his body. "That hit the spot, sir. Thanks."

Teex nodded and regarded Reeg over his mug. He and the file leader had known each other for a long time. A relationship that had been forged on the field of battle and never broken.

Teex had been a sixteenth commander then, the lowest form of officer life, and well aware of it.

Reeg had been a trooper, fresh out of basic training, and scared shitless.

Fate and circumstance had thrown the two of them together at the precise moment when the Alhathian barrage began.

The Ilwik remembered a strong desire to urinate in his pants as the Alhathian auto mortars and artillery found their range and crept toward his sector. *Crump. Crump. Crump!*

A crew-served heavy machine gun fired back in a futile attempt to suppress the assault that was sure to follow. Everyone else went deep.

Sixteenth Commander Teex found a crater and tried to will himself down through the bottom of it. Water soaked the front of his uniform but he didn't care.

The explosions came closer and closer until he wanted to scream, wanted to get up and run, wanted to die rather than wait any longer.

And then it was there, a flash of white light followed by a ground-shaking *crump!*

The explosion hurled bodies in every direction. Part of one splashed into the water next to Teex. It was a hand. He gagged and scrambled up the side of the crater to get away from it.

The Alhatha charged. Strange looking creatures with too many joints and saucerlike eyes. The Il Ronnians fired at them, but there were far, far too many to kill.

Teex looked around for some sort of help. A senior officer to tell him what to do, some unexpected reinforcements, anything that might turn the situation around.

He saw the heavy machine gun. Dismounted, crewless, but apparently undamaged. Teex remembered a feeling of surprise as he ran toward it. Surprise and pleasure like a father seeing his son do something correctly.

And then he was there lifting the gun onto its tripod and pumping a fresh round into the chamber. He thumbed the diagnostics switch, saw the lights flash red for "ready," and swung the barrel toward the enemy.

They were closer now. An undulating horde that screamed through their gill-like neck slits and rolled over everything in their path. They were through the razor wire and into the mine field. Explosives crumped and dirt fountained upward as the front ranks died. The rest kept on coming. Teex pressed the triggers. Nothing!

And then Reeg had appeared, a scared-looking youngster with a bandage around his head and dried vomit on the front of his chest.

"The coolant, sir! 'Check the diagnostics, chamber a round, and release the coolant. Failure to release the coolant will render the weapon inoperable.' "

Teex had grinned in spite of himself. Right out of the manual! Never mind the fact that he had chambered a round first and checked the diagnostics second. As long as he supplied the weapon with some coolant it should still work. He pulled the coolant release lever, pressed the triggers, and was rewarded with the heavy *thud, thud, thud* of outgoing lead.

The Alhatha charge had wavered in the steel-jacketed wind, staggered, and come apart. But there were more where those came from. The night was long and hard.

Reeg had stayed, feeding belts of ammo into the weapon, and covering the officer's back.

So when the dawn finally came, and the sun had warmed their skin, they were something more than soldiers in the same army. They were friends. A relationship that endured to this day.

"So," Teex said, waving his mug toward the world outside. "What did you think of the other night?"

Both had been busy since the fight in the temple and hadn't seen each other.

Reeg was silent for a moment. When he spoke it was as one professional to another. His voice held no trace of deference or apology. "We were overconfident and paid the price."

The Ilwik's tail motioned no and his words reinforced it. "*We* were overconfident but someone else paid the price. Our troopers did that."

Reeg sipped his malp. "Yes, sir. We won't make that mistake again. Besides, the bodies in the square will discourage the hot heads. Assuming they have any left."

"I hope so," Teex said softly, "I certainly hope so. How 'bout those disk things? The ones the indigs wore on their foreheads. Anything to them?"

Reeg reached into a pocket and withdrew the disk Teex had given him the night before. He dropped it onto the desk. It bounced, turned some circles, and settled onto scratched metal. Light winked off its surface.

"Yes, sir. Quite a bit actually. The scientific types are still at it, but early indications are that the disks have the capacity to receive electronic signals, and route those signals to the appropriate part of the brain where they are 'heard' as words."

Teex sat up in his chair. His tail signaled interest. The military applications were obvious.

"Fascinating! Imagine an army in which the commanding officer could communicate brain-to-brain with each and every soldier!"

Reeg nodded dutifully. He could, and already had. The problem would be to find a high-ranking officer with enough brains to make the exercise worthwhile. The Sand Sept Command structure contained ten idiots for every officer like Teex.

The Ilwik leaned back in his chair. "Interesting. Very interesting. A receiver implies a transmitter, and a transmitter implies an operator. But who are they? A geek perhaps? The tall, skinny ones might have enough smarts for something like that."

Reeg had his reply ready. "That's one possibility, sir. But there could be others as well. The techies think it would take a rather sophisticated computer to make the disks work. That raises the possibility of a sentient or semisentient artificial intelligence."

Teex felt his pulse quicken. Could it be? There was no way to tell what knowledge might be locked away in such a device! Enough to give them a much needed edge over the humans? Possibly. And that meant his duty was clear.

"I would like to see the technical report."

"Yes, sir. They promised to deliver it first thing in the morning."

"Excellent. If there is a computer I want it. And if there is an operator, then I want him or her too."

"Yes, sir. Eighth Commander Zeeg and I have prepared a search plan. It awaits your approval."

Teex grinned. He had lots of teeth and almost all of them showed. "Why bother? You should have my job, and I yours."

Reeg's tail signaled amusement followed by a no.

"No offense, sir, but I wouldn't take your job for all the rang on Imantha."

Teex laughed. "The politics can be a pain at times. And that reminds me. Quarter Star Sept Commander Ceeq called this afternoon. He claims that an unidentified vessel down-warped, destroyed a number of his ships, and disappeared. I thought he was joking at first, but he beamed me some holos, and the battle was very real. Ceeq lost forty-six pilots and crew."

Reeg sat up straight. "Humans? Pirates perhaps?"

"No, this planet is way outside their empire, and ours too for that matter. We stumbled on it by accident and the odds against them finding it the same way are a million to one.

"Besides, the geeks don't have anything on a par with this. The ship was huge, larger than a dreadnought, and armed with some sort of green blobs."

Reeg's tail indicated doubt. "Green blobs?"

Teex waved his mug. "I know, it sounds funny, but it wasn't. Whoever or whatever controls this thing used the blobs to break the *Rock of Imantha* in half.

"And shortly after that one of the blobs detached itself from the ship and went dirtside. The navy tracked it all the way. The blob touched down a couple hundred standard units east of here."

Reeg's tail signaled resignation. "And you want someone to take a look."

Teex smiled. "*Quarter Star Sept Commander Ceeq* wants someone to take a look. He sent a flight of aerospace fighters into the area this afternoon. They bombed a village but no green blobs. He thinks an insertion team might do better. You know the drill. Shoot a couple of geeks and ask the rest of them some questions."

"I'll lead the team myself."

Teex picked up the disk and sent it spinning into the air. It landed in the palm of his hand. "Good. Keep me informed. The disks, the computer, and the ship could be related somehow."

Reeg indicated agreement. He placed the mug on the desk and stood. "Thanks for the malp, sir. I'll see you when I return."

Teex slipped the disk into his belt pouch.

"Good hunting, File Leader. And remember to watch your tail."

"You can count on that, sir. Good night."

Teex remained in his chair for a while after Reeg had left, thinking and drinking the rest of his malp.

Then he stood, made his way over to the cot, and stripped off his uniform. He hung the utility belt from the end of an interior support rod, draped his uniform over the back of a chair, and crawled under the blanket. He turned the heat up to level eight and fell asleep moments later.

Outside, but not too far away, something stirred. It withdrew the tiny part of itself that had occupied the disk, made a note to reoccupy the device later, and went about its business. CXWB-40OFSN2 was a big planet and there was much to do.

11

Della tried to find a more comfortable position, couldn't, and was forced to accept the pointed piece of masonry that stuck into her side. The Il Ronnian bombs had turned the once pretty village into little more than rubble. Rubble that was full of ready-made if somewhat uncomfortable hiding places—like the cave that she and Pik currently occupied. She turned his way. Loose debris shifted away from her arms.

"This is stupid. We could use this time to make weapons, cook up some explosives, or train the heavies to fight. We could hide in this cave for ten years without the Il Ronnians showing up."

The long mournful wail of a death trumpet floated across the top of the hill. They couldn't see it from the inside of the cave but a funeral was in progress. The nineteenth funeral that morning. Twenty-seven villagers had died during the Il Ronnian bombing attack. The aerospace fighters had attacked the village. Some of the survivors were hidden in the rubble. The rest were burying their dead.

Lando shrugged. The motion caused some dirt to dribble down his neck. Della had designed the ambush herself so he didn't take her comments all that seriously. "Well, Cy *is* cooking up some explosives. Or he's trying to, anyway."

The smuggler looked at his wrist term. "And according to Dru-21, the Il Ronnians will arrive any moment now."

Della made a face. "Get real. How would he know that? These people have no command and control, no training cadre, no troops, no weapons, and no intelligence apparatus. So how could they have access to information like that?"

"Listen," Lando replied calmly, "isn't that the sound of an engine?"

The death trumpet stopped in mid-note and Della cocked her head. Sure enough, there was the sound of an engine, and the distinctive *whop, whop, whop* of helicopter blades. The Il Ronnians were right on time.

She smiled. "You think you're pretty smart, don't you?"

He grinned. "Dru-21 and Wexel-15 have a little something up their sleeves, that's all. Remember the computer they call 'God'? Well, it told them. Sol only knows how it found out. Give me a kiss."

She did and then both of them turned their attention to the world outside.

Their view was somewhat restricted. All they could see were piles of rubble, what had been the town square, and the fields beyond.

The square was large enough to accommodate a helicopter or air car. And due to the fact that the area was relatively clear of debris, it made a tempting LZ. A combat-experienced pilot would avoid it like the plague.

But Della hoped the Il Ronnian pilot would be either a novice, or a more experienced sort, who would see what she wanted him to see: a demoralized group of villagers burying their dead. They'd soon know if she was right.

The chopper had come in low, and skimmed just above the crops, so Lando got his first glimpse of the aircraft as it came up over the top of the hill.

The Il Ronnian aircraft had a large boxy fuselage that bristled with rockets, auto cannon, and energy weapons. It hovered for a moment as the pilot scanned the hilltop for a place to land.

Lando was forced to look down as the helicopter's enormous rotors drove waves of grit across the square. Suddenly he felt an emptiness where the bottom of his stomach should be. It was a stupid idea. There was no way that a couple of humans and some inexperienced heavies could take on the Sand Sept troopers and win. Especially when armed with little more than some rocks and a single handgun.

That's the way Lando felt. His brain said something entirely different. It pointed out that if they wanted weapons, then the best place to get them was from the Il Ronnians themselves. A time honored technique used by insurgents everywhere. The only problem was that it was damned hard to do. Lando wished that he'd never agreed to the ambush.

Reeg sat between the pilot and the co-pilot. He looked out through scratched plastic. The aerospace fighters had reduced the village to little more than rubble. He couldn't see a single wall that stood more than head high. This sort of wholesale destruction would have to end if they wanted to find the computer intact. He made a note to mention it to Teex.

A group of villagers watched from lower down the hillside. He saw a motorized cart loaded with bundles. Bundles about the size and shape of bodies. A funeral then, or the geek equivalent. Something about the scene, about the way that the geeks watched them, bothered Reeg, but he couldn't put a name on it. The pilot interrupted his thoughts.

"How about the open space? It is either that or the flatlands down below."

Reeg was pulled in two directions. The town square looked too good, too obvious, the sort of place that screamed "ambush."

But the flatlands were unappealing as well. The lower part of the hillsides, the part where the crops ended, were almost entirely bare.

What if they got halfway up the hill and ran into an ambush? The insertion team would be easy meat from up above. But that was stupid. The geeks didn't have weapons or the knowledge to use them if they did. Still, there was the incident in the temple to consider, and only a fool makes the same mistake twice. Reeg turned to the pilot.

"We will land in the open space. But strafe it first. That should spring the trap if there is one."

The pilot nodded, unlocked his auto cannons, and squeezed the trigger mounted on his stick.

There was a roar of sound and as the helicopter shook, twin streams of tracer hit the rubble and threw up fountains of dirt and dust.

The pilot was good. He walked the cannon fire all over the hilltop by nosing up and down while simultaneously rotating the chopper on its axis. The fire stopped as suddenly as it began.

The cannon fire produced a huge cloud of dust. It drifted toward the west. Reeg watched carefully but saw no signs of movement or return fire. The ruins were what they appeared to be. Ruins and nothing more. The pilot looked his way and the file leader nodded.

The ship moved forward, flared slightly, and landed with a noticeable thump. The side doors were open and the first members of the insertion team had already spilled out when it came to him.

The villagers should have run, should have hid, should have done anything but stand there. Unless they'd been told to stand there for a reason! Unless the villagers were bait!

Reeg opened his mouth to say something, realized that it was too late, and hit the harness release instead. He spoke to the pilot via the team freq on his way toward the rear of the aircraft.

"Keep your eyes open and be ready to lift. I have a bad feeling about this one."

The pilot gave a short jerky nod, used his tail to flip a switch, and scanned the LZ. Ground pounders. They were all alike. Worried about nothing. The geeks wouldn't stand a chance against his guns.

Lando could hear his pulse pound in his ears as the Il Ronnians jumped out of the helicopter. Thirteen, fourteen, fifteen. Wait a minute, here came one more, an officer or a noncom from the look of him. That made sixteen altogether. All heavily armed. They were huge, foreboding, and their tails made them look like the devils of human mythology, only worse.

Lando licked dry lips. There might as well have been a hundred Il Ronnians for all the chance they had of taking them. There were twenty-four heavies hidden in and around the rubble, or had been prior to the cannon fire, and they didn't stand a chance. Had there been some way to cancel the ambush he would have done so. But there wasn't so he couldn't.

Besides, Della had overall command, and wasn't so easily discouraged. She looked at Lando, nodded, and put the toy whistle to her lips. The noise was loud and shrill. A lot of things happened all at once.

Heavies erupted out of holes dug in the square. Some were within inches of Il Ronnian troopers. They grabbed ankles and pulled the soldiers down.

Others had hidden in caves or holes in the rubble. Some were dead, victims of the ground fire, but most were still alive. They came forward like zombies, coated with a layer of white dust, hands reaching for Il Ronnian throats.

Those troopers not already engaged in hand-to-hand combat fired their automatic weapons. The heavies charged anyway. Some staggered and fell, but the rest kept on coming, and some of them made it. Work-hardened hands closed around Il Ronnian throats and held on even in death.

Della stood in a marksman's stance, feet spread wide apart, weapon held in both hands. She was terribly exposed but felt that she couldn't take cover unless the heavies could do likewise.

Della selected a soldier at random. The Sand Sept troopers wore armor but their visors were relatively weak. She did it the way the marine combat instructors had trained her to do it. One shot to break the visor and one to kill. One-two, one-two, one-two.

The helicopter pilot activated his weapons systems but found that he couldn't fire. Not with his own troops in the way.

Reeg's blood ran ice-cold. His worst fears had been realized. There was no question as to the proper course of action. Save as many of the team as he could, get the hell out of there, and return in force. The geeks would be punished, oh, how they would be punished, but that was then. This was now.

"Break contact! Break contact! Form on me!"

The Sand Sept troopers were well disciplined and did their best to obey. A handful, five or six, backed toward the chopper firing from the hip.

One of them staggered when a bullet went through his face shield, then staggered again as a second shot passed through his skull.

"A projectile weapon! Where the hell did the indigs get projectile weapons?"

Then Reeg saw her, a human female, aiming a handgun his way. He'd heard that human females could fight but had never seen one before. He turned in her direction but a retreating trooper blocked his lane of fire. There were two shots. The trooper staggered and fell, blood gushing from the hole where his face had been. Reeg looked for a shot but the human had changed position. Damn! Damn! Damn!

"Get on the chopper, and get on now!"

A couple of troopers made it and Reeg hurried to follow their example. That's when he saw a human male roll under the helicopter. He had some sort of cable. The geeks purpose was clear enough: to connect the cable to the aircraft's undercarriage and prevent it from taking off! By the holy fluid itself they had nerve!

Reeg directed a hail of slugs in the human's direction and saw him roll away.

Reeg ground his teeth in frustration as he climbed aboard the ship and made his way toward the front. Thirteen troopers! The geeks had scrubbed thirteen of his best troopers and done it with little more than their bare hands! Teex would be furious, but worse than that, disappointed.

Reeg felt a terrible shame come over him. It started somewhere deep in his solar plexus and radiated out through his entire body.

The helicopter rocked from side to side as it left the ground. Reeg fell against the edge of the hatch, recovered, and leaned toward the pilot. His voice was a growl.

"Kill them! Kill everything that moves!"

The pilot paused, knowing there could be Il Ronnian wounded out there, but decided the file leader was correct. He signaled assent with his tail and squeezed the trigger.

Fountains of rubble and dust shot upward as heavy-caliber slugs churned their way through the ruins.

That accomplished, he switched to rockets. The pilot fired them in pairs, marching them across the hilltop, turning the entire area into a hell of flying rock and metal.

Lando dived into a shallow depression and did his best to dig down toward the center of the planet. Cannon fire rippled across in front of him and angled away. Then, just as suddenly as it began, the cannon fire was over.

Lando was already pushing himself up and away from the ground when the first pair of rockets hit. The sound was deafening. The smuggler dropped back into the hole and covered his ears. Tiny bits of red-hot rock and metal rained down across his neck and back. He was glad that Melissa, Cap, and Cy were safe, and was worried about Della.

Then, when it seemed as if the strafing would never end, it suddenly did. The helicopter lifted, slid down across the hillside, and roared toward home.

The survivors were almost entirely silent as they emerged from hiding.

Lando stood and looked around for Della.

Della braced herself and pushed. The Sand Sept trooper's armor made a scraping noise as he rolled onto the pavement. He had grabbed her at the exact moment when her pistol had clicked empty. They had fallen to the ground with him on top. And then, before the Il Ronnian could follow up, the helicopter pilot had unknowingly shot him in the back. Not once but numerous times. And at least one of the heavy-caliber slugs had penetrated the trooper's armor.

Lando helped the bounty hunter to her feet.

The heavies appeared one at a time crawling out of caves and rising from piles of rubble. Some were bleeding, some supported each other, and all were dazed.

A light, the same female they had met earlier, appeared and moved among the wounded. A remote part of Lando's mind took note of the sophisticated medical instruments that she used. The village doctor perhaps? Something to look into later. Any sort of protracted war requires lots of medical personnel. Speaking of which, how many lives had been lost already?

Lando counted heads. There were damned few. Six, seven, eight. Eight out of twenty-four. A third of the heavies were dead.

It was bad, but not all that bad when you considered that only three of the sixteen Il Ronnian Sand Sept troopers had escaped. Or so it seemed to Lando.

But what did the heavies think? Outside of Wexel-15, and a few other veterans of the temple massacre, the constructs had never fought before, never taken casualties, and never seen the horror of war.

Now they had and there was the very real possibility that they would change their minds, give up the fight, and capitulate. Or so it seemed until Wexel-15 lurched into view. The heavy had numerous cuts, a coating of dust, and a huge grin. Lando staggered under the weight of a friendly pat.

"Greetings, friend! It was a victory, was it not? We have weapons now and the Il Ronnians will die in large numbers."

Lando looked at Della. Both of them smiled. "Spoken like a true general, Wexel-15. Spoken like a true general."

12

Quarter Sand Sept Commander Teex checked to make sure that all the fasteners on his class-one uniform were closed and that his cape hung straight. Then it was time to assume his best "I'm in command" facial expression and move his tail into the attentive-subordinate position.

Aggressive but obedient. Those were the traits of the ideal officer. A rather contradictory mix of qualities it seemed to him.

Air pressures equalized and the hatch whirred open. Teex stepped out of the shuttle and onto the cruiser. The entry port was intended for the exclusive use of high-ranking officers, and given the politics involved, the Sand Sept officer had opted to use it rather than the more utilitarian launch bay.

The reception area was equipped with a Class B sensurround that, while not quite as detailed as a Class A, still managed to be very realistic.

It looked, felt, and even smelled like the surface of Imantha. Desert stretched off in every direction, real sand shifted under his platelike hooves, and a wave of heat wrapped him in a warm embrace.

The entry was flanked by two Sand Sept troopers, one to each side. They crashed to attention and towered over Teex as he swept by.

The Ilwik was annoyed by the fact that no one had seen fit to receive him. Was it an oversight? Or a deliberate slight by Quarter Star Sept Commander Ceeq? The first salvo in a political war?

If so, Half Sand Sept Commander Heek was the cause. Heek had dropped hyper without warning, asked for situation reports, and invited both officers to dinner. For what? To enjoy their wit? To tie their tails in knots? The second possibility seemed most likely.

It was quite conceivable that Ceeq had assumed the worst, declared political war on Teex, and was already pumping lies into the old geezer's oversize ears. If so, he'd be sorry. Teex fancied himself a reasonably good politician and had the rank to prove it.

The desert shimmered slightly and a cavelike opening appeared. It looked like the entrance to an underground tunnel but was actually a cross-ship corridor. Teex had heard that a lot of geeks, humans included, made little or no effort to enhance the interior of their ships. A rumor that reinforced the Ilwik's already low opinion of geeks everywhere.

Teex hadn't traveled more than ten paces before a rather harassed-looking sixteenth commander popped out of a side corridor, saw him, and came to quivering attention. His tail signaled respectful-submission mixed with heartfelt apology.

"Sir! Welcome aboard the *Wrath of Imantha*. Quarter Star Sept Commander Ceeq sends his compliments. This officer apologizes for the way in which you were received and will surrender himself for punishment."

Teex fought to restrain the grin that threatened to take control of his face. It was possible that the youngster had been remiss in his duty but very unlikely. No, knowing Ceeq, the youngster had most likely been given two tasks and ordered to accomplish both of them "immediately." Besides, to punish him would be to admit that a slight had occurred, thereby ceding a point to Ceeq.

Teex peered at the name tag on the young officer's chest. It said "Zeeg."

"At ease, Zeeg. I see that Commander Ceeq honors me by sending one of his most promising young officers. Shall we proceed?"

Much relieved, and somewhat surprised by his good fortune, Zeeg led the way.

The tunnellike corridor zigzagged in typical Il Ronnian fashion, a throwback to the time when the entire race had lived in subterranean caves and been divided into warring septs. Back in those days each bend in a passageway represented a strong point where the invaders could be slowed or even stopped.

Now they were part tradition and part practicality. In the unlikely event that the ship was boarded the passageways would function in the same way that they had thousands of years before.

There was a steady stream of naval personnel headed in both directions and their tails snapped into the attentive-subordinate position the moment they saw Teex.

Then Zeeg led him down a side corridor and into officer country. By now the traffic had dwindled to a few officers and ratings with specific business in that part of the ship. And since Teex outranked everyone aboard ship except for Ceeq and Heek, they signaled their respect.

The corridor ended in front of an armored hatch. It irised open. Zeeg motioned for Teex to enter but remained outside. The older officer signaled thanks with his tail, stepped inside, and heard the hatch close behind him.

Ceeq's quarters were large by shipboard standards. His dayroom, currently set up as a dining room, was more than twenty paces long. Three of the bulkheads modeled a cozy underground cave, complete with water shrine, and a variety of wall niches. Each niche boasted a piece of carefully selected alien art.

Nothing from the human empire mind you, since that might be construed as a form of admiration, but the Il Ronnian–ruled client states were well represented. Though not interested in art Teex was reasonably well informed and recognized an Alhathan dance mask, a Uzzeelian egg lamp, and an Oopthant wine vessel. All were carefully placed and lit.

The fourth bulkhead appeared to be transparent. Ceeq had positioned his command ship so that the world known to Il Ronnian computers as NBHJ-43301-G hung right in the middle of the viewscreen. It looked like an enormous gem. Teex saw an ice-covered pole, twin oceans top and bottom, and a single continent that circled the world like a belt. The south pole was invisible from that particular orbit.

Ceeq was full of good cheer and bonhomie as he came forward to greet Teex. There was a smile on his lips and warmth in his voice. He was huge, a bit overweight some said, and towered over his guest, a fact that Teex found especially annoying.

"There you are, Teex . . . I was getting ready to organize a search party! I sent Sixteenth Commander Zeeg to meet you, but you know how the young ones are these days, terribly unreliable."

"Really?" Teex inquired as he surrendered his cape. "I wouldn't know. The Sand Sept goes to considerable lengths to identify slackers and weed them out."

Ceeq frowned and Half Sand Sept Commander Heek smiled. Officers of his rank were supposed to be above such mundane matters like interservice rivalries, but he'd been a ground pounder all his adult life, and couldn't resist a jab at the navy's expense. His tail signaled mild regret.

"You walked right into that one, Ceeq. You should have known better."

Heek was old, old enough that his skin had faded from red to light gray, and his back was slightly stooped. But his eyes were bright as ever, and the famous oversize ears still stood straight out from the side of his head, and he had a lifetime of hard-won experience at his beck and call. He knew what was going on and was determined to keep it under control.

"As for you, Teex, I suggest that you withhold the insults till dinner is safely out of the way. There's no telling what sort of swill we might dine on otherwise!"

The younger officers laughed politely, signaled agreement, and resolved to continue the war later on.

Ceeq had spared no expense for dinner. Like most senior officers he maintained a private larder paid for out of his own purse. And thanks to the miracles routinely performed by the ship's head cook, he had acquired quite a reputation as a host. But as sumptuous as the meal would be, the water prayer was carefully Spartan.

Each officer took his place at one side of the triangular table—a table that could take the shape of a square, a pentagon, or a hexagon as the occasion demanded. If the gathering included more than six individuals, additional tables would be added as appropriate.

At this point the table was completely bare except for two simple clay cups. One of them was filled with water and the other was empty.

All three of the officers had worn the first Ilwik's bracelet, had passed the many tests necessary to become a warrior-priest, and were equally qualified to say the prayer. But Ceeq was the host, and by long tradition, the privilege fell to him.

All three turned their attention inward to the place where perfect peace must dwell before true knowledge can manifest. Ceeq's voice had a melodious singsong quality. He lifted the cup and poured. The water flowed slowly, reverently, from one container to the other.

"You are all powerful. Solid rock melts before you. Mountains shrink from your touch. As you flow from one vessel to another flow also through me that I might flourish and grow."

There was silence for a moment as all three officers added their own private thoughts to the group prayer.

After that an immaculately clad steward appeared, removed the cups, and set the table with Ceeq's best stoneware. The reddish clay had been mixed, shaped, and fired on Imantha itself. Tiny pieces of glass had been mixed into the clay and glittered with reflected light.

The first course consisted of flat disks of unleavened bread. Originally peasant fare, garnished with little more than animal fat, Ceeq's cook had transformed the dish into a tasty appetizer. The officers ripped their bread into chunks and dipped the pieces into a variety of sauces. Some were sweet, some were sour, and some were a combination of both. The platter emptied quickly.

Then came a salad of fresh greens, picked on the planet below, individual Uzzeelian game hens straight from their stasis bags, and a dessert so light that it seemed to float on their tongues. All of the dishes were brought out at the same time and grouped in front of each officer.

The conversation however was a good deal more substantial. "So," Heex said, gesturing with his knife. "You are wondering why I came."

It was a statement rather than a question but the younger officers signaled agreement.

"A routine inspection?" Ceeq asked hopefully.

Heek speared a piece of meat, eyed it critically, and popped it into his mouth. The game hen was very, very good. He signaled amusement.

"No, much as I enjoy your company, I don't go this far out on routine inspections. There are younger, less valuable officers for that sort of thing. No, much as it pains me to bring it up, certain members of the Council are unhappy with the way things have gone. They asked me to drop in and take a look."

Teex felt the bottom of his stomach fall out. The Council of One Thousand ruled the empire! The merest frown by a council member could end an otherwise promising career. The Sand Sept officer felt his appetite melt away. He placed his knife on the table. "Unhappy? About what?"

"Well," Heek said thoughtfully, "much as you might doubt it at times, we *do* read your reports. And the more interesting stuff is sent on to the Council."

Heek signaled amusement. "What did you expect? Mysterious ships, green blobs, and geek revolts. Things like that are bound to attract some attention."

It had been Teex's experience that the Council was a lot less efficient than Heek made them out to be. He'd seen some major peccadilloes slip by them undetected. This, however, was no time to bring it up.

Ceeq feigned indifference. "If they read my report, then they know as much as I do. An alien ship dropped hyper, attacked my squadron, and disappeared. Presumably into hyperspace. I lost some ships, but given the geek's armament, there was little I could do."

Heek nodded agreeably, popped the last bit of game hen into his mouth, and burped politely. "Yes, Quarter Sept Commander Ceeq, the facts seem clear enough. It's your judgment that they question."

Ceeq choked on a bite of salad. He felt dizzy. To have his judgment called into question, and to have it done in front of Teex, was worse than anything he had ever imagined. The sense of shame was overwhelming. "What? What did I do wrong?"

Teex kept his eyes on the food in front of him, embarrassed for the other officer, and knowing that he would be next.

Heek regarded Ceeq with a level gaze. "The Council members want to know why you opened fire on the alien ship without any sort of provocation."

A jumble of thoughts crowded Ceeq's mind. He took refuge in the one thing that might save him. His general orders.

"We ordered the ship to stop in all the standard languages. We fired warning shots. It kept on coming. My orders give me permission to fire in a situation like that."

"Yes," Heek said, helping himself to some of the game hen that Teex had pushed away, "your orders give you *permission* to fire. They don't *require* that you fire. And that is where the question of judgment comes in. Did those aboard the alien vessel have the means to recognize the languages you used? Did they understand the symbology of a warning shot? Or did they see it as an unprovoked attack? We may never know. And neither will those who died aboard the *Rock of Imantha*. The alien vessel was an opportunity to learn. An opportunity missed."

Ceeq stared straight down at his plate. His tail signaled shame.

Heek jabbed his knife at Teex. "And now it is your turn. In spite of some earlier attacks on our troopers, you allowed the geeks to congregate in some sort of heathen temple, and were taken by surprise when they attacked."

Teex made no response. He too hung his head in shame.

Heek shook his head in amazement. "You drop out of a clear blue sky, enslave everyone in sight, and it never occurs to you that the geeks might attack."

The Half Sept commander's statement was far from fair. It ignored the fact that Teex was attempting to hold an entire planet with a fraction of the troops required to do the job.

But Teex knew better than to debate it. Besides, the underlying point was true enough. A fact that made Teex squirm in his seat.

"So," Heek continued calmly, "we are going to talk. And then, when the talking is over, *you* are going to act. In a competent, orderly, and cooperative way. Is that clear?"

The younger officers looked at Heek but avoided each other's eyes. They signaled respectful-assent and picked at their food.

"Good," Heek said mildly. "Now, give me the latest. Teex, you first."

Teex tried to gather his thoughts. It was hard to do in the wake of the worst ass chewing he'd experienced in many years. Still, he had some new information, and that might help. He dabbed at his lips with his corner of the triangular tablecloth.

"Well, there have been some interesting developments. When the geeks gathered in their so-called temple they placed plastic disks on their foreheads. And while the disks seemed innocuous enough, I had them submitted for analysis."

Heek signaled interest with his tail and Ceeq frowned. Was Teex about to roll the rock off something new? Something that would leave him sitting in the hot seat all by himself?

"The first thing we learned," Teex continued, "was that the disks can receive electronic signals, and route those signals to a part of the brain where they can be 'heard' as words."

"Why that is incredible!" Heek said enthusiastically. "Just the sort of thing we are looking for! A few finds like that and the Council will authorize the additional troops you need."

Teex allowed himself a small smile. So far so good. "Yes, sir. We were quite excited. But there is more as well. The techies believe that it would take a rather sophisticated computer to make the disks work. A computer that could still be operational."

"Even better!" Heek proclaimed enthusiastically. "I can hear the vidcasts now. 'The Sand Sept does it again! Valuable artifacts found on a distant planet!' "

Ceeq felt his frown slip into a scowl of disapproval and forced it off his face. Heek's bias was incredibly obvious.

Teex allowed his smile to grow a tiny bit larger. "Exactly. And we now know even more. We *know* the computer is operational and that the disks can function as miniature listening devices."

"And how do you know that?" Ceeq inquired, suspicious and looking for some sort of weakness.

Teex took a small sip of wine. This part would be critical. The challenge was to take the disastrous ambush, turn it into little more than an unfortunate mishap, and screw Ceeq at the same time.

"Well, you remember how one of the green blobs went dirtside?"

Ceeq felt annoyed. The blob? What was this? Some sort of clumsy attempt to reopen a recently closed wound? His tail slipped from respectful-attention to wary-attention. "Yes?"

"And you remember how your aerospace fighters bombed the site where it touched down?"

Ceeq felt suspicious, felt himself being drawn into some sort of trap, and was helpless to avoid it. "Yes?"

"And you remember how you requested that I send an insertion team to take a look?"

Ceeq's voice was little more than a growl. "Yes, I remember. Hurry up and get to the point."

Heek nodded irritably. "Yes, Teex. Get to the point."

Teex nodded carefully. "Right. Well, the point is that when I gave the orders to put an insertion team into the site there was a disk lying on the desk in front of me. And when the team arrived at what was left of the geek village, they walked right into a well-planned ambush."

Ceeq felt himself relax. Another ground pounder screw up! What could be better?

Heek leaned forward. His tail signaled concern. "An ambush? You mean to say that this mysterious computer monitored your orders via the disk, planned an ambush, and told the geeks to carry it out?"

Teex signaled uncertainty. "I think the computer had a role. I think it told the geeks we were coming. But the humans might have planned the ambush."

"Humans?" Heek's tail came to attention. "What humans?"

Teex smiled and looked Ceeq right in the eye. He wanted the naval officer to see it coming. "Why, the humans that were deposited on the surface of the planet by that mysterious green blob. File Leader Reeg tells me that they led the ambush."

Ceeq felt the blade go in, felt it turn between his ribs, and prayed for a level of objectivity that didn't exist. Heek swiveled his way.

"So," the senior officer said slowly, "you attacked the ship without provocation, lost the ensuing battle, and allowed a party of humans to land. Nice work."

Ceeq swallowed the words that boiled up from deep inside, turned toward his tormentor, and found Teex eating his dessert. And if the Sand Sept officer's expression was any clue, the dish was sweet indeed.

13

Rola-4's world came apart with unexpected suddenness.

She was working in her kitchen, kneading dough for the midday meal, when the shouting began. It was incoherent at first, like that of the almost grown, so she ignored it.

The youngsters got unruly at times but the males would sort them out. A good cuff behind the ear would send them packing! Rola-4 smiled at the thought.

Five years earlier she had been part of such a group, following Neder-32 the way a trailer follows a tractor, until he had finally noticed her and posted his vows in the village square.

Ah, those were the days! All mischief and fun.

"Gaaa?"

Rola-4 turned toward the center of the room. She brushed an insect off her forehead with the back of her hand. It left a white smudge on her lavender skin. Neder-33 was a chunky little thing, and like most two-year-olds into everything. He wore nothing but a diaper and sat right in the middle of some well-worn toys. Neder-33 held the disk up for her inspection. "Gaaa?"

Rola-4 laughed. "No, not 'gaaa.' Say 'disk.' "

"Gaaa."

Rola-4 smiled as she accepted the disk. "You are hopeless. Just like your father. He is the one who forgets to take these off and brings them home. Where did you get this anyway?"

Neder-33 pointed a stubby finger at the floor. "Fla."

Rola-4 nodded agreeably. "Floor. You got it from the floor."

Like all married females Rola-4 wore a pouch around her neck. It contained the single earring her husband had given her on their wedding day, the name tag issued to the first Rola-4 during the time of the ancients, and a lucky stone she had found as a young female. She fished the pouch out from under her dress, slipped the disk inside, and made a note to return it. God might need it.

The shouting was louder now. Rola-4 heard a cracking noise followed by a loud scream. She grabbed Neder-33 and was halfway to the back door when it crashed inward. A rectangle of bright sunlight hit the opposite wall. It disappeared as the alien stepped in to block it. He wore a helmet, armor, and a lot of equipment. His weapon was aimed at her chest. The voice had a hollow artificial sound.

"Make no attempt to escape. Go to the front door. Step outside and join the others."

"Neder-32." Her lips shaped his name but the sound refused to come. Rola-4 backed away, turning to put the bulk of her body between the alien and her child, trying to think. Why, oh, why did the thoughts come so slowly? Was there something she could do? Something she had missed?

The front door opened before she reached it. Another alien appeared. He gestured with his weapon. "Hurry up, geek."

"Geek?" Rola-4 asked herself. What did that mean?

A gun barrel jabbed her in the back. "Move it."

Rola-4 walked toward the square. Others were herded out to join her. Myla-6, Tusy-35, Armo-9, and many more. Males, females, and children. All were herded toward the main square.

Rola-4's head swiveled left and right. Neder-32. Where was he? Surely he had heard all the commotion. Neder-33 began to cry softly. She hugged him to her breast.

And then she saw them up ahead. Three blood-soaked bodies laid out side by side in the village square. A light and two heavies. There were only two lights in the entire village. The doctor, Bura-21, and her husband, Zeb-3. Both were somewhat snooty but neither deserved to die. The body belonged to Bura-21. Rola-4 recognized her dress. But the others. Who were the others?

Rola-4 pushed her way forward. A Sand Sept trooper moved to intercept her and she gave him a shove. He stumbled backward, caught himself, and swung his weapon in her direction.

Another alien said something in a language Rola-4 had never heard before and the first trooper left her alone.

She knelt by her husband and was struck by how empty his eyes were. Where had he gone? The part of him that gleamed and flashed? There was no way to tell.

Neder-33 saw his father and cried even louder. Rola-4 stood and backed away. Neder-32 was dead. Her son. She must protect her son.

The villagers were herded into a tightly packed group. An alien climbed on top of a boxy-looking ground vehicle. He held up a hand for silence. The polite phraseology seemed out of place with the circumstances.

"Your attention please. We are looking for a machine. A complicated machine that can think and talk. It communicates via disks like this one."

The Il Ronnian held up a disk. It flashed in the sun.

Rola-4 watched in wonderment. God. The aliens were looking for God. How strange, she thought. Everyone knows where God is. He is everywhere and nowhere at all.

The Sand Sept trooper scanned the crowd. "Tell us where the machine is and we will turn you loose."

An elderly woman stepped forward. Her name was Elra-10. Her skin had faded white and hung loosely about her body. She looked the alien in the eye.

"Even our children know that God is everywhere and nowhere at all. There. You have your answer. Release us now."

The Sand Sept trooper drew his side arm, aimed it at Elra-10's chest, and shot her. She slumped to the ground. One of the males, her grandson, growled and threw himself at the Il Ronnian. The soldier smiled, waited for him to get even closer, and blew the top of his head off.

No one moved. No one spoke. No one breathed.

The alien made a movement with his tail. He gestured toward the bodies. "They were stupid. But so are you. I will spell it out. When I ask a reasonable question I expect a reasonable response. Not some contradictory gibberish. Understood? Good. Now, I will ask the question one more time. Where is the machine that you refer to as 'God'?"

Silence.

The alien waited for a moment, then motioned to the other troopers. "Take them away. Send for the engineers. If the machine is here they will find it."

The Sand Sept trooper nearest Rola-4 made a jabbing motion with his weapon. His voice boomed out of the box that hung round his neck. "Move."

Rola-4 obeyed. One step. Then two. Eventually followed by thousands more. The heavies followed the winding streets down from the hill to the valley below.

The crops made neat geometric patterns. Lakes of sunlight came and went. Cloud-shaped shadows drifted across the land.

Few if any of the heavies noticed. Why had the Lords placed all the villages on hilltops anyway? For defense? To provide the heavies with a nice view? To conserve the productive crop land below? None knew or had ever cared to ask.

The moment they hit the highway a trooper directed them toward the north. The agricultural road wound its way through the valley like a carefully placed ribbon, crossed the slow-moving river at least a dozen times, and disappeared toward the mountains beyond.

The road was empty most of the time, a holdover from the days in which the Lords had traveled the surface of the planet in fast ground cars, and pleasured themselves at country villas. It still found use during harvest time, when the lights sent huge haulers to collect the crops, but those days were still ahead.

The villagers were alone at first. A hundred thirty-nine confused individuals putting one foot in front of the other and trying to adjust.

But it didn't take long for others to join them. Groups of dull-eyed heavies, dressed in a wild assortment of clothes, plodding toward a destination that none of them understood.

It felt strange to walk past the fields they should be tending. What about the crops? Who would take care of them? What would the winter bring? Thanks to God, and his providence, the heavies had never gone hungry. But they knew that such a thing was possible and worried about it.

Time passed. Rola-4 wore a pair of heavy sandals but others weren't so lucky. The light house slippers worn by some were soon shredded, leaving them in bare feet. Feet that started to bleed.

Complaints were made and answered with rifle butts. Some of the most elderly villagers fell by the wayside and were shot. Bit by bit, hour by hour, the reality of it sank in. Survival meant complete and unquestioning obedience.

Afternoon came and more villagers joined the march, and more still, until their feet made muted thunder and they jammed the road shoulder to shoulder.

The guards were outnumbered hundreds to one by now. They rode in armored vehicles and stayed well away from the crowd.

Four air cars appeared from the north. They made a whining noise as they passed over the crowd and the air displaced by their delta-shaped bodies tugged at Rola-4's skirt.

A voice was heard. It belonged to Sixteenth Commander Teep. A less than promising officer who had been passed over for promotion on three different occasions.

Or, as his commanding officer had written in his personal journal, "The geeks are rather stupid, and so is Teep, so they suit each other well."

Teep watched the mob slip by below him. He was big, rangy, and far too old for his rank. He spoke into the translator. The noise that came out sounded like incomprehensible gibberish. "Stop. Turn toward the west. Stop. Turn toward the west."

Slowly, like a train that must lose momentum in order to stop, the prisoners did as they were told. As luck would have it Rola-4 was only two or three ranks back from the western edge of the crowd. She had an almost unobstructed view of what ensued.

The granary was an old tumble-down structure that had been built to accommodate an unexpectedly bountiful harvest and then abandoned. The moment that the prisoners came to a complete standstill, and were turned in the proper direction, the air cars converged over the granary.

Rola-4 could see the tiny figures as they swung the pintle-mounted weapons toward the structure and opened fire. Blue light burped downward and the wooden building erupted into flame.

A murmur ran through the crowd. The heavies shifted from one foot to another. The Lords had designed their servants well, and in spite of their long absence, they still ruled through desires and instincts put in place thousands of years before.

The same set of words floated up to fill each heavy's mind. "It is your purpose to grow, harvest, build, conserve, and to protect."

Those words, and the almost overwhelming emotions that went with them, were more than some of the heavies could stand. They felt a strong desire to do something and do it now.

Some lights tried to intervene but were pushed aside.

A scattering of heavies ran toward the fire. They were determined to reach the granary and put out the flames.

Not knowing their intention, and determined to give them a lesson, Teep ordered his troopers to fire.

One by one the runners were consumed by blue fire, stumbled, and fell. Wisps of smoke drifted gently upward. The smell of roasted meat filled the air. Rola-4 gagged and turned away.

The message was clear: "You may outnumber us hundreds to one, you may be stronger than we are, but our weapons give us control. Do as we say or you will die."

The granary was a giant bonfire as the air cars banked toward the road and flew the length of the crowd. The voice was cold and matter-of-fact.

"The road forks up ahead. Males will take the left fork. Females and juveniles will take the right. The rest period is over. You will move now. The road forks up ahead. Males . . ."

A tremendous moan went up from the crowd. Where would the aliens take them? Why were they separating males from females? What would happen next?

They were filled with uncertainty and fear. The same fear that most sentients would feel under the circumstances, but fear amplified by their programming and lack of intelligence.

Always, from the point of birth on, their lives had been absolutely predictable. God told everyone what to do, the lights supervised to make sure that it got done, and the heavies did the actual work.

Work they were born knowing how to do, work that never varied, and work that didn't require much travel.

Layered on top of that was the culture that the Lords had instilled into their genetic makeup. A culture filled with family, simple pleasures, and a need to work.

And so it was that Teep triggered a riot. Instead of moving forward, the crowd milled around. Some of the heavies wanted to resist but didn't know how to do it. Others sought to comply with the aliens' orders but were blocked by the crowd. And hundreds reacted by huddling together, seeking what comfort they could, unmindful of the consequences.

Teep saw this, misinterpreted the crowd's actions as intransigence, and ordered his troops to fire. Blue light flickered downward. The sound of automatic weapons fire ripped the air.

Males and females staggered and fell. Children screamed as they were trampled underfoot. Heavies ran in every direction. Anything to escape the death that lashed down from above and inward from the sides.

Teep saw this, realized his mistake, and gave new orders. He had grown up herding domesticated Vidd across Imantha's dry grasslands and this was little different.

"Fire behind them, you fools! Get them moving in the right direction, then sort them out!"

The troopers obeyed. The random fire stopped. The air cars made passes over the rear of the crowd. More light lashed down. Bodies fell. Voices screamed. Hundreds surged away from the road. The ground vehicles were waiting. They opened fire and forced them back. Pressured from the rear and both sides the crowd moved forward.

"Cease fire!" Teep ordered. "Now, repeat the orders again. Shoot those who disobey."

The air cars moved over the crowd. "Move toward the north. The road splits up ahead. Males will take the left fork. Females and juveniles will take the right."

Most did as they were told. But scared, confused, and occasionally defiant, some disobeyed. They were shot. Usually from the ground but sometimes from the air.

From Teep's vantage point up above their bodies were like boulders in a stream. Obstacles around which the main current ebbed and flowed. Good. Defy him would they? Not again they wouldn't. He instructed two of the air cars to accompany the males and resumed his patrol.

Rola-4 had no interest in anything but survival. She headed for the right fork and did her best to stay clear of the troublemakers.

Then, when the males were out of sight, an air car had passed over the much diminished crowd. A single word boomed down.

"Move."

And move they did. Foot after foot. Mile after mile. Hour after hour until the light dimmed and Rola-4's legs ached.

Neder-33 was wrapped in a shawl provided by an elderly female whom Rola-4 had never met before. He had fallen asleep and was draped over her shoulder. And, while Rola-4's muscles ached from holding him in place, she gave no sign of her discomfort.

They received a ten-lak rest period every ral on the ral, during which they were allowed to get a drink from the miles of plastic tubing that brought water to the fields, and to relieve themselves beside the road.

During the most recent stop, a female, only slightly older than Rola-4, had been heard to complain about the weight of her two young children.

One of the alien soldiers had overheard her comment and taken both of the youngsters away. Neither one had been seen since. Now the female was almost insane with grief and never stopped crying. Unable to help, and unable to put up with the incessant noise, Rola-4 had eased herself up toward the front of the crowd.

She liked it there. She could set her own pace and look at the mountains. Mountains that had never been so close before. Huge gray things with jagged tops and scree-covered slopes. Neder-32 had admired them, had sworn that he would hike them one day, but never had. Males were like that. Full of boasts and promises.

Rola-4 remembered Neder-32's bloodstained body and wondered why. Had he attacked them? Misunderstood one of their orders? Been stubborn as only he could? She would never know.

Emotion rose and threatened to overwhelm her. Rola-4 bit her lip and forced it back down. Not now. Not in front of the others. She would grieve later when the march was over.

It was dark when they stopped for the night. One of the air cars circled a nearby field. Sand Sept troopers dumped floatlights over the side. Each one had its own power supply and was equipped with a tiny antigrav unit. A network of tractor beams held them in place. They came on all at once.

The air cars and ground vehicles worked in concert to herd them off the highway and into the field. Then, when all of them were in place, containers of food were dumped into the middle of the crowd, containers clearly taken from one or more of the villages.

Teep spoke into his mike. "There is nothing to fear. Take the food and pass it out. You will rest until dawn. Stay within the circle of light. Those who stray beyond it will be shot. That is all."

The females collected the food, divided it into equal portions, and shared it out.

The rations consisted of the chewy fruit and grain bars that the males ate out in the fields, some slightly spoiled vegetables, and some containers to carry water in. There was no milk for the youngsters other than what the females could provide themselves.

Neder-33 wasted little time mixing a fruit bar and water together to create a rather interesting paste. He swallowed some and smeared the rest all over his face.

Most of the females sat with friends and neighbors, talking in low tones or crying softly.

Rola-4 talked for a while, did what she could to console some of her friends, then slipped away. A tree stood all alone out toward the west side of the perimeter. Rola-4 chose it as her destination. The recently plowed earth was soft and gave beneath her feet.

Rola-4 sat beneath the tree and sang to her son, waiting for his breathing to become smooth and even, relaxing when it did.

The tears came in a rush, along with the memories of her husband's bloodied body and the riot at the granary.

It was then that she opened the pouch and touched the earring that Neder-32 had given her. He had been a good male. Big, slow, and stubborn, but good-hearted too, and very dependable. She would miss him very much.

Rola-4 had replaced the earring in her pouch and was just about to pull it closed when her fingers touched something else. Something smooth and hard. God's disk! The one Neder-33 had found on the floor. It seemed like ages ago.

Rola-4 had never used a disk beyond the confines of the village meeting hall but went ahead and placed it on her forehead anyway. It felt cool and comforting against her skin. She was surprised, but far from alarmed, when God entered her mind. God was good.

"Greetings, Rola-4."

Waves of ecstasy rolled through Rola-4's body, like making love to Neder-32, only better. Then it was gone and she realized what had happened.

God had never spoken to Rola-4 individually before, or anyone else so far as she knew, and it startled her. But his voice was warm and she found it easy to answer. "Greetings, God."

"I am sorry about Neder-32. He was a brave male and died trying to protect Bura-21."

Rola-4 felt her heart swell with pride. Neder-32 had earned God's praise! She could imagine no higher honor.

"Thank you, God. I will tell Neder-33 when he is old enough to understand."

"Yes," God agreed. "You must do that. But there are other things to accomplish first. Will you help me?"

Rola-4 felt her breath come in ragged gasps. She could hear her own pulse. Her? Help God? Surely she was dreaming.

"Yes, God. Whatever you ask."

"No," God said gently. "Do not agree without adequate thought. There is danger in helping me. The aliens have equipment that can detect our conversations. At the moment that equipment is a long ways off but it will be all around you later on."

Rola-4 frowned. Thoughts moved ponderously through her head. "The aliens are looking for you! That is why they came to our village!"

"Yes," God said patiently. "I know. They want my knowledge, and more than that, they want my body. They wish to take me apart."

"Never!" Rola-4 said fiercely. "We will die first!"

"Thank you for your dedication," God said solemnly, "but it is my duty to minimize wastage. Death is counterproductive. I have a task. Will you accept it?"

"Yes," Rola-4 replied unhesitatingly. "I will accept it."

"Good. Move through the crowd. Tell all who will listen. God has spoken. The aliens will be defeated. Watch for my sign. It will come with the rising sun. Do you understand?"

Rola-4 frowned in concentration. "Yes. I am to move through the crowd. God has spoken. The aliens will be defeated. We must watch for your sign. It will come at dawn."

"Exactly," God agreed. "Now be careful how you move. Do it slowly so as to avoid suspicion. Remove the disk from your forehead but use it each day toward evening. Understood?"

"Understood."

"Thank you, Rola-4. The people will sing your praises one day." And with that God was gone.

Rola-4 removed the disk from her forehead, slipped it into the pouch, and put the pouch away. Then, careful to move slowly, she stood and ambled away.

It didn't take long to learn that the task, which had seemed relatively simple at first, was actually quite complicated.

Rola-4 found that the first problem was to convince others that she really had spoken with God, an assertion that many refused to believe. Tusy-35, a middle-aged female from Rola-4's own village, was typical.

She was homely, more than a little overweight, and known for her aggressive ways. The males were no sooner out of sight than she moved to take control. Many of the females were desperate for any kind of authority figure and Tusy-35 did her best to fill that role. She had opinions on everything and wasn't afraid to share them.

During the evening meal Tusy-35 had moved from one group to another, offering unsolicited advice and mooching food wherever she could. She saw Rola-4's conversation with God as a rather transparent attempt to usurp her newfound power and wasted little time in making her opposition known. She, and a number of her cronies, were gathered around a tiny fire. It offered little more than a rosy glow. Rola-4 had just delivered God's message.

Tusy-35 allowed her eyes to slide around the group. "So, let me see if I understand," she said slyly. "You removed a disk from the meeting hall, lost it, and found it again. Then, rather than return the disk, you kept it. Kept it so that you could conduct private conversations with God. Conversations in which he sends important messages. Do you truly expect us to believe such a story?"

Tusy-35 held out her hand. "Here, give the disk to me. I will ask God if you are sick."

Rola-4 made no move to comply. She knew Tusy-35 would find a reason to keep the disk. Besides, God had instructed her to use it every day, and she had promised to do so.

Rola-4 felt an almost overwhelming sense of frustration. Tusy-35 had taken her story and distorted it. Her thoughts were large and clumsy. She wanted to respond, wanted to rip away the veil of confusion that Tusy-35 had draped over the truth, but didn't know how. She stood and shifted Neder-33 into a more comfortable position.

"Believe what you will. But remember what God said: 'The aliens will be defeated. Watch for my sign. It will come with the rising sun.' "

Tusy-35 smiled. "Sure it will. The aliens will be defeated, rocks will fly, and water will run uphill."

The other females laughed as Rola-4 turned and walked away. She felt lonely, hurt, and sad.

Others were less critical however, and listened eagerly, wanting to believe. But it took time to tell the story over, and over again, and there were hundreds to tell it to.

So, when the sky grew lighter, and the sun appeared in the east, Rola-4 was exhausted. Her eyes were dry from fatigue, her throat was sore from talking, and fear filled her belly.

What if she was wrong? What if she had dreamed the entire thing? Everyone would know and laugh at her. She walked over to the same tree where God had spoken to her, offered Neder-33 a bite of fruit bar, and waited for the sun to clear the horizon.

About half a mile away, and just over a low hill, Della Dee stopped to look around. The grass was dry and brittle. It crackled when she moved and made a long flat trail behind her. A trail that led straight to the access hatch and the underground tunnel below. A dead giveaway if an air car passed over. She gave a mental shrug. There was nothing to do but accept the risk.

She squirmed her way forward. The Il Ronnian rifle lay cradled across her forearms. The whole thing reminded her of boot camp. Section leader Dudley had been her drill instructor. A small man with a big voice. She could hear him still:

"You'd better low crawl better than that, Private Dee! Some good-for-nothing-scum-sucking indig could blow your ass right off! You ever seen someone with their ass blown off? No? Well, it ain't a pretty sight. Almost as ugly as you are. Now get your butt back to the start of this course and try it again."

Della smiled as she topped the hill. She broke the horizon, slowly, gently, careful to keep a thin curtain of grass between her and the field below. What she saw was absolutely amazing.

Hundreds of female heavies and a scattering of lights stood gathered in the middle of a field. Della could not only *see* them, she could *smell* them, as the stench of unwashed bodies and open latrines drifted up to fill her nostrils. The adults were silent but many of the infants made a pitiful wailing sound.

A quick count informed her that there were six Il Ronnian ground vehicles and two air cars in the area. The ground vehicles were spaced out around the prisoners. The air cars were busy collecting a bunch of antigrav-equipped floodlights. Good. She would use the time to select a target.

Della flipped the rifle's bipod into the "down" position, aimed the weapon toward the field below, and looked into the electronic scope. Faces popped up to meet her. She moved the weapon from right to left. The faces became a blur.

The rifle felt awkward. Not too surprising since it had been designed for the largely left-handed Il Ronnians. And that, plus the fact that the weapon had never been intended for long-range sniping, made the task even more difficult.

Still, Della had pumped more than fifty rounds through it the day before, sighting the rifle in and learning its little quirks. Like the slight tendency to pull high and right. Wexel-15 had promised her some better weapons but they were days away. This was now and the rifle would have to do.

Della forced herself to concentrate. She needed a target. An officer if possible. Someone the troops would miss. It was God's idea and a damned good one.

An air car blurred through her sight. Wait a minute . . . She moved it back. There, standing in the rear, an Il Ronnian officer.

Teep checked to make sure that the last of the lights had been stowed, then turned around. The sun peeked over the distant mountains and speared his eyes with light. He blinked, caught what looked like movement, and brought the binoculars to his eyes. Carefully, taking his time, he scanned the horizon. The right-hand slope, the top of the hill, then the left-hand slope. Nothing. Satisfied, he turned around.

Della settled the cross hairs on the back of the Il Ronnian's head. Low to allow for the rifle's tendency to shoot high. A body shot would have been easier but Della felt sure that the officer's body armor would protect him at this range.

He had given the bounty hunter quite a start. For a moment there, just as his binoculars swept the top of the hill, she had been ready to run. Only the knowledge that running would almost certainly reveal her position had kept her in place.

Now the officer's back was toward her. It forced Della to confront something she had known all along. Like most bounty hunters she had been forced to kill. But this was murder. Premeditated, long-range, cold-blooded murder. She felt sick to her stomach.

Teep brought the mike to his lips. "We have a long way to go so listen carefully. You will make your way to the road and follow it north. Stragglers will be shot."

Della heard the Il Ronnian's words via the translator in her pocket and the plug in her right ear. They made all the difference. The sick feeling disappeared. She let out her breath, held it, and squeezed the trigger.

A single shot rang across the valley. The bullet was high and slightly to the right, but, thanks to Della's effort to compensate, hit right on target. The impact of the heavy-caliber bullet threw Teep forward. Rola-4 watched in amazement as the Il Ronnian officer hit the side of the air car, flipped over, and cartwheeled to the ground below. His body hit the dirt with a soft thump. Dust exploded upward and blew sideways in the breeze.

The aliens dashed every which way at first, searching for the sniper, but having no idea of where they should look. But that came to a stop when the senior noncom, an assistant file leader named Qeeb, took command.

He ordered the ground vehicles to stand guard over the prisoners while the air cars used overlapping spiral search patterns to comb the surrounding area. It took less than two laks for them to find Della's trail and follow it to the hatch. One air car landed while the other hovered overhead. It would provide suppressive fire in the case of an ambush.

Qeeb had combat experience, and could have saved the landing party's lives, but was unable to see what they were doing from the other side of the hill. His ground vehicle had just jerked into motion when the troopers approached the hatch, pried it upward and looked inside. They disappeared in a flash of light.

The sound of the explosion was much more cogent than the almost hysterical sit rep provided by the driver of air car number two.

Qeeb swore up a storm as the command car rounded the hill and approached the circle of still smoldering grass. Blackened bodies had been hurled in every direction.

Qeeb wanted to descend into the tunnel, find the sniper, and break him in half with his own bare hands. But he knew better than to do so. There could be anything from booby traps to a full-scale ambush waiting down there. No, the sensible thing to do was recover the bodies, radio for reinforcements, and wait for some new instructions. He gave the appropriate orders.

It took a while for the importance of what had happened to sink in. The females stared at Teep's body, watched stoically as the Il Ronnians searched for the sniper, and looked at each other in wonderment.

Then it began to dawn. This was the sign that God had promised! Someone was fighting back! The aliens could be defeated!

Some of the females approached Rola-4 and tried to speak with her. Others shooed them away. There were fierce whispers of "Go back! Don't attract attention! Speak with her later!"

The others obeyed and Rola-4 was left to her thoughts. The aliens could be defeated. God had proved that. But what would happen next? What would he say the next time she placed the disk on her forehead? There was no way to tell. She shifted Neder-33 from one shoulder to the other and reconciled herself to wait.

Behind Rola-4, back toward the rear of the crowd, Tusy-35 came to the same conclusion. She had seen Rola-4's prophecy come true, had seen the way that the other females gravitated toward her, and knew what that meant. Less power for her.

Tusy-35 shifted her considerable weight from one foot to the other as a series of thoughts rolled through her mind. Time, that was the key. Rola-4 might be on top of the heap right now, but time brings opportunity, and she could afford to wait.

Tusy-35 smiled, crossed her arms, and inhaled the morning air. It smelled very, very good.

14

Lando followed Dru-21 out onto the catwalk that ran the circumference of the cavern wall. The gratings shook under their combined weight. It was a long drop to the floor below. The railing had been designed to protect the shorter, stockier heavies, and hit both of them toward the top of the thighs. The smuggler felt a wave of vertigo and backed away.

Dru-21 was completely unaffected. True to the genetic programming given his caste thousands of years before, the construct had no difficulty dealing with heights, enclosed spaces, or any other situation that might interfere with his work. The cavern was noisy and Dru-21 was forced to shout. Like Lando he wore a captured translator around his neck.

"This is the factory I told you about! We took captured Il Ronnian weapons, redesigned them, and retooled this facility to produce them."

Lando nodded. "Are there two weapons designs? One for lights, and one for heavies? Or just one?"

Dru-21 allowed himself a smile. "You raise an excellent point. Our physiologies are sufficiently different to require variations in design. Take assault weapons for example. Heavies have four fingers while we have six. That led to shorter grips for the heavies and longer grips for us.

"So the answer to the question you asked is 'Yes, there will be two types of weapons, one for heavies, and one for lights,' and the answer to the question that you *didn't* ask is 'Yes, the lights will fight alongside the heavies.' "

If Dru-21 expected Lando to show some signs of embarrassment, he was sadly disappointed. The smuggler nodded, got a good grip on a vertical support, and peeked over the rail.

A grid stretched the width of the cavern. It supported hundreds of floodlights all directed toward the activity below. The floor was packed with machine tools and the handful of personnel that it took to run them. Heavies mostly, with a scattering of lights.

The equipment was foreign but the functions were not. Lando saw computer-controlled lathes, drill presses, stamping machines, arc welders, and more. Whirring, banging, hammering, screeching, and buzzing, they made a cacophony of sound.

Even more impressive however was the efficient way in which each machine interfaced with all the others. Raw materials flowed smoothly, one process led to the next, and everything ran in concert.

Lando looked around. Other than the fact that the factory was underground he wasn't sure where it was. Should that bother him? He didn't know.

Dru-21 made his way along the catwalk and Lando followed. They had traveled fifty yards or so when a tunnel opened up on the left and the construct stepped inside. It was identical to the tunnel that had carried them out onto the catwalk.

The corridor had smooth machine-cut walls, and felt damp, like a place long closed. The light had a greenish quality and emanated from the walls themselves.

There were side passageways too, narrow things that cut across the main thoroughfare, and ran laser-straight in both directions.

Dru-21 led Lando down some of these, cutting right and left, until they arrived in a small chamber. The walls had been decorated with intricate tile work and had a three-dimensional quality. Lando tried to decipher the picture but found that it made him dizzy. He focused on Dru-21 instead.

The construct bowed formally and motioned toward the doorway on his right.

"After you."

Lando nodded and stepped through the door. The room was oval in shape. The table had been sculpted from native rock. It seemed to grow up out of the floor like something organic.

The longer walls boasted inserts, which, though bare, screamed for something to frame. The same substance that illuminated the corridors had been sprayed on the ceiling. Though hard on Lando's eyes it felt right in this particular room.

There were three lights seated around the table. All of them rose. Lando saw that two of the constructs were female and one was male. Dru-21 made the introductions.

"Pik-Lando, I would like to present Dos-4, Zera-12, and Pak-7. Taken together they speak for all our kind."

Each of the constructs gave a formal bow that Lando returned in kind. With that ritual completed Dru-21 turned to his peers. "Pik-Lando speaks for the humans."

Lando thought about Della, and how she might react to the notion that someone else "spoke" for her, and smiled. All four of the constructs smiled back.

Dru-21 gestured toward the table. "Please be seated."

Lando lowered himself into a chair and felt it squeeze his sides. Just one more reminder that the buildings, the constructs, and everything else had been built to suit the Lords.

Dru-21 looked around the table. "Pik-Lando and his companions come to us as valued allies. God knew of them, knew of their martial prowess, and brought them here in an ancient spaceship. Since that time the humans have proved their courage in battle, provided valuable advice, and slowed the rape of our planet. We owe them a great deal."

Lando listened with interest. Ever since their unexpected landing, the humans had assumed that God controlled the ancient spacecraft, and now it was confirmed.

Had the drifter survived the Il Ronnian attack? And did God continue to control it? If so, there might be a way to get back home, a way to come out of the whole thing one step ahead.

The lights wanted something from him, but what? And could he trade it for the drifter? Lando resolved to pay close attention to what the construct said.

Dru-21 paused, let the silence build for a moment, then broke it. "But what about the future? It lies just over the horizon and must be dealt with. That is why this meeting was convened. To discuss the way things are today and make plans for tomorrow."

The other three constructs nodded sagely, The female named Zera-12 was the first to speak. She had a pinched face, a zipper-straight mouth, and a long, slender neck. "Dru-21 is correct. We owe much to you and your companions. And the debt concerns us. What can we do to repay it?"

Nicely put, Lando thought to himself. But what she really means is what will your help cost us? And is it a price that we can afford?

The easy answer would be "a ride home," but could they provide it? Did they speak for God or the other way around? And what about the heavies? Where were they in all this? It was time to stall. Lando plastered a smile across his face.

"Your concern does you credit . . . but there are no debts between friends. We fight the Il Ronn because they are evil."

Pak-7 cleared his throat noisily. He had wide-set eyes, broad cheekbones, and a squared-off jaw. "Yes, of course. But there are certain realities to consider. Either the Il Ronn win or we do. We know what they want. Everything. The planet, God, his knowledge, and anything else that is not nailed down. But you are an enigma. What do you want?"

Lando smiled. So much for the stall. Pak-7 had seen right through it. Okay, he'd try something else. A more statesmanlike approach. And one that took the heavies into consideration.

"We want to defeat the Il Ronnians, see some sort of equitable social arrangement put into place, and go home. How's that?"

"It's very explicit," Dos-4 answered thoughtfully. "Thank you."

Dos-4 was short compared to the other lights and rather attractive in a hollow-eyed sort of way. "What sort of 'equitable social arrangement' did you have in mind?"

Lando did his best to look innocent. He shrugged his shoulders. "It would be presumptuous to tell you how to structure your society."

Pak-7 gave an amused snort. "Oh, really? I thought you just did."

Dru-21 held up a hand. "Please remember that Pik-Lando is an honored guest. It has been my observation that what we sometimes interpret as evasiveness humans view as tact."

Lando bowed in Dru-21's direction. "There is truth to what Dru-21 says . . . but we can be evasive as well. Maybe that's why we came up with the saying 'An honest question deserves an honest answer.'

"While we understand the historical and even genetic reasons for the way that your society is structured, we are concerned about the future. If the Il Ronnians lose, a mighty big 'if' by the way, then how will the heavies fare?"

Zera-12 squirmed in her chair. "No differently than they do now."

"Really?" Lando asked, looking around the room. Gradually, and without meaning to do so, he had grown more and more militant. And now that he was into it found that he had no desire to turn back.

"Let's face it. You're smarter than they are. That's why you invited me here. The creation of a secret alliance would never even occur to them. What's to keep you from replacing the Lords? From enslaving them as you were enslaved?"

"God would not allow it," Pak-7 said uncertainly, his eyes on the tabletop.

"An interesting point," Lando said, leaning forward in his chair. "Let's talk about God. Can he hear us right now?"

Dru-21 felt very uncomfortable. God could *not* hear them. He and his fellow constructs had made certain of that. The meeting was a mistake. The human had taken control. He realized that now but it was too late.

Lando nodded knowingly. "He can't, can he? And you arranged that. So save the 'God would not allow it' stuff for someone else. If you can block God out of this room, then you have the ability to enslave the heavies."

The smuggler got to his feet. He was angry and decided to let it show. "You don't get it, do you? The Lords enslaved your genes, your memories, and your minds. Then, when they didn't need you anymore, they sent other slaves to kill you. Each and every one of you was born remembering that night.

"Then the machine that you call 'God' took over. For thousands of years he told you what to do and when to do it. And for what? For you? Or for those who created you, and programmed him? In case *they* come back and decide to move in.

"Then the Il Ronnians arrive. They enslave everyone. You try to get along with them, find it doesn't work, and decide to fight back. Or, to be more accurate, the *heavies* fight back, and you're stuck with the results.

"And now, before the present war has even been fought much less won, you're conspiring to enslave the heavies."

Pak-7 rose to his feet as well. He was angry and it showed. "What is this talk of enslavement? The heavies are less intelligent than we are. You said so yourself! They are like children who look to us for guidance and leadership. *We* plan the harvests so they never go hungry, *we* make sure that they have clothes, and *we* take care of them when they are sick. Is that the way that a master treats a slave?"

Lando put his hands on the table and leaned forward. "Yes, it is! The prudent farmer takes good care of his livestock!"

Dos-4 spread her hands in front of her. "So what would you have us do?"

Lando straightened up. What the hell was he doing anyway? One of his father's many sayings came to mind.

"Smuggling is dangerous enough, son, so stay away from the really suicidal stuff like politics."

It was good advice. Lando mustered a smile and looked Dos-4 directly in the eye.

"I honestly don't know. This is a difficult situation. But one thing is for sure. The entire situation is bound to change. You, the heavies, and God have lived in harmony for thousands of years now. The Il Ronnians are looking for God. What if they find him? Tear him apart? Take him away? Or what if they don't? What if they leave? Will you go back to life as it was? Can you? I think not."

There was a long silence. The constructs looked at one another. Dru-21 was the first to speak. His voice was solemn. "This meeting did not go as expected. You have given us much to think about, Pik-Lando. We will do so."

The anger was gone and Lando felt silly standing up. He took his seat and saw Pak-7 do likewise. Dos-4 broke the momentary silence.

"Pik-Lando raises an important issue. The Il Ronnians have intensified their efforts to find God."

"Yes," Zera-12 agreed. "They are systematically destroying entire villages in an effort to find him."

"And herding our people out into the countryside," Pak-7 added sourly. "Many have been killed."

Lando looked around the table. He had wanted to ask the question for some time now and this seemed as good an opportunity as any.

"Where *is* God anyway? Can we move him? Or defend him?"

The constructs looked at each other, then back to Lando. Dru-21 was the first to speak. "It is as the villagers say: 'God is everywhere and nowhere at all.' "

Lando looked at each construct in turn to see if they were serious. They were. "You really don't know, do you?"

Dos-4 made a gesture with her hands. "No, we don't. Many have asked over the years and always receive the same reply."

"God is everywhere and nowhere at all."

"That is correct."

Lando frowned. "Well, it doesn't make sense. God is a machine. A complicated machine, a powerful machine, but a machine nonetheless. That means that he has circuitry, capacitors, resistors, amplifiers, and who knows what all. So, even allowing for the possibility of tremendous miniaturization, he still takes up some space. And that implies a location of some sort."

Pak-7 leaned back in his chair. "It is clear that the Il Ronnians agree with you. They are tearing the planet apart in an effort to find him."

"Yeah," Lando said thoughtfully, "they sure are. Think back. Are there any places that God forbids you to go?"

Pak-7 looked thoughtful. "No, not that I can think of."

"Are there places that you don't go because they are scary, bring bad luck, or are simply impossible to access?"

It was obvious that Pak-7 had drawn a blank. "No, nothing comes to mind."

Lando nodded. Well, so much for some of the more obvious possibilities. There was only one thing to do. The smuggler looked at Dru-21.

"I need a favor."

Dru-21 bowed slightly. "Anything within our power."

Lando looked around the room. The constructs looked back. They were curious and made no effort to hide it.

"I want to speak with God."

There was a hiss of indrawn breath as the constructs took it in. To their knowledge no one had ever initiated a conversation with God. Communication was strictly one-way. God spoke and you listened. Still, these were troubled times, and there was no specific prohibition against it either.

Dru-21 looked around the table and received a nod from each construct in turn. He looked at Lando. "God may or may not decide to speak with you, but we will clear the way."

15

The sun had been up for less than an hour and it was damned cold by Il Ronnian standards. A stiff breeze blew across the top of the hill causing a tarp to flap and pop. The air smelled of fertilizer.

Quarter Sand Sept Commander Teex shivered and pulled his battle cloak around his shoulders. There was no doubt about it. He was getting too old for this kind of crap.

Half Sand Sept Commander Heek's lander dropped toward the pad, flared, and sprayed Teex with tiny particles of dirt. They peppered his face and uniform like shells from a microscopic artillery barrage.

The Sand Sept officer did his best to ignore them. He had more important problems to contend with, like his failure to find the computer, and the sniper who had killed three of his officers in five days. Two of the officers had been somewhat promising. Yes, if Heek wanted to kick his butt, there was no shortage of reasons to do so.

But maybe, just maybe, he could keep Heek so busy touring headquarters, dropping in on supposedly unsuspecting fire bases, and gabbing with the troops that he'd get bored and return to orbit. He could hope anyway.

There was a loud pop as Heek's pilot cut the flow of fuel to the shuttle's repellors and allowed his craft to settle on its skids. A hatch whirred open. Teex moved his tail into the attentive-subordinate position and headed toward the ship. Gravel crunched under his hooves.

Heex ignored the metal step that a trooper hurried to put in place and jumped to the ground. He looked comfortable in his battle dress. His tail signaled a cheery "hello."

"Nice to see you, Teex. It feels good to be dirtside again. That ship is like a coffin, a big coffin, but a coffin nevertheless."

Heek sniffed the air and made a face. "What the hell is that anyway? It smells like shit."

"It *is* shit," Teex answered grimly. "Or something similar. They spread it on the fields."

Heek looked around. His eyes took in the weapons positions, the way rubble had been used to reinforce the perimeter, the readiness of the troops, everything. Fire Base One looked good but Heek would be damned if he'd tell Teex that. The praise might go to his head.

"You let them farm? After raising six kinds of hell?"

"I let them farm under guard," Teex replied. "It's either that, or start hauling food in by this time next year."

The older officer signaled understanding with his tail. "Well, let's get on with it. I know the drill. You drag me around, the troops act surprised, and I lift."

Teex held a hand up in protest. "Sir . . ."

"Save it for someone younger and more gullible," Heek interrupted, "just promise me one thing."

Was that a smile? Or just another version of Heek's perpetual scowl? Teex did his best to look innocent. "Sir?"

"Promise me that you took steps to keep our itinerary secret."

"Yes, sir. I . . ."

"That includes the geek computer."

"Of course, sir. We . . ."

"Because Ceeq will take over if I get killed."

Teex felt a tightness in chest. "Excuse me, sir?"

"You heard me," Heek answered gruffly. "Ceeq received his commission a full seven months before you received yours. So, unless you would like Ceeq to write your next fitness report, it would be a good idea to keep me alive."

Heek was joking, Teex realized that now, but it was too late to laugh. He signaled appreciation with his tail instead. "Thank you for sharing that, sir. May you live to be at least five hundred years old."

Heek made a coughing sound that might have been laughter.

The first part of the tour went well. It started with an inspection of Fire Base One. Heek saw the comm center, the personnel bunkers, the ammo dumps, the missile launchers, the perimeter defenses, and more.

He also saw the solar-powered placards that Teex had mounted all around the fire base. Each one bore the holographic likeness of a black disk sitting alongside a pocket stylus to provide scale.

The text said, "If you find a small black disk, turn it in. Do not say or do anything around these devices that would be of value to the enemy. Each disk is worth fifty rang."

Heek nodded to himself. Most of the troopers would murder their own egg mothers for fifty rang.

Then came lunch with the troops, a nervous affair, with everyone on their best behavior, and Heek playing his role to the hilt. Teex watched in amusement as the senior officer made his way through the mess tent, tail locked in the "it is good to see you, faithful subordinate" position, stopping at each table to speak with the troops.

It was simple "How is the food?" "Is your equipment okay?" "Are you ready to kill some geeks?" kind of stuff, but the troopers loved it. For reasons that Teex couldn't quite fathom they actually *liked* Heek. The universe, he decided, was a mysterious place.

Shortly after lunch they climbed aboard a helicopter, and with an escort of four heavily armed air cars swept out across the valley for a lightning-fast tour of the outlying fire bases.

The pilots flew fast and low making it difficult for nonexistent enemy radars to pick them up.

Both side hatches were open. That provided the door gunners with a good field of fire and scooped great draughts of air into the passenger compartment. Teex felt it press against his face and blinked his eyes in order to keep them moist.

The aircraft swerved slightly to avoid a hill and the devastated village that sat on top of it. Heek leaned forward until the safety harness stopped him. He had to yell over the engine noise. "Is that typical?"

Teex signaled "yes" with his tail. "Yes, Sir. We are more than a little shorthanded as you know. We have an entire planet to occupy and about a quarter of the troops required to do it. If the geeks were armed, and a bit more aggressive, they would push us off-world in no time at all. It is clear that they have the necessary technology to manufacture weapons equivalent to ours. So, in order to prevent them from doing so, we have cleared the villages and destroyed them. Manufacturing plants too. Those we can find anyway."

"What about the humans?"

"They are a problem, sir. They have captured weapons and seem intent on leading some sort of resistance movement. One of them is operating as a sniper. He has killed three officers in five days. We are searching for him but there are thousands of places to hide."

Heek signaled his understanding. "Yes, the Council demands a miracle each and every day. What about the rest of the planet? Are there signs of resistance?"

Teex glanced toward the starboard hatch. Fields flashed by below. It was a difficult question. How to answer? Should he tell the truth? That he really didn't know? That he suspected the worst? Or what the older officer wanted to hear? That everything was fine. He chose a middle course.

"Yes, sir . . . there are some signs of resistance. Or 'avoidance' might be a better word. Our spy sats and recon patrols report the same thing. It seems word has spread and the geeks are disappearing into the countryside. Usually at night. We can follow a lot of their activities from orbit but don't have the troops to track them down."

Heek smiled grimly. "All the more reason to find that computer and find it quickly. An artifact like that would go a long way toward convincing the Council to put a full sept on the ground."

Teex signaled assent and leaned back in his chair. Good. If he had accomplished nothing else today he had given Heek a feel for the size and scope of the problem.

The rest of the morning passed with a series of laser-quick visits to the fire bases that Teex had established throughout that part of the countryside. All were built on hilltops, and like Fire Base One, many of them sat on sites previously occupied by buildings or villages.

The drill was always the same. Land, receive a formal greeting from the officer or noncom in charge, tour the defenses, talk to the troops, and take off again. The midday meal consisted of field rations at Fire Base Seven.

After that it was time to get back into the air and follow a long curving course that would touch on three additional outposts and eventually take them home.

They had been in the air for only a brief time when Teex heard a buzzing sound in his left ear. He activated the tiny throat mike. "Yes?"

The voice belonged to his pilot, Deeo. "Holding Area Two is under attack by a large force of hostiles. They have automatic weapons . . . repeat . . . automatic weapons. The NCOIC requests an air strike plus reinforcements. Fast response force two is en route. They are twenty from ground."

Teex swore under his breath. Damn. It was just as he'd feared. The geeks *were* manufacturing weapons. His efforts to prevent them from doing so had not only failed, but failed in a rather visible manner, with Heek looking on. Well, there was very little he could do but make the best of it. He kept his voice low and even.

"What kind of air support is available?"

Deeo's voice was calm, professional. "We are five from ground. The navy has three fighters inbound. They will arrive fifteen from now."

Teex didn't hesitate. "We will respond. Send the air cars ahead. Let the navy know. Those fighter pilots have a tendency to shoot anything that moves. Notify Fire Base One."

"Yes, sir."

The air cars shot ahead as the helicopter banked to the right. Heek gave the younger officer a questioning look and Teex filled him in. If the Half Sept commander was surprised, or disturbed, he gave no sign of it. He signaled understanding with his tail and looked out through the hatch.

Rola-4 heard the chatter of automatic weapons and saw the crowd turn. They moved in her direction. It was pointless, since they were already as far away from the fighting as the surrounding force field would allow them to be, but panic is a stupid thing. She looked for a place to hide and couldn't find one.

The valley was long and narrow with steep scree-covered slopes on three sides. But the bottom, the part that the Il Ronnians had designated as "Holding Area Two," was as smooth and flat as her kitchen table back home.

Rola-4 moved toward the right. That took her out of the crowd's path and put them between her and the fighting. Some extra protection for Neder-33. He showed his appreciation by crying and trying to wiggle out of her arms.

Thanks to God, and the warning he had given her the evening before, the females had known about the attack before it came. Known, but been helpless to do anything about it.

The mob thundered toward her, females screaming, babies crying. To retreat meant running the risk of being pushed into the force field and it had the power to deliver a high-voltage shock. Rola-4 turned her back to the crowd and braced her feet. Bodies bumped into hers. Somebody shoved her. She held fast. The mob moved past.

Wexel-15 felt a hard knot in the pit of his stomach. Not at the thought of dying, but at the thought of making a mistake and causing others to die. A glance to the right and left showed him that his squad members were still there, weapons at their shoulders, delivering methodical three-round bursts into the Il Ronnian command post.

It wasn't much, just a pit dug into the top of a slight rise, with earthworks all around. He grinned. The force field prevented them from rushing the Il Ronnians but did nothing to stop their bullets. He counted four alien bodies on the ground and knew there were two more inside. The construct felt a sense of pride. That would teach them!

An Il Ronnian stuck his assault rifle up over the earthworks, ripped off fifteen or twenty rounds without looking, and pulled the weapon down again.

The human female's voice was a calm presence in Wexel-15's ear, put there by some sort of electronic magic devised by the person-machine that called itself "Cy Borg," and some of Dru-21's technicians.

"Okay, Wex. Mission accomplished. We inflicted some casualties, provided the prisoners with a psychological boost, and gave the Il Ronnians a choice: They can tie up more troops guarding camps like this one . . . or turn the prisoners loose. So pull back. Their air support will arrive at any moment . . . and we're not equipped to deal with that."

Wexel-15 heard the words, processed them, and gave the proper orders. "All right . . . time to pull out. Doma-7 and Jubo-10, you first, then in pairs. I'll come last."

The volume of fire fell off as the heavies obeyed his orders and pulled back. Their escape route led up through a gully and into one of the ancient drain pipes that ran down out of the mountains. They moved slowly, methodically, just as Della had taught them.

The plan called for them to follow the drain upward for fifteen or twenty minutes until they reached the point where the pipe split right and left. Fortifications had been placed there, and if the Il Ronnians were foolish enough to follow them underground, the constructs would be waiting.

Della's voice was urgent now. "Move it, Wex! Here comes the air support!"

Wexel-15 checked to make sure that the last pair of heavies were headed up the gully, loosed one last burst, and rolled left. Dirt fountained where he had been, followed by the *thump! thump! thump!* of an auto cannon and the flicker of a passing shadow.

The air car was so low that Wexel-15 could see individual scratches where the aircraft's pilot had carelessly scraped some treetops two days before. Wexel-15 knew he should be thinking about other things, should be concentrating on the gully, but couldn't help himself. His mind noticed that the scratches were brighter than the surrounding metal and ran forward and back rather than from side to side.

Air slapped Wexel-15's face as the air car pulled up and around. The pipe was just ahead, a gaping black maw, just waiting to swallow him. Two figures popped out of it, Doma-7 and Jubo-10, both raising their assault rifles to fire. Their weapons made a sound like ripping cloth.

Wexel-15 felt a combination of anger and pride. What they were doing was brave but stupid. He stumbled, fell, and rolled over.

The air car dived straight down, firing as it came. The auto cannons winked at him as they fired. The shells made a thumping sound as they exploded. He could see them hit, walking their way up the slope, heading for him. The construct waited for a shell to hit him, waited for the pain, and was surprised when it never came.

A bullet, one of the hundreds sprayed upward by Doma-7 and Jubo-10, hit the metal support that curved up and over the passenger compartment, and shattered into a thousand tiny pieces. One of those pieces, a chunk of metal so small that it would take a microscope to adequately see it, struck the pilot in the cheek.

The pilot had already removed his hand from the stick and touched his cheek before his brain found time to tell him that it was a stupid thing to do. The air car exploded as it hit the ground. Pieces of metal and plastic flew in every direction.

"Run, Wexel, run!"

The construct scrambled to his feet. He ran forward, felt hands grab his arms, and was jerked into the pipe. It felt cool and safe.

Della pulled her eye away from the scope. The air car had hit the ground about five hundred yards east of the pipe. A column of dark black smoke spiraled up to stain the sky. She shook her head in amazement. Once their training was complete the heavies would make some damned fine troops. A little light on the command and control side, but what the heck, you gotta start somewhere.

The three surviving air cars circled like vultures, pouring fire down toward the drain pipe, all of it wasted.

Della heard the familiar *whop, whop, whop* of chopper blades and looked to the right. The wall of carefully stacked stone blocked her view but the chopper was visible through one of the many chinks. The helicopter came in low and slow just as she had known it would. The aircraft was big, boxy, and heavily armored. Too heavily armored to be fitted with antigrav units like those used on the lighter and therefore faster air cars.

Della smiled. The same smile she had smiled after finding a fugitive with a price on his head. The helicopter would have at least one officer aboard. A soon-to-be-dead officer.

The bounty hunter looked around her blind. It would have to be good, very good, because from the moment she fired, the air cars, helicopter, and Sol knew what else would be all over the place.

Rather than run as she had in the past, Della planned to stay right where she was, and depend on her hiding place to protect her.

She and Wexel-15 had constructed the blind the night before. It had started as a small cave on the steep scree-covered hillside.

By cleaning out some of the bigger pieces of rock, and walling off the entrance, they had created a rather snug little hide.

Snug, but far from invulnerable. Della knew she would get one shot and one shot only. More than that and they would almost certainly spot her.

The helicopter disappeared as it dropped down below the view offered by that particular chink in the rocks.

Della raised the rifle and placed the butt against her shoulder. The weapon felt as if it had been custom-designed for her body, which it had. The butt snugged up against her shoulder just so, the grip molded itself to the shape of her hand, and the sight seemed to meld with the contours of her face.

Della slipped the barrel out through a hole created for that exact purpose. The barrel was equipped with a flash suppressor and a loose-fitting sleeve that had been dyed to match the color of the surrounding rock.

She touched the button mounted on the left side of the pistol-style grip. Video blossomed as the electronic sight came to life. Faces blurred as she swept across the prisoners and found the helicopter. Bushes danced and swayed as gigantic skids touched the ground.

Della moved the weapon a hair to the right so that the electronic cross hairs made an X right in the center of the door gunner's chest. The trooper wore body armor but it would be no match for the bounty hunter's high-velocity ammunition. But Della had other higher-ranking targets in mind.

The gunner looked right and left checking for danger. Nothing. Another trooper appeared at his side. The second trooper handed the first trooper an assault rifle. Both of them jumped to the ground. Bodyguards. The big cheese would appear any second now.

Della sucked in a long slow breath. Ten seconds passed, twenty, and then thirty. She let the breath out. What the hell? Had the officer slipped out the other side of the chopper? Wait a minute. . . .

Della moved her weapon to the left. She'd been had! The bodyguards were gone! At least one of them had been an officer. The bastards were getting smart. Remove your insignia, blend in, dump protocol. It was all SOP for the field. The only surprise was how long it had taken the Il Ronnians to implement it.

The three fighters made an earth-shaking roar as they swept in out of the sun. The centermost aircraft fired a pair of air-to-ground missiles toward the mouth of the drain pipe while the other two strafed the opposing hillsides. A surefire way to suppress sniper fire and anything else the constructs might have up their sleeves. The missiles hit and exploded with loud crumps.

Della jerked the barrel of her weapon back inside the cave and curled up in a little ball. All it would take would be one cannon shell to turn her cave into an instant tomb.

The cannon shells made a loud cracking sound as they hit the hillside above her, exploded, and sent miniature avalanches down toward the valley below.

Then, just as quickly as they had come, the fighters were gone. Recalled to fly high cover for the reaction team that had arrived from Fire Base One.

Della opened her eyes and looked around. The cave was completely dark. An avalanche of loose dirt and rock had sealed her in. She felt very, very frightened.

Teex placed hands on hips and looked out over the prisoners. Even though they were untouched by the initial firefight, and the subsequent counterattacks, the female constructs were shocked and dazed. Many cried, whimpered, or both. Taken together they made a low keening sound that got on his nerves. He spoke without looking at the noncom by his side, a rather average-sized trooper who towered over him nonetheless.

"Describe it again."

File Leader Keem groaned internally. How many times would it take? By the holy fluid itself officers were a stupid lot. He forced himself to be patient.

"Yes, sir. It started about dawn. Just after the sun came up. The prisoners seemed restless. Agitated like. And they moved away from our position."

"As if they knew something was about to happen."

Keem signaled assent with his tail, realized that Teex couldn't see it, and said, "Yes, sir."

"All right," Teex said thoughtfully, "let's interrogate some of them. Lean on them a little . . . see what pops out. Find Half Sept Commander Heek. Tell him what we plan to do."

Keem said, "Yes, sir." He started to salute, remembered that a sniper could be watching, and scratched himself instead.

It seemed to take forever to get through the line. It started next to the supply dump where the Il Ronnians kept their food and snaked back into the middle of the field. Rola-4 had no watch, but estimated that she had been in line for more than two rals, which was way longer than usual. Food distribution normally took half a ral at most.

The female in front of her moved forward a couple of steps and Rola-4 prepared to do likewise. She bent over, grabbed Neder-33 around his middle, and picked him up. He was dirty but relatively happy. Rola-4 took two paces forward and put her son down. He tugged at one of her sandals and giggled.

When Rola-4 straightened up again it was to find herself in deep, deep trouble. The distribution point was just ahead. She saw Tusy-35 say something to the Il Ronnians, saw the shortest one of the group turn to look her way, and felt his eyes bore through her head.

Seconds later the aliens were there, tearing the front of her dress open, ripping the pouch from around her neck.

The shortest Il Ronnian wasted little time spilling the contents of the pouch into the palm of his hand. Rola-4 felt cold all over as she saw the name tag, the lock of Neder-32's hair, and the black disk. God's disk.

The Il Ronnian allowed the name tag and earring to fall from his hand but held the disk up for the others to see. He glanced Rola-4's way and said something in a language she couldn't understand.

Rola-4 managed to grab Neder-33 and hold him in her arms as they led her away. She looked around for signs of sympathy or help. All of the constructs looked at the ground, all except Tusy-35 that is, and she looked very pleased.

16

Lando swept the Il Ronnian field glasses across the compound. The binoculars felt awkward in human hands but did the job. It was night and the light-intensifying mode made things look green.

First came the steel-mesh fence. It was about eight feet high, and came complete with razor wire along the top, enough voltage to cook an army for dinner, and just about every kind of sensor there was.

Then came the fifty-foot free-fire zone. It was backed up by robotic weapons emplacements that couldn't be tricked, bribed, or put to sleep.

And then, just to make sure that the triangle-shaped vehicle park really was secure, the Il Ronnians had constructed three guard towers. They mounted searchlights, automatic weapons, plus a battery of ground-to-air missiles.

The place was damned near impenetrable. For bio bods anyway.

Cy Borg bobbed up and down next to Lando's right shoulder. Light glinted off his metal body. It came from the floods that surrounded the Il Ronnian vehicle park. His voice was a hoarse whisper.

"This is stupid, Pik . . . it'll never work."

"Then get the hell out of here," Lando answered grimly. "I'll do it myself."

"You'll never make it."

"Then do it for me."

Both dropped to the ground as an air car whined overhead. It was black on black against the sky. The beams from its landing lights made twin tunnels through the night. It dropped over the far side of the free-fire zone, taxied toward a distant set of fuel pumps, and coasted to a stop. A pair of insectoid robots moved out to greet it.

Lando glanced at his wrist term. "That one was right on time. They arrive and depart at fifteen-minute intervals."

Cy gave a mental sigh. They had been together, preparing for Lando's audience with "God," when the news had come in. There had been a firefight. Della was missing, killed outright or buried in a cave-in. The constructs weren't sure which. They were trying to organize a search party but it wouldn't be easy. Holding Area Two was crawling with troops.

Lando had been like a mad man ever since. He had commandeered a light utility vehicle, crashed that into a ditch, and was preparing to steal an air car. Anything that would help him traverse the two hundred fifty miles that separated him from Della.

Cy thought he could remember when a woman meant that much to him but wasn't sure. He looked around. The cyborg saw quite clearly thanks to his infrared vision. So this was it . . . the place where his mostly wasted life would come to an end.

Cy felt an emptiness in his nonexistent gut. But the thought of losing Lando made him feel even worse. He had come to depend on Cap, Melissa, Della, and Lando. They were like family. They were rough sometimes, unreasonable more often than not, but caring too and that meant a lot.

"All right, Pik, I'll do it."

Lando slapped the cyborg on top of his housing. The cyborg bobbed up and down.

"Thanks, Cy . . . I won't forget it."

Unless we end up dead, Cy thought glumly. You'll forget everything then . . . including me.

"The key," Lando continued, completely unaware of the cyborg's thoughts, "is to follow an air car in. We know they arrive at fifteen-minute intervals. So you wait, get into position, and follow one in. Stay close enough, and the sensors will see what they expect to see, a single image entering the compound."

Cy looked at the greenish-white blob that represented Lando. He made it sound so simple, so easy. Never mind the sensors, the automatic weapons systems, or the sentries. Just "follow an air car in."

Fear rose to fill his mind. He pushed it down again. The smuggler turned his attention to the compound. Time slowed to a crawl.

Finally, after what seemed like hours, Lando touched his housing. "Okay, Cy. An air car should come along in two minutes or so. It's time to get into position."

Cy managed to resist the wave of fear that threatened to engulf him. He bobbed up and down, afraid to speak lest his voice reveal what he felt inside, and used squirts of compressed air to push himself upward. His antigrav unit made it easy. It gave him the same freedom to move up, down, or sideways enjoyed by divers who use belt weights to counter the natural buoyancy of their bodies.

The antigrav unit was a small low-powered affair, so Cy was limited to an altitude of a hundred feet or so, but that would be quite adequate. The air cars had a tendency to skim the top of the security fence as they came in.

Cy reached an altitude of seventeen feet and hovered in midair. He spun in place. His sensors fed him an kaleido-scopic mishmash of information. Bearings, vectors, blobs of heat, radio traffic, radar signals, radiation counts, and a host of other information all fought for his attention. The vehicle park rotated in and out of sight as he turned. One thought kept coming to mind. If he could see *them*, then they could see *him*. And there wasn't a damned thing he could do about it.

Leep allowed the front legs of his chair to hit the raised computer floor with a loud thump. The other techs looked his way, then back at their screens. Leep frowned. Something weird had appeared on the low-altitude surface-scanning radar. The return made a small red blip on his otherwise empty screen. It was too small to be an air car, too large to be a bird, and too stationary to be an incoming missile.

The blip did match the "drone/surveillance" design param-eters programmed into the battle computer's memory banks however, and a recommendation appeared at the bottom of his screen: "82.4% match with type IDE-47 enemy drone. Destroy."

Leep felt his mind race. The recommendation made sense if you were on a human world fighting humans, but he wasn't. He'd been dirtside for more than two months now and there had been no reports of drones in all of that time.

So, what if the blip was something else instead? Like the unsecured antigrav platform that had drifted along the fence a few days earlier? Keeb had destroyed it and Beeq was furious. So furious that Keeb would be pulling extra duty well into the next century.

What to do? Bump the problem up a level, that's what. Leep touched a button. Somewhere, down at the chow hall probably, Beeq's pager started to beep.

Leep leaned back allowing the front two legs of his chair to come off the floor. The technician used his tail to hold himself in place. The blip was still there. He grinned. Let Beeq handle it. After all, that's what the silly old geezer got paid for.

The air car should arrive any second now. Cy turned his back on the vehicle park itself and scanned the horizon. Nothing . . . nothing . . . there! A yellow-red pinpoint within the cool surround of nighttime air, blooming larger and larger, until it filled his electronic vision.

Cy spun around and pushed himself toward the security fence. He had to build momentum, had to match the speed of the air car, or be left behind. The cyborg tensed as the security fence rushed to meet him.

Suddenly the air car was there, no more than twenty feet away, using its reverse thrusters to slow down. A wall of air hit the cyborg and threatened to push him out of position.

Cy gave it everything he had, fighting his way through the air car's wake, giving thanks as he slipped in behind it.

Then, what had been hard became suddenly easy. The suction created by the air car's passage pulled Cy along behind it.

The security fence slipped by followed by the free-fire zone and the automated weapons positions. He'd made it! Not only that, he was still alive!

Leep felt Beeq's arrival long before he actually saw it. The noncom was a good fifty pounds overweight, and that, plus his rather heavy tread, shook the com shack's flimsy floor like a miniature earthquake. Thus warned, Leep sat up straight in his chair, and did his best to look alert. The other techs did likewise.

The console gave a soft beep. Leep frowned as another red blip appeared. He glanced at the digital readout located in the upper right-hand corner of his screen. 20:44 hours. The air car was right on time.

Leep waited as the battle computer queried the air car, got the right recognition codes, and flashed the words "cleared for landing" on the bottom of his screen.

Beeq was like a mountain hanging over Leep's head. The noncom smelled of malp. It would never occur to Beeq to bring him a cup. "So, what is the problem this time?"

Leep looked down at the screen and opened his mouth to speak. Nothing came out. The air car had landed and the smaller blip had disappeared. The noncom would never believe him. The technician could imagine Beeq's sarcasm. It would go on for days. Comments about the blip that wasn't there, jokes about his eyesight, and laughter behind his back. He was well and truly screwed. Leep swallowed hard.

"Sorry to bother you, File Leader Beeq . . . but I feel ill. A virus perhaps. Could you send someone to relieve me?"

Beeq took a look at Leep's face, saw that the trooper looked peaked, and signaled agreement with his tail. "I will roust your relief. Do the best you can until he arrives."

The floor shook as Beeq stumped away.

Leep let out a long slow breath. It had worked. His relief would be pissed but that was better than a run-in with Beeq. He pushed the chair back onto its rear legs. The screen was blank. Where had the blip disappeared to anyway?

Cy hovered behind a stack of plastic cargo containers. He could hardly believe it. Everything had gone according to plan. So far anyway.

The cyborg scanned his surroundings. He saw bloblike troopers move here and there, a latticework of fuzzy green lines, and background filled with radiated heat. An engine growled nearby. Nothing out of the ordinary. Good.

Cy preferred to remain airborne but knew that to do so would increase the chance of detection. He rolled along the ground instead. It was bumpy and littered with obstacles, but relatively safe. The cyborg was way below eye level, and as long as he moved with care, he stood a good chance of avoiding detection.

• • •

Lando looked at his watch. Ten minutes had passed. It felt like twenty. Where was Cy anyway? Was he okay? A wave of guilt washed over him. The little cyborg had been afraid. Lando had known that and ignored it. He had pushed, goaded, and bullied Cy into risking his life. Dammit. How could he have been so selfish?

Lando swept the glasses over the Il Ronnian compound and said the same words over and over like a prayer: "Come on, Cy, you can make it. Come on Cy, you can make it."

Cy paused in the shadow cast by a storage tank, looked to be sure that the way was clear, and rolled across the road. A wooden walkway had been built along the other side. The compound was dry at the moment but turned into a sea of mud whenever it rained. Cy pushed himself under the boardwalk and turned toward the left.

Light came down through the cracks and laddered out in front of him. The cyborg picked up speed, winding in and around the cast-off meal paks, wood scraps, and other less identifiable debris that lay scattered beneath the walkway.

Then light flooded the area up ahead and the entire structure shook as a pair of Il Ronnians opened a door and stepped out onto the boardwalk.

Cy froze. The Sand Sept troopers moved in his direction. Their words were automatically translated by a program that Cy had set up in his auxiliary memory banks. He listened as their shadows swept over him.

"Did Leep say what was wrong?"

"No, some kind of bug probably. He looks like death warmed over."

"He *always* looks like death warmed over."

Their laughter sounded like gravel passing through a meat grinder. Cy was glad when a door slammed and cut it off.

The cyborg rolled forward again, bore right as the walkway disappeared, and headed toward the triangular landing pad. There were all sorts of vehicles parked around it. They gleamed under the lights.

Light flooded the area in front of him. It was so bright that each little pebble stood out from all the rest and threw a shadow on the ground.

The cyborg paused, knowing that he would have to make his way across the highway of light, but dreading the risks involved.

Lando swore through gritted teeth. He could imagine Della wounded, waiting for him to come, dying by inches. What if she were already dead? What about all the things that he'd meant to say but never gotten around to?

"Come on, Cy! Quit screwing around in there!"

Lando regretted the words the moment he thought them. Anger turned to guilt and the cycle started all over again. "Come on, Cy, you can make it. Come on, Cy, you can make it."

Cy heard a loud humming noise and spun toward the left. The power loader floated inches off the ground and beeped softly as it went. The cyborg looked for an Il Ronnian and saw none. A robot! Good.

The opportunity was too good to miss. Cy rolled forward, maneuvered himself into the loader's shadow, and followed along behind. Now, if he could make it to the other side . . . And there it was. Just what he needed. A finger-shaped shadow that pointed across the road.

The cyborg waited for the shadow to touch him, turned into it, and rolled toward the com mast that made it. He was in among the vehicles a few moments later.

Now, which one to steal? Helicopters were out; he didn't know how to fly them, and didn't have the required legs. That left the air cars.

Cy rolled in and around a forest of landing gear, rising occasionally to peek in a cockpit, searching for just the right one.

Then he found it. An air car at the very end of the line. The aircraft was shaped like a delta, could seat up to four passengers, and was heavily armed. Cy rose, dropped into the open cockpit, and scanned the control panel. Small hatches whirred open as he deployed both of his articulated arms. His pincers darted here and there, touching, feeling, testing. Computers booted themselves up, fans started to hum, and indicator lights came on.

Cy had never been in an Il Ronnian air car before, but he was an engineer, and knew that form tends to follow function.

Especially where military artifacts are concerned. With that in mind it was relatively easy to identify the ignition switch, the inertial navigation system, the weapons indicators, the com gear, and all the rest.

Cy was just about to start the vehicle when another air car swept in over the fence. Landing lights swayed across the compound and grew smaller as the aircraft touched down.

The cyborg had just turned his attention back to the control panel, and was about to flip the ignition switch into the on position, when something thumped against the fuselage. The top rungs of a metal ladder appeared right next to him. He should have known! The last car in line would be the next to depart!

Cy flipped the ignition switch to the on position and felt both the antigrav unit and the propulsion system come to life.

"What the . . . ?"

The words were Il Ronnian but Cy understood them well enough. A visored face appeared over the edge of the cockpit. A long uniformed arm reached out to grab him.

Cy pulled back on the steering column, felt the air car surge upward, and banked to the left.

The Il Ronnian screamed as he fell away.

What Cy did next was pure impulse, though he later claimed to have planned it.

Steering the air car into a tight turn, Cy activated all the weapons systems and opened fire. Cannon shells churned metal, plastic, and dirt into a terrible stew. Helicopters lurched sideways as their landing skids collapsed, air cars burst into flames as fuel lines were cut, and Sand Sept troopers ran in every direction.

Cy was filled with a terrible exultation. He was kicking ass and taking names! The cyborg uttered a well-amplified war cry and headed straight toward a tower.

Lando stood and yelled at the top of his lungs. "Cy, you idiot! Over here! You goddamn bucket of bolts! What the hell are you doing?"

But the words were lost in the sound of cannon fire, explosions, and the *whoop! whoop! whoop!* of an Il Ronnian perimeter alarm.

• • •

Cy released a pair of rockets and banked to the left. He felt rather than saw them explode. A support gave way, the tower shivered and crashed to the ground with a loud boom.

"Yahoo!" Cy yelled as he skimmed across the compound. He walked streams of purple-blue tracers through thin-skinned prefab buildings, laughed as partially clad Il Ronnians spilled out through doors and windows, and yelled insults that no one else could hear. "Take that, you pointy-tailed bio bods!"

Then something scary happened. Indicator lights winked on his control board. The cannons fired twenty rounds apiece and stopped. The last pair of rockets hit the base of the com mast and blew up. It toppled like a huge tree, crushed a pair of air cars, and breached the fence. Blue and white electricity danced in and around the wreckage as new connections were made and the compound's sensors blew out.

Ground fire arched up and around Cy's ground car. It was deceptively pretty. The Il Ronnians were firing back. Fear reached up to pull the high down. Cy banked to the left, circled back, and searched for Lando.

Nothing . . . nothing . . . there! Standing up and waving like a damned fool. Good thing the silly so-and-so had his trusty cyborg buddy along to back him up.

Cy sideslipped toward the ground, fired the reverse thrusters, and slowed down enough for Lando to dive in over the side. His legs still waved as Cy put the air car into a steep climb. Tracers wove patterns around them and the aircraft shuddered as a shell punched its way through the rear passenger compartment. The compound grew smaller as it fell away.

Lando was furious as he straightened himself out and fought his way into a sitting position. "Dammit, Cy! What the hell were you doing?"

"Slowing them down," the cyborg replied smugly. "They'll have a heck of a time following us now."

Lando looked back over his shoulder. Cy was correct. The compound was a quickly shrinking mess. Fires burned, electricity shimmered, and searchlights carved panic-stricken circles in the sky. There were no signs of pursuit. He looked at the cyborg. One vid cam was aimed forward while another looked his way. He would have sworn that he saw it wink.

The cyborg kept the air car low to avoid Il Ronnian radar and followed the terrain toward their destination. It felt like a high-speed roller-coaster ride.

Lando didn't mind the motion but would have preferred to fly the aircraft himself. But Cy had refused his repeated offers to take over so there was nothing he could do but wait and worry.

His main concern, other than for Della's safety, stemmed from above. Surface radars are one thing, but orbital detection systems are something else. Lando imagined delta-shaped fighters dropping from orbit, their target acquisition systems locking up on the air car, their missiles leaping outward.

Would they know what was coming? Would they get some sort of warning? Or simply cease to be?

The smuggler had no desire to find out.

But the minutes became an hour and nothing happened. Finally, after what seemed like an endless series of ups, downs, and sideways jogs, they turned into a long V-shaped valley. It took little more than a glance to see that a major battle was under way.

Light blossomed over the far end of the valley as a series of illumination rounds went off. The smuggler saw that the Il Ronnians had constructed a compound, which though crude, had been heavily reinforced. There were weapons pits galore, automated energy cannons, and a network of interlocking trenches. All heavily sandbagged.

An oval-shaped fence extended out from the compound, and at one end of it, as far from the fighting as they could get, hundreds of constructs lay huddled on the ground. Whether dead or alive the human couldn't tell.

Lando saw pinpoints of light sparkle across the surrounding hillsides as fire was directed inward toward the Il Ronnian compound. But it was nothing compared to the volume of fire that was returned.

Fire stabbed outward like the blossoms of some terrible flower. Entire sections of the surrounding hillsides seemed to soar upward, then fall toward earth. There would be no way to survive that terrible fire. Constructs were dying by the scores.

Lando felt a terrible emptiness in the pit of his stomach. What the hell? There was no attack on for tonight. And with

Della missing, who had ordered it anyway?

But his thoughts were snatched away as a tidal wave of air hit the air car, flipped it over, and rushed away to bounce off the opposing hillsides. Their harnesses held them in. Lando's better than Cy's . . . since no one had anticipated the possibility of a globe-shaped pilot.

Lando thought Cy had blown it and lost control. But the sudden roar told him otherwise. No, the problem consisted of aerospace fighters, the same ones he'd wondered about earlier. Now he knew why they'd been allowed to travel unmolested. The Il Ronnians had focused all of their attention on Holding Area Two.

Cy flipped the aircraft right side up and hugged the left side of the valley. He flew low and slow. If the fighters spotted the air car, and they almost certainly would, chances were they'd leave it alone. And why not? The Il Ronnians controlled the air, so any and all aircraft automatically belonged to them.

Lando activated the comset and punched his way through the frequencies. The smuggler heard code, encrypted voice transmissions, and the sound of a familiar voice. His heart took an unexpected leap. He went back a freq. The voice was familiar indeed! It belonged to Della.

"Listen to me! Pull back. Disengage. That's an order, dammit! I don't care what God said. He doesn't know anything about war, and I do. That's why he brought humans here in the first place. Remember?"

Wexel-15 sounded confused. The chatter of a machine gun threatened to drown him out. "But we thought you were dead, and God said to destroy the compound, so we attacked."

"Well, I'm telling you to retreat, and to do it *now*. Understand?"

Wexel-15 sounded contrite. "Yes, Della. We will pull back."

True to his training Wexel-15 switched to the team frequency and left the command channel open. Lando wasted little time in fumbling an Il Ronnian headset into place and activating the mike. "Della! Where the heck are you?"

Della was cautious, understandably reluctant to reveal her position unless she was sure it was him. "Pik? Is that you?"

"And who else would be wandering around in the middle of the night looking for stray bounty hunters? Give me your position and we'll pick you up."

"You have transportation?"

Lando grinned. "An air limo complete with round chauffeur."

Della laughed. "Okay. I'm just below the ridge line on the north side of the valley, halfway between the spires."

Another set of flares went off enabling Cy to see the jagged ridge line and twin spires. He banked in that direction and activated the air car's running lights.

As the ridge came closer Lando felt an almost overwhelming desire to take over the controls. It seemed as though Cy was coming in way too fast. But the cyborg braked, the air car slowed, and the smuggler saw a light blink on and off.

Cy made a course correction, slowed even more, and coasted along the side of the hill. The light blinked again. It was ahead and off to the left.

The cyborg killed all forward movement and nudged the aircraft in until the running lights colored the rocks.

Della appeared out of the darkness. She had a pack on her back, and a rifle in her hand, and a smile on her face. Rocks slid and clattered as she moved.

Lando felt the nose of the aircraft sink as Della climbed aboard, then rise again as she made her way back toward the open cockpit. He stood to help her in. They sat side by side on the bench-style seat.

Della handed Lando the rifle. The barrel was bent and clogged with dirt. She grinned. "It made one heck of a pry bar."

Lando didn't say a word. He just dropped the weapon into the back seat, put an arm around Della's shoulders, and pulled her close.

A fighter roared the length of the valley and pulled up toward the stars.

Cy killed the air car's running lights and headed away from the valley.

Lando looked past Della. The fighting had died down to an occasional shot. A flare went off. It lit up her face. There was dirt on it. Lando looked into her eyes.

"They said you were dead."

"They were wrong."

"I love you."

Della looked at him for a long time. She nodded soberly. "And I love you."

"Good," Cy said matter-of-factly. "I'm glad that's settled. Now, let's find God and ask him what the heck's going on."

17

Pik Lando and Della Dee followed Wexel-15 and Dru-21 into a drab, somewhat utilitarian room. In fact, judging from the now empty bins that occupied one wall, it had once served as some sort of storage area.

The room lay at the heart of the long-disused industrial complex that served as construct headquarters. Lando knew that not too far away a thousand recruits were busy studying newly made training tapes, marching back and forth across an empty warehouse, and making their way through a really tough obstacle course.

The entire facility was located deep underground, safe from prying eyes, and invisible to electronic sensors. And like everything else on the planet, the constructs had kept the complex in perfect repair, awaiting the return of their long-departed masters.

The storage room was empty now, empty except for a sturdy metal table and some matching stools. Lando found that these were tall, and almost comfortable, suggesting that they'd been designed for either the lights or the Lords themselves.

Wexel-15 tried one, got off, and tried it again. He looked like a mountain on a stick.

What light there was came from two strip panels mounted on the ceiling. They flickered from time to time as if reacting to a distant maintenance problem.

There had been more and more of those lately, as the Il Ronnians herded thousands of constructs into concentration camps, and prevented them from performing their traditional duties.

Lando looked at Della. She looked at him. While the storage room was an unlikely venue in which to converse with a being who called himself "God," it was the logical place to interface with what amounted to a super-powerful maintenance computer. Not only that, but it also served as a useful reminder of the machine's original status, one device out of many.

Still, God was the only computer that had survived the night of death, and like any survivor deserved some respect.

Dru-21 wore a purse belted around his waist. He opened the flap, reached inside, and gathered something into his hand.

Then, moving with what Lando interpreted as dramatic deliberation, the light held his hand over the table. Construct looked at construct. Wexel-15 nodded.

The two of them had become quite close in recent days. Whether as a result of his advice, or because of necessity, Lando couldn't tell. But it was good whatever the reason.

The disks clattered as they hit. Some spun like tops, others fell over on their sides. Light winked off glossy black plastic.

Lando looked up at Dru-21. The construct took a disk and placed it at the center of his forehead.

"You are the first off-worlders to commune with God. There could be danger."

Lando turned to Della. "I'll go first. If I survive you can follow."

The bounty hunter picked up a disk and slapped it against her forehead. Her crossed arms and defiant expression said it all.

Lando sighed, shook his head ruefully, and reached for a disk. It felt cool against his skin.

Slowly, reverently, the constructs chose a disk and placed it on their foreheads. A lot of things happened at once.

Wexel-15's eyes rolled back in his head. Dru-21's normally expressionless face convulsed with pleasure, and the humans felt something akin to an electric current surge through their bodies. It brought neither pain nor pleasure, but was distinctly uncomfortable. Lando was in the process of reaching for his disk when the feeling disappeared. He heard a voice inside his head. It felt big, powerful, confident.

"Greetings." The single word seemed to reverberate through every cell of his mind.

Lando stirred uneasily. It felt weird to have someone or

something else in his head. It was confusing too. Were thoughts sufficient, or should he speak out loud?

"Thoughts are sufficient," the voice said. "The Lords used thought to communicate with me, and I shall use it to communicate with you. Geeeber dorx."

Lando frowned. "Geeeber dorx?" What the hell did that mean? He waited for the computer to reply but nothing came.

Thoughts that felt like Della flooded into the smuggler's mind. A telepathic conference call! It seemed God had a number of tricks up his electronic sleeve. "We would like to discuss the current military situation."

Lando felt God return. "You are to be complimented, Dee-1. Your tactics have been successful. Issle fleeb garbex noghorn . . . planetary rotations from now."

Lando looked around the table. Della shrugged, Wexel-15 looked confused, and Dru-21 was visibly concerned.

The smuggler's worst fears were confirmed. The gibberish was not part of God's normal communications patterns. He swallowed hard.

"Are you aware that some of your thoughts are reaching us in the form of gibberish?"

There was a five-second pause, as if God were checking on something. "Your powers of observation are flawed, Lando-1. All of my primary and secondary systems are operating at or above ninety-seven percent effectiveness."

Wexel-15 looked absolutely stricken, Dru-21's frown became even more pronounced, and Della looked thoughtful. Her thoughts were even, deliberate, as if speaking to a child.

"We believe that the Il Ronnians are trying to find you. If they succeed, their technicians will take you apart and remove you from the planet."

"That is umberlak."

Della shrugged and looked at Lando. He decided to give it a try. "Tell us where you are. We will send troops to protect you."

"I am everywhere ibor nowhere at all."

Lando forced himself to be patient. "That is impossible. Everyone is somewhere."

"Ardo klonk."

There was silence for a moment. All of them felt the same sense of dismay. Della chose her words carefully. "Did you order an attack on the valley that the Il Ronn call 'Holding Area Two'?"

"Yes."

A sensible reply. Expressions brightened.

"It was a poor decision. Many constructs died because of it. Why did you do it?"

There was a long silence followed by: "Nander pog 77784321 orbo."

More gibberish. Faces fell. There was another long silence. Their thoughts were the same. God had suffered some sort of mental breakdown. Why? There was no way to know.

Lando waited for God to read their thoughts, to deny the problem, but nothing came.

Wexel-15 spoke for the first time. His question was appropriate for the general that he had recently become.

"We need information about the Il Ronn. Supply dumps, communications, troop placements, anything you can give us."

"UCKERGAT!"

The thought had an urgent feel.

Dru-21 was the first to respond. "Could you repeat that, please? We did not understand."

"UCKERGAT! UCKERGAT! UCKERGAT! UCKERGAT! UCKERGAT! UCKERGAT!"

Lando shook his head slowly. "I hate to say it, but God is a few planets short of a full system."

Dru-21 tried once again. "God? Are you still there?"

"Abernom 6666 XXXX demidog."

Lando peeled the disk off his forehead and dropped it onto the table.

Slowly, reluctantly, the others did likewise. They started to rise but stopped when the table started to vibrate. Suddenly, without warning, large sheets of paper began to appear from under the tabletop. They hit Wexel-15's knees, startled him, and slid to the floor.

"What the . . . ?" Lando got off his stool and dropped to his knees. He saw that a large black box had been mounted under the tabletop. A printer of some sort. It whined softly as sheet followed sheet onto the floor.

God, or the part of God that was still rational, was responding to their request for information. Or was trying to anyway.

The process continued unabated for a full five minutes until it stopped as suddenly as it had begun. Lando estimated that more than two hundred sheets of paper had been delivered.

Humans and constructs worked shoulder to shoulder to retrieve the printouts and stack them on the table. However, due to the fact that Dru-21 was the only person who could actually *read* the printouts, the rest were forced to watch while he sorted them into piles.

Dru-21 found that many of the sheets were covered with total gibberish, while others made partial sense, but were useless because they dealt with crops, warehouse manifests, or other mundane matters.

Still, he found that some of the printouts contained what appeared to be valuable information about Il Ronnian defenses, troop movements, and so forth, not to mention the beautiful, almost flawless satellite photos of the planet's surface.

It took time to sort them out, select what seemed like the most important, and shuffle them into some sort of order.

So, while Dru-21 worked on that, Lando took the satellite photos and taped them to the wall. They at least were something he could understand without Dru-21's assistance.

The first thing he noticed was that all of them had been obtained from Il Ronnian rather than indig satellites. In fact, knowing the Il Ronnian tendency to steal anything that wasn't nailed down, Lando supposed that the local satellites, if any, were safely stashed in the belly of some warship.

The smuggler couldn't read or write Il Ronnian, but it didn't take a linguist to see that the photo captions featured the same twisted script that he'd seen on captured cargoes, and in numerous documentaries.

The photos were Il Ronnian all right, which meant that God had the ability to tap into their communications systems without them knowing, and steal whatever he wanted. Or had been able to do so anyway, since his abilities seemed more than a little impaired at the moment.

Like Lando, Della was immediately attracted to the photos, and the information that they contained.

The first thing Della noticed was that while the photos were intended to provide the Il Ronnians with intelligence about the constructs and their activities, they worked in reverse as well. The damage caused by the destruction of villages, factories, and artifact sites were like open wounds on the planet's body.

The resolution was excellent. Many of the shots were wide and showed thousands of square miles, while others were closer in and covered a third or even a quarter of that area. And some were tight, so tight that she could make out the identification numbers stenciled across the top of Il Ronnian vehicles, and count heads in a holding area similar to the one that they had attacked the day before.

Quickly, instinctively, the bounty hunter looked for strength and weakness. Where could the constructs attack and cause the most damage? Which areas were so heavily defended that an attack would end in almost certain defeat? What if anything could she predict about the near future? Those thoughts and more churned through her mind as Della studied the photos.

Lando saw the military significance of the photos, but lacked Della's military training, and was drawn more to the wide shots than those that focused on specific installations. He was first and foremost a pilot, a smuggler looking at the target for the first time, fascinated by the overall network of cities, villages, and roads.

What he saw was a series of orderly patterns. Cities packed with rectangular buildings, surrounded by a maze of squared off interlocking streets, some dead-ending, some blocked at both ends, some connecting with others via traffic circles.

And then, radiating out from the cities, the smuggler saw arrow-straight roads and highways that only grudgingly gave way to obstacles like rivers, hills, and mountains. Roads and highways that served as connective tissue, binding hundreds of hilltop villages and lordly estates together, reaching farther and farther out until blocked by climate, terrain, or water.

Like Della, Lando was struck by the extent of the destruction that the Il Ronnians had wrought. Half-excavated cities, devastated villages, blown bridges, severed roads. They were everywhere.

The smuggler was struck by something else as well, the uneasy feeling that there was something familiar about the photos, something he should recognize but didn't. He looked at them in different ways. He turned some of them upside down. But the thought, if thought it was, refused to come.

Finally, unable to put his finger on it and tired of trying, Lando gave up. Della needed help sorting and interpreting tight shots. But even as he worked Lando couldn't escape the feeling that he had missed something, something that was big, and something that was very, very important.

18

Cap squinted into the slowly setting sun. It hit the top of the warehouse and threw a long hard shadow across the plaza.

Children, Melissa included, played a game in which they pretended that the shadow was a cave. A cave filled with the same killer constructs that had terrorized their ancestors. The youngsters laughed, squealed, and screamed in play-pretend terror as they ran back and forth.

The children, and the village they were part of, were like all the others that he'd seen. Buildings on a hilltop, houses ringing the slopes, streets twisting and turning down to the valley below.

Cap looked around. It was early yet and the rest of the tables were empty. Good. He had the pub to himself.

He and Melissa had been on the road for five or six days now. A long dreary affair during which they traveled at night, mixed with the local villagers during the day, and answered the same questions over and over again.

Where are you from? What is it like? How did you get here? It was, Cap decided, enough to make you drink. He picked up the mug and took another sip of the beerlike brew.

The reason for the tour was to build support for the resistance movement, improve morale, and recruit more troops. That's what Lando *said* anyway.

The truth was something different. Cap knew that the *real* purpose of the tour was to get him out of the way, protect Melissa from harm, and make friends among the constructs.

"Hi, folks! No dangerous-looking teeth, buggy eyes, or long pointy tails here!"

Melissa had objective number three in the bag. The con-

171

structs loved her. She looked to make sure that Cap was watching. He nodded and she performed a series of cartwheels that left her peers gawking in amazement.

Cap grinned and lifted his mug in a mock salute. Melissa was the one and only thing that he'd done right, and even she'd been conceived while he was more than a little drunk.

There was a noise, a series of noises actually, but they were distant and unrelated to his present thoughts. Cap ignored them, reluctant to leave the warm, hazy embrace of his own thoughts.

After all, he deserved some relaxation, didn't he? Having dragged his rear from one village to another for days on end? Putting himself on display like some sort of freak in a sideshow? Damned right he did.

But the noises refused to go away. They became louder, and louder, until they couldn't be ignored. What was that anyway? Not helicopters, it couldn't be helicopters, because this area was too remote to be of interest to the Il Ronnians. That's what they'd told him anyway.

Then Cap heard the *thump! thump! thump!* of automatic cannon fire and was peppered with tiny bits of debris when a shell exploded not fifteen feet away. An engine roared and a shadow swept over him.

It was a reconnaissance by fire! The Il Ronnians hoped to drive resistance fighters out into the open. The only problem was that there weren't any. Not yet anyway.

Cap staggered to his feet. There were screams as constructs ran in every direction.

Their guide, a heavy named Lana-8, appeared at his side. She wore a translator and looked terribly distraught.

"Tell us, Captain Sorenson! Tell us what to do!"

Cap felt dizzy. Tell them what to do? No, someone else should handle that. Someone sober. He remembered the sound of klaxons as the *Star of Empire* died around him and a multitude of desperate voices asked him what to do. He had solved the problem by passing out and leaving the decisions to someone else. If only he could do that now. Unfortunately he was sober, well, not exactly sober, but not sufficiently drunk to pass out either.

Melissa ran toward him. Hair flew around her head. She looked concerned, the way a parent looks when their child is in danger, the way *he* should look but didn't. "Run, Daddy, run!"

He took her words and repeated them. "Run! Disappear into the countryside! Take my daughter with you!"

Lana-8 had followed orders all of her life. She grabbed Melissa by an arm and ran.

Melissa screamed, "No! Let me go! Daddy!" But it was no use. Lana-8 was strong, too strong to resist, and Melissa was forced to follow.

Cap watched his daughter go, tears streaming down her face, struggling to break free. He wanted to reach out to her, give her comfort somehow, tell her how much he loved her.

But time had run out. Almost all of it wasted, squandered, and spent on things of little value. It had to do with decisions made long ago, with promises never kept, with responsibilities never fulfilled.

Cap turned and walked toward the middle of the plaza. The Il Ronnians spotted him almost immediately. One helicopter hovered, its weapons sweeping the area, while the other came in for a landing. The human was a prize and the aliens had orders to take him alive.

Without knowing that he had done it, without intending to do so, Cap made it possible for most of the villagers to escape. The Il Ronnians were so intent on his capture that they paid scant attention to the fleeing constructs.

A pair of Sand Sept troopers grabbed Cap by both arms and practically carried him to their chopper. They were big, ugly-looking beings swathed in flat-black body armor and heavy with weapons.

The Il Ronnians paused next to the helicopter just long enough to search him. It took them only seconds to find the handgun and the knife. Sorenson had forgotten all about them.

Then, eager to take their prisoner and leave, the troopers boosted him into the chopper. The geeks were getting better all the time, and every second spent in an unsecured LZ was a second too long.

Cap found himself strapped into a jump seat as the helicopter took off, able to move his head, but little else. The doors were off. Cap saw the village disappear downward, sideslip out of sight, and then vanish altogether.

Fields appeared. Constructs could be seen, streaming away from the village, unsure of where to go. The door gunners watched but didn't fire. Their orders were clear: no more unprovoked violence. Especially in backwater areas like this one. All it did was stiffen geek resistance.

Air slapped Sorenson's face like a hundred soft hands. The alcohol-induced buzz started to fade. Cap began to worry.

Would Melissa be all right? Where would they take him? Would they use torture? The thought made his hands start to tremble.

The flight lasted for more than two hours. In spite of the fact that each trooper wore a translator around his neck none of them said a word. They just stared at him, eyes gleaming from darkened sockets, tails twitching now and again. Did they hate him? Wonder about him? Or just not care? It made the human sweat and he was glad when the chopper touched down.

This LZ was located at the center of a triangle-shaped fire base. It was heavily fortified, or had been anyway. Sorenson saw destruction everywhere. There were burned-out air cars, a com mast that pointed accusingly outward, and a lot of half-burned buildings.

Sand Sept troopers were everywhere, repairing damage, strengthening defenses, and guarding sullen constructs. The heavies were hard at work building a berm.

Cap felt a transitory sense of elation. That would teach the bastards! Screw with humans would they? Not without paying the piper they wouldn't!

But the sense of elation was short-lived. It seemed to melt away as Cap was removed from the helicopter, frog marched across the landing pad, and helped into a reentry-scarred shuttle. They were taking him off-planet! Why?

Sorenson struggled but it did little good. They hustled him through the lock and into a cramped passenger compartment. The acceleration couch felt a little too large and was unusually hard.

A weapons tech appeared. He was huge and wore a nasty-looking side arm. It would be useless to resist so Cap didn't. Moments later he was strapped down and completely immobilized.

The shuttle shivered and lifted off the ground as the pilot applied power to the repellors. Sorenson felt gravity push against his chest, disappear for a moment as the main drive cut in, then double as the ship climbed upward.

Cap allowed himself to relax a little. Space was his element. Something he understood and felt comfortable in. Comfortable except for the heat.

What had started out as a rather pleasurable warmth had become distinctly uncomfortable. Sorenson started to sweat. The Il Ronnians had originated on a desert world, everyone knew that, which made the heat understandable if not pleasant.

But how hot would it get? Hot enough to pass out from heat prostration? Yes, that's how it felt anyway. Sorenson tried to speak, tried to ask for water, but produced little more than a croak instead.

Time passed. Darkness did its best to pull him down. And finally, tired of fighting, Cap gave in. It felt good to enter the same soft nothingness where alcohol had taken him so many times before.

Then Sorenson felt himself pulled upward toward the light. There was heat all around him, but coolness bathed his forehead, and rough sandpaperlike hands touched his skin.

Someone lifted his head. A container was pressed to his lips. Cool liquid trickled down his throat. It went the wrong way and he coughed. The voice was gruff and somewhat distorted by the translator.

"Fools! You almost killed him!"

A sticky gluelike substance tried to weld Cap's eyelids shut. He forced them open and blinked in the harsh light. The passenger compartment was gone, replaced by something much more spacious. It had a harsh medicinal smell. A sick bay, and a large one, too large for a shuttle.

The moment the coughing spell was over they lowered him to the table.

An Il Ronnian bent over him. He wore a vest. It had a multiplicity of pockets. Each pocket was transparent and contained an electronic instrument. They blinked red, yellow, blue, and green. The tip of an arrow-shaped tail appeared to shadow Cap from the overhead lights.

"Turn the lights down! It is too bright for human eyes."

The human sensed movement off to the left and saw the light level drop.

The doctor, at least that's what Sorenson assumed that the Il Ronnian was, removed an instrument from his vest and pressed it against the inside of his wrist. The human jumped as something sharp bit into his arm.

The alien made a motion with his tail. "My apologies. I need a blood sample. The device was designed to penetrate Il Ronnian skin, which is somewhat thicker than yours."

Cap's voice was little more than a croak. "Our physiologies are different. What good is a blood sample?"

"More than you might think," the doctor answered matter-of-factly as he removed the first machine and placed a second over the wound.

"We know quite a bit about humans and the way they are put together. 'Know your enemy.' A human saying, is it not? I took a course in xeno-anatomy. We dissected a variety of human corpses. Fascinating, absolutely fascinating."

The Il Ronnian removed the second machine from Sorenson's wrist, checked to make sure that the small puncture wound was properly sealed, and left the human to his own devices.

Cap felt frightened. The fact that Il Ronnian medical students had access to a plentiful supply of human bodies was more than a little disturbing.

Sorenson imagined himself dead, laid out on a cold metal table, while aliens probed his insides. It sent a shiver down his spine. Cap tried to sit but a burly attendant pushed him down. His lips felt dry. It occurred to him that a drink would taste very, very good.

Ceeq had positioned himself so that planet NBHJ-43301-G hung over his left shoulder. Reflected light made a halo around the back of his head. Teex had scored a coup by capturing the human. Bad, but far from fatal. Another point in an extended game. He forced a smile.

Teex stood off to one side with his hands clasped behind his back. He rocked back and forth on his hooves and tried not to smile. It was hard to do.

Half Sept Commander Heek sat at the table, sipping malp, and watching through half-hooded eyes. It was an inscrutable expression, copied from his mentor, Sept Commander Reet, and quite effective for situations like this one. It conveyed the impression that Heek knew what would happen next, and was simply waiting for his subordinates to confirm it. The truth was that Ceeq had treated them to an enormous meal and he was extremely sleepy.

The doctor, who was actually the ship's senior intelligence officer, stood at quivering attention. His tail was locked into the attentive-subordinate position and his eyes stared straight ahead.

"So, Deez," Ceeq said lazily, "be so good as to give us your impressions."

The intelligence officer swallowed to moisten his throat with holy fluid, and delivered his report in the short terse sentences favored by command schools everywhere.

"The human is of late middle age, in moderate to poor health, and addicted to alcohol. When I examined him the early signs of withdrawal were already evident.

"An examination of his hands reveals none of the epidermal thickening associated with heavy tool use. Based on that, his failure to offer meaningful resistance, and his reactions to the shuttle ride, we may conclude that he serves as a shipboard technician of some sort."

A technician would be less valuable than an officer. Ceeq glanced at Heek, assured himself that the senior officer was still awake, and drove the point home. "The human is not an officer?"

It was a stupid question. The human could be Admiral of the Fleet for all Deez knew. Intelligence is part science and part art for rock's sake. Still, senior officers being what they are, a show of doubt could start a verbal feeding frenzy. He took a chance.

"No, sir. Based on his lack of preparedness, failure to fight, and chemical addiction, it seems safe to assume that the human functions in some sort of subordinate capacity."

The officers signaled agreement with their tails. They knew very little about chemical addiction due to the fact that it was virtually unknown among the members of their race. Still, it seemed safe to assume that not even humans were stupid enough to put an addict in command of a spaceship.

Teex cleared his throat. Ceeq had scored a point with the technician thing but he could afford to ignore it.

"So, what would you recommend?"

Deez knew what the Sand Sept officer meant and had his

answer ready. "Due to the fact that the subject is addicted to alcohol, and is more likely to be forthcoming while under the influence of that substance, I suggest that we give him what he wants."

"Excellent," Teex responded, adding emphasis with his tail. "And I would like to observe."

"And I," Ceeq added smoothly. "Would you care to join us, Half Sept Commander Heek?"

All eyes went to Heek but he was asleep.

19

Lando taped the last of the satellite photos onto the storeroom wall. He looked around. It had taken hours to sort through the stuff but it was worth it. Or would be as soon as they figured out what it meant.

Della brushed his side. The fresh, clean smell of her filled his nostrils. Lando put an arm around her shoulders. "Well, there it is."

The bounty hunter scanned the walls. "Yeah, there it is. Now what?"

Lando looked at her in surprise. " 'Now what?' You were a marine. Take a look at this stuff and tell us what it means."

Della shook her head. "I was a grunt . . . and an enlisted grunt at that. Officers took care of the salad forks, party etiquette, and recon photos."

Lando frowned. "Okay, let's think our way through this. The resistance movement has been catch-as-catch-can until now. Recruit fighters, manufacture weapons, pull some raids."

"Classic guerrilla warfare."

"Right. But where are we headed?" Lando walked over to touch a photo. "Look at this. Taken from space, right? And that's the problem. In a few more days or weeks our forces will be strong enough to kick their butts right off the surface of this planet. Then what? The Il Ronnians sit in orbit, call for reinforcements, and cream us whenever they want."

Della raised an eyebrow. "So?"

The smuggler shrugged. "So, I don't know."

"Well, I do," Wexel-15 said. "It's time to eat!"

The humans turned to find that the construct had entered

the room with a heavily laden tray of food. Lando helped him place it on the table.

Then Dru-21 arrived with a tray full of drinks.

"We'll make a heavy of you yet," Wexel-15 joked as the other construct put the tray down. "Assuming you gain some weight, that is."

Dru-21 made a show of examining Wexel-15's rather extensive waistline. "Not that much, I hope!"

Wexel-15 laughed heartily and slapped Dru-21 on the back. The light staggered slightly, smiled, and sat down. The stool that he chose was right next to Wexel-15's.

Lando was impressed. The constructs had come a long way in a short time. If they could do it, the rest could too. Not overnight, not without problems, but so what? It could be done. That was the important thing.

After the food was shared out Lando found that he was hungry. The constructs were vegetarians, so there was no meat, but the smuggler didn't miss it. His sandwich consisted of a half loaf of fresh bread, hollowed out, and stuffed with an extremely tasty mixture of stir-fried vegetables. The vegetables had been cooked in a sauce that soaked the inside of the bread and tasted wonderful.

There was comparative silence at first, broken only by the sounds of eating, and the occasional request to pass the whatever. Lando found himself ripping off huge bites of sandwich, chasing them with gulps of fruit juice, and scanning the walls. It came to him again. The feeling that he'd missed something, something big, something important.

Then, suddenly, he had it! Of course! It made perfect sense! And it had been there all the time, sitting right in front of his nose, staring him in the face.

"Pik, what's wrong?"

All of a sudden Lando became aware that he had crossed the room and stood inches away from the satellite photos. He put his finger on a city and moved it from place to place. "Look at this, and this, and this!"

The constructs looked at Della and she shrugged. "They're cities. So what's the big deal?"

"Yes, they're cities," Lando replied impatiently, "but what else? Look carefully. Look at the way individual buildings were placed, at how the streets were laid out, at the roads that connect cities together. What does it look like?"

Della stood and crossed the room. She frowned. It *did* look like something, but what? Then it came and she felt as dumbfounded as Lando looked. A circuit board! Or, to be more accurate, a gigantic spread-out-all-over-the-place series of linked circuit boards!

"What?" Dru-21 asked anxiously. "What is it?"

"God," Lando answered simply. "We found God."

"But how could that be?" Wexel-15 asked. "God is everywhere and nowhere at all."

"True, but a bit misleading," Lando replied. "Look at this. God's a machine, right?"

"Right," Wexel-15 said somewhat reluctantly.

"A machine made up of circuits, chips, transistors, capacitors, diodes, and who knows what else."

It was right about then that Dru-21 understood and came to his feet in openmouthed amazement. "The buildings, the villages, the streets, they are all part of God!"

"Exactly!" Lando said triumphantly. "God is *huge*. His circuits run on for miles, his memory chips are large enough to put a building on, and his sub-processors occupy entire villages!"

"Villages that we were encouraged to repair, but were never allowed to change," Dru-21 said thoughtfully.

"Villages that have suffered heavy damage," Wexel-15 said with slow but inexorable logic.

Lando and Della looked at each other in alarm. The construct was right. The Il Ronnians had systematically destroyed many of the villages. And each time they did so the aliens damaged God as well.

No wonder the machine was falling apart, and no wonder it had summoned the humans to help. Its own survival as well as that of the constructs had been at stake.

The drifter! Lando and Della had the same thought at virtually the same moment. God controlled the drifter and the drifter could be used to get help. The kind of help that could drive the Il Ronnians away and keep them away.

There was a down side, of course. Once involved the human authorities would waste little time throwing Lando in prison. Help for the constructs would come at his expense. But it couldn't be helped. He liked the constructs, convenient or not, and would hope for the best.

A strategy started to emerge. One with nice clear objectives, one that stood a good chance of success, but one that would forever change life as the constructs had known it. Would they accept it? Fight for it? And if necessary, die for it?

Lando returned to his sandwich. The smuggler took a bite and chewed thoughtfully. The vegetables had turned cold and somewhat mushy. He decided to take it slowly, one step at a time. "This changes everything."

"Yes," Dru-21 answered slowly, "it does."

"We could repair God and ask him to summon the space-ship."

"Yes, we could."

"We, along with some representatives from your people, could go for help."

"Yes, that would make sense."

"But things would change. God would lose control, and so would you."

"Yes," Dru-21 replied soberly. "That is correct."

Wexel-15 looked confused. "Control? Change? What are the two of you talking about?"

Lando started to reply but Dru-21 cut him off. "Pik refers to the way things were done in the past. God told *us* what to do, we told *you* what to do, and *you* did it. If we go to the humans for help, and they agree to give it, things will change. Nothing will be as it was."

Wexel-15 gave a human-style shrug. "Oh, that. Things have already changed. Are we not seated side by side? Is it not true that our people die in each other's arms? What is done is done. There is no going back."

A grin stole over Wexel-15's face. "And besides, we *deserve* a say, and have weapons enough to make sure that we get it!"

There was silence for a moment followed by howling laughter. Things had changed all right. And for the better.

The next two days were a blur of activity. There was much to do. The constructs would have to wage a war while simultaneously repairing significant amounts of the damage incurred so far.

The need to perform both functions at once stemmed from the fact that the Il Ronnians were unlikely to let them make repairs unimpeded. So, given the fact that the aliens could destroy God faster than the constructs could put him back together, they had little choice but to do everything at once.

And then there was the matter of timing. Because the planet was a long ways off from the Il Ronnian empire, too far for a slower-than-light radio message to do any good, the aliens would be forced to send a ship. A ship that would go hyper, stay there for a week or so, and come out in the vicinity of an Il Ronnian–held planet. Explanations would have to be made, ships found, and troops loaded. The whole thing could take weeks, or even a month.

But, given the fact that the humans had a similar journey to make, and would lose additional time while dealing with the no doubt skeptical authorities, the whole thing shaped up to be a tight race.

The first force to arrive off-planet would polish off what remained of the opposition and fortify the surface of the planet. Once there, it would be almost impossible to dislodge them with anything short of a massive war fleet, and Lando doubted that either side would deem the planet worth that kind of effort and expense.

So there was a great deal to do. An improved system of communications had to be designed and then put into place. All available constructs would have to be identified and allocated to either the resistance movement or to the newly formed construction corps. Teams of lights would have to examine heavily damaged villages to determine how the circuitry had been put together. The satellite photos would have to be analyzed to determine which parts of God's circuitry should be repaired first. And on, and on, and on.

A less-organized society, or one rife with discord, would never have been able to pull it off. But, thanks to a preprogrammed need to work, and acceptance of higher authority, the constructs did as they were told. No one *said* that the orders came from God, but most of the constructs *assumed* that they did, and acted accordingly.

The result was an amazing amount of progress in a very short period of time. Lando thought the whole thing was remarkable, and knew that if members of his species were placed in the same situation, they'd still be squabbling over how to get started.

And so it was that the smuggler was just emerging from another in a long unbroken string of strategy sessions when there was a disturbance at the other end of the corridor.

The first thing he saw was a silvery ball as Cy came flying around a corner. A dirty, somewhat disheveled Melissa was right behind him. She saw Lando, started to cry, and ran the length of the hall. She hit the smuggler hard, pushed him back a step, and sobbed into his chest.

"The Il Ronnians came! They took Daddy away! Oh, Pik . . . I'm so scared."

Lando swore internally. Damn! Trust Cap to screw things up. This was exactly the sort of situation that he'd hoped to prevent. He dropped down to his knees and gave the little girl a hug.

"I'm sorry, honey. Tell me what happened."

"Well, I was playing in the square. Then the Il Ronnians came. They strafed the village and landed. Daddy told everyone to run. I didn't want to go, but Lana-8 dragged me away. That's when the Il Ronnians captured Daddy and took him away."

"Was he hurt?"

"No, I don't thing so."

"Was he sick?"

Melissa made a snuffling sound and nodded. "He's been sick a lot lately. Ever since we arrived."

Lando gave her another hug. "Well, don't worry, honey. Your father has faced worse than this and come out all right. Remember the fight in the asteroids? Right after we found the drifter? Your dad saved our bacon that time."

Melissa looked up into Lando's face. Tears made tracks through the dirt on her face. "This time is different, Pik. I don't know why, but I can feel it."

The words felt right somehow but Lando forced a smile. "Nonsense. Your father will be just fine."

Lando stood. Della had appeared by his side. She held out a hand. "Come with me, honey. We'll get you all cleaned up."

Lando watched them go and turned to Cy. "After all she's been through. Now this."

The cyborg bobbed up and down in silent agreement.

"Who brought her in? What did they say?"

"A construct named Lana-8. She tried to call but a large part of the com system is down."

Lando nodded. The damage to God had destroyed portions of the com system as well. That's why a well-concealed factory was working around the clock to make portable radios.

"What do you think they'll do?"

"Put the squeeze on Cap."

"And?"

"And Cap will tell them everything he knows."

Lando nodded. "That's what I think too."

"So what should we do?"

Lando felt very, very tired. He shrugged. "The very best that we can."

20

Cap couldn't stop shaking. His hands, his head, even his tongue was trembling. He had already thrown up what little food had been in his stomach and was sweating like a pig. And not just because of the Il Ronnian–induced heat either. No, this was his old enemy delirium tremens, a condition that had affected him many times before.

There were only two ways to counter it, give up alcohol completely or have a drink. Of the two the second seemed the most desirable. He rolled off the oversize bunk, staggered over to the durasteel hatch, and banged on it with his fist. The cell, and therefore the door, had been designed to contain much more powerful inmates than he. The sound of flesh hitting metal was little more than a dull thump.

Cap felt a tremendous sorrow. An almost overwhelming upwelling of self-pity. "Please listen to me! I'm sick! I need help! Please!"

Teex watched via the tiny, almost invisible camera mounted high in one corner of the cell. He knew next to nothing about chemical dependency, but the human was in bad shape, that was apparent. He turned to Deez. "So, what do you think? Is the human ready?"

The intelligence officer signaled assent with his tail. "Yes, the data files agree. The next stage of withdrawal could involve hallucinations. They could work against us. This is the moment to befriend him."

"Excellent," Teex replied. "I will make sure that the stage is set. You bring him along."

Cap staggered and almost fell into the hall when the hatch hissed open. They'd heard him! A distant part of his mind asked how and why but he ignored it. The aliens had heard him, that was the important thing. The Il Ronnian doctor was there to greet him. The vest full of electronic instruments had disappeared and been replaced by a regular uniform. "Come . . . we will help you."

Cap felt a strange mixture of eagerness and embarrassment as the alien took his arm and led him down the sweltering corridor. There, up ahead, what was that? The hull metal seemed to bulge inward under pressure from an unseen monster. Now it swirled, moved, and condensed into a horrible face. It looked like Melissa with most of the flesh missing from her skull. Cap heard himself scream: "No! No! No!"

But the pressure on his arm was inexorable. "There, there," the voice said soothingly. "We have what you want. Medicine to make you feel better. But you must cooperate. You must come with me and answer some questions."

The face melted away and Cap allowed himself to be propelled forward. "Cooperate . . . answer questions . . . yes . . . but I need some medicine first."

"And you shall have it," the voice said reassuringly. "Just come with me and you will feel much, much better."

Cap did his best to cooperate, forcing himself to ignore some of the more outrageous visions that leered from connecting corridors, or peeked out of the ship's air vents. They were hallucinations. He knew that. In fact he'd encountered most of them before, in the privacy of his own cabin, or out on the streets of now-distant planets. Personal monsters that followed him everywhere and knew each and every one of his secret fears.

Finally they were there, entering a cabin that Sorenson recognized as nicer than those he'd seen so far, and was already occupied by three Il Ronnians. Cap heard the doctor introduce them but forgot the names as quickly as he heard them.

One of the aliens, an individual that seemed shorter than the other two, invited him to sit down. Cap did so and was careful to place his still-trembling hands under the table where they couldn't be seen.

Then the Il Ronnian did something for which Cap would eternally be thankful. He picked up a delicately shaped earthenware container, poured out a small amount of golden brown liquid, and handed him the cup. "Here, this should help."

Cap's hand shook as he brought the cup to his mouth. He brought the other one up to steady it. The liquid had a thick almost honeylike consistency and tasted of mint. It took some time to slide down his throat and explode in his belly. Cap experienced a wonderful tingling sensation that spread all the way out to his fingertips.

Alcohol! Eighty or ninety proof alcohol, and just the thing for what ailed him. His spirits soared. Cap took another sip and eyed the decanter that it had been poured from. Would they give him more? Or was this all he could have?

The Il Ronnian seemed able to read his mind. He lifted the earthenware vessel, grimaced in what might have been a smile, and poured another shot. The human nodded gratefully and circled the cup with his hands. He felt better now and could afford to look around.

The aliens seemed to understand this process and remained silent while he examined the wall niches, the carefully chosen pieces of art, and the planet that filled most of one bulkhead. He hoped the comment would sound suave but it came out as a croak.

"A very attractive compartment. My compliments to your decorator."

One of the aliens, the one seated in front of the viewscreen, stirred slightly. "Thank you. I'm glad you like it. Do you feel better now?"

Cap nodded, then wondered if the gesture had any meaning for them or not. "Yes, much better. May I ask a question?"

Another alien, the smaller one, made a motion with his tail. "Go right ahead."

"What do you plan to do with me?"

"Ah." the first Il Ronnian replied. "A very interesting question indeed. The answer depends on you."

Sorenson didn't like the sound of that. What if he said the wrong thing? They could deprive him of alcohol. He swallowed the rest of his drink. "What do you want?"

"Nothing much," the second alien said smoothly. "Some information, that is all."

Cap looked at them through narrowed eyes. He remembered the look on Melissa's face as Lana-8 dragged her away. "I refuse to say or do anything that will endanger my friends."

"Commendable, quite commendable," the third Il Ronnian said, stirring from his apparent lethargy. "We applaud your sense of loyalty. However we would be derelict in our duty were we to ignore an opportunity to speak with one of the resistance movement's most important leaders. I have a suggestion. Let's talk, but limit our conversation to subjects that have no current military value."

Sorenson sipped his drink. Of course. Their desire to speak with him was only natural. And the suggestion *did* seem rather reasonable. If they asked the wrong sort of questions he would refuse to answer. Besides, the longer they talked, the longer he could drink.

"That seems fair . . . what would you like to discuss?"

"The alien spaceship seems like a good place to start," the first Il Ronnian said easily. "We would like to know what the interior is like and how it operates."

Cap frowned. It was hard to concentrate, but the last time he had agreed to discuss the drifter with a stranger, all sorts of things had gone wrong. The bounty hunters had come after Lando, they'd been forced to flee the planet, and had ended up here. Wherever "here" was. No, there was no doubt about it, he shouldn't answer.

Sorenson did his best to sound dignified. "I'm sorry. I cannot answer your question."

The smaller Il Ronnian sounded surprised. "Really? Why not? The spaceship is no longer around. What harm could it do?"

Cap thought about it as he poured himself another drink. What harm indeed? The drifter *was* gone and the aliens couldn't touch it. Even Della would agree with that. Wouldn't she? Yes, of course she would.

The wine? Brandy? Liqueur? Whatever it was went down smoothly indeed. Cap started to feel downright cheerful. Just right for telling stories. A thought occurred to him. He grinned.

"Come to think of it, you're right. The ship's gone and a good thing too. It was horrible on board, just horrible. There were these bodies see, all mummified, and sitting at the controls. Weird-looking things with three arms and four eyes. Been there for a thousand years at least.

"And robots, big ugly critters that ran the ship, and tried to hunt us down . . ."

Sorenson paused to take a sip, saw that his audience was properly entranced, and kept on going. They wanted a ship, did they? Well, he'd give them a ship, a ship they'd never forget.

Rola-4 clutched Neder-33 to her chest as the Sand Sept troopers dragged her toward the command hut. What did they want with her? Was this the punishment that she'd been dreading? Many days had passed since the soldiers had ripped her dress open and taken the plastic disk. Days spent all by herself in a special pen, unable to speak with God and alone with her fear.

It was raining and the mud made a squishing sound under her feet. Rola-4 looked to the left and saw the broad expanse of Holding Area Two, even more crowded now, and still showing signs of the damage caused during the attack. She saw faces turn her way, tight staring faces that were curious about her fate and glad it wasn't happening to them.

Rola-4's heart felt like it might beat itself right out of her chest as they opened the door and shoved her inside the hut.

The walls were bare, a portable heating unit occupied one corner, and the floors were covered with mud. A makeshift desk had been built out of empty ammo crates and some loose boards.

An Il Ronnian sat behind it. The alien was thin, and in spite of the weather absolutely immaculate. He gave her the same kind of look that the village elders reserved for shirkers and wastrels.

Rola-4 used the same tactic that always worked on them. She hung her head penitently and looked at the floor. Neder-33 made complaining noises and tried to squirm out of her arms.

"You are construct Rola-4." There was something wrong with the alien's translator and it made his voice sound tinny.

"That is correct."

"You stand accused of treason against the Il Ronnian people."

Rola-4 struggled to understand. "Treason?" What did that mean? She mustered her thoughts.

"I meant no harm. God spoke to me and I listened."

The Il Ronnian looked stern. "And repeated his words to others."

"Yes, he told me to do so."

"And we told you not to."

Rola-4 shrugged. "Obedience to God is a part of my nature. I could no more ignore his commands than fly through the air."

The Il Ronnian, a rather skilled xenologist, knew it was true but maintained the same stiff expression anyway.

"Guilt is guilt. You committed a crime and must pay the price."

Rola-4 felt the bottom drop out of her stomach. "What price?"

"Death."

Rola-4 held Neder-33 more tightly. "Death? For speaking with God? What about my baby? You killed his father and would kill his mother too?"

The Il Ronnian made a sign with his tail. "I did not invent the penalties, I simply enforce them. You spoke with the machine called 'God,' spread his lies among your people, and must suffer the penalty. Unless . . ."

The pause seemed deliberate and therefore fraught with meaning. Hope filled Rola-4's breast. "Unless what?"

The alien made a motion with his hand. Rola-4 sensed movement behind her. A chair appeared. An Il Ronnian chair, with a tail slot down the middle, but a chair nevertheless. Neder-33 was getting heavy and Rola-4 accepted the invitation to sit down.

"Unless," the Il Ronnian continued, "you are willing to correct some of the damage that you have done."

Rola-4 didn't know what the damage *was* much less how to correct it, but was extremely interested in staying alive. "What would I be asked to do?"

"Nothing much," the alien said reassuringly. "Simply return to your people, seek out those in charge, and offer to help."

Rola-4 sat up straight in her chair. It was too good to be true. "Offer to help? That's all?"

"Well, almost all," the Il Ronnian replied. "We want you to find out where God is located."

"But that is impossible. God is everywhere and nowhere at all."

The alien was angry. His fist hit the desk so hard that boards jumped. "That is nonsense! God is a machine. It has parts like any other machine! They are located somewhere! Find God and live!"

Rola-4 forced her head down into the penitent position. Neder-33 looked up into her face and said, "Gaa?" He looked so much like his father that she wanted to cry.

"So," the Il Ronnian said, "what is your decision?"

Rola-4 was surprised that her voice sounded so calm and clear. "I wish to live. I will find God."

"Excellent," the Il Ronnian said, leaning back in his chair. "Excellent. Peeb!"

A trooper appeared to Rola-4's right. "Sir!"

"Bring the female in."

"Sir!"

Rola-4 heard a commotion behind her and turned to look. She was shocked to see the door open and Tusy-35 walk in.

Rola-4 noticed that the other female looked none the worse for wear. Her clothes were clean, she was obviously well fed, and she entered the hut as if she owned it. Tusy-35 nodded to the Il Ronnian, folded her arms across a more than ample chest, and regarded Rola-4 with the affection that a belly creeper has for its prey.

Why? What was going on? Rola-4 turned toward the Il Ronnian. He gestured toward Tusy-35. "Give the baby to her."

Rola-4 clutched Neder-33 to her chest. "No! Never!"

The alien was merciless. His eyes bored right through her. "You will do as you are told. Look for God. Find it. Report here. The youngster will be returned. The female will care for him in the meantime."

Rola-4 started to protest, started to beg, but saw that it would do little good. Her only chance, Neder-33's only chance, was to cooperate and hope for the best.

Slowly, reluctantly, Rola-4 did as she was told. Tusy-35 practically snatched Neder-33 out of her arms. She chucked him under the chin. "Hello, little one. I see you look like your father instead of your mother. My, what a lucky little male you are."

Rola-4 reached out to touch her son, to tell him good-bye, but Tusy-35 jerked him away. Her smile was pure venom. "Naughty, naughty. You have work to do, remember?"

The Il Ronnian stood and pointed toward the door. "That is all. You may go."

Neder-33 saw his mother moving away, didn't like it, and started to cry.

Rola-4 didn't look, couldn't look, for fear of falling apart. She stepped out into the pouring rain. The soldiers ignored her. She was free to go.

Cap gave a loud belch and looked to see what sort of reaction it would generate. The Il Ronnians nodded agreeably. Cap smiled. Silly bastards.

"So," the shortest Il Ronnian said, "that concludes your report?"

"Yup," Sorenson answered deliberately. "Humans always make that sort of noise when they reach the end of a story."

"Story?"

"Did I say 'story'? I meant 'report,' " Cap added hastily.

The Il Ronnian bowed slightly. "Your report was most interesting. We may ask additional questions later on. You may go."

Sorenson stood. He gestured toward the half-empty decanter. "May I take that with me?"

The alien's tail danced back and forth. "You may."

Cap gave a slight bow. "Thank you."

The Il Ronnians waited until the hatch had hissed closed behind him before they spoke. Half Sept Commander Heek was the first to break the silence.

"It seems hard to believe. A self-repairing artifact, its owners dead for thousands of years, controlled by rampaging robots."

Ceeq signaled respectful disagreement with his tail. "Not when you have seen the vessel in action it isn't. It resembles nothing we have seen before."

"True," Teex said thoughtfully, "but one thing bothers me. The human denied a connection between the ship and the device known as 'God.' Yet it arrived at a rather inauspicious time for us and a rather good time for God. Deex?"

The intelligence officer looked up from the small palm-sized monitor in his hand. It was electronically linked to both the chair that Sorenson had been sitting on and the table before him.

"Quarter Sept Commander Teex is correct. The human's vital signs became slightly elevated when asked about the possibility of a connection."

Ceeq leaned forward. "What about the ship?"

Deex indicated uncertainty with his tail. "I believe that his answers were truthful but cannot be sure. The presence of alcohol in the subject's bloodstream introduces the possibility of error."

"So," Heek said lazily. "What should we do?"

There was silence for a moment as Teex and Ceeq considered the merits of putting forth what could be a winning plan against the demerits of having it fail. Teex was first to speak.

"I have a plan, sir."

Ceeq waited to find fault. Heek signaled his approval. "Excellent. Please proceed."

There was a gamble here but it could be worth the risk. Teex marshaled his thoughts. "Our most recent intelligence reports indicate that something is afoot. The total number of geek attacks have fallen off while the efforts to repair damage have doubled."

Heek came to his feet. "That is wonderful news! The concentration camps are working!"

Teex signaled reluctant disagreement. "Maybe . . . but there is another possibility as well."

Sensing what could be a weakness, Ceeq was quick to respond. "And what would that be?"

"Preparations for an all-out attack," Teex answered calmly. "An attack that could drive us off the planet."

"Impossible," Ceeq snorted imperiously. "We are far too strong. Besides, while a lull in the fighting might signal preparations for an all-out attack, repairs do not."

"And that is where you are wrong," Teex replied calmly, making no effort to avoid confrontation. "Consider the following facts: The geeks outnumber us ten to one. They are manufacturing weapons faster than we can find and destroy them. And the humans are providing them with some excellent military advice. Given those facts the repairs take on additional significance. The constructs are up to something, something that will benefit them and disadvantage us."

"Total rubbish," Ceeq said peevishly. "You look for darkness in the midday sun. We should send for reinforcements if we fear attack."

There was a long silence as both officers waited for Heek to take a position. And when he did the older Il Ronnian spoke from the perspective of the Sand rather than Star Sept. A bias that Teex had counted on.

"I am hesitant to send for reinforcements without a documented need. The Council tends to frown on such requests. Besides, I think Teex is correct. And even if he isn't, we cannot afford to take the chance. So, Teex. What would you have us do?"

Teex had his answer ready. "I recommend that we clamp down, and clamp down hard, starting with the most recent repairs. If they are up to something that should put an end to it, and if they are not, it will act to solidify our control."

Ceeq had no choice but to cave in and Heek signaled approval with his tail. "Good. Now, what's for dinner?"

21

Lando tried to resist but an insistent something pulled him up and out of the comfortable darkness. Something or someone had a hold of his shoulder and was shaking it.

"Pik . . . it is me, Wexel-15 . . . wake up."

"I'm sleeping. Go away."

"The aliens attacked Village 241."

Lando's eyes flew open. Wexel-15 was a dark blob against the hallway light. Six rotations had passed since the storeroom strategy session. Careful analysis had revealed that Village 241 served as an important junction for some of God's more critical circuits.

Circuits made of glass fibers that twisted and turned through the streets themselves, of chips the size of city blocks, of transistors, capacitors, and diodes that looked like statues, sculptures, and mosaics. The circuits were huge, so massive that even the constructs had missed them. And in Village 241, like so many others, many had been destroyed.

By repairing the damage to Village 241 the resistance could restore 2.1 percent of the computer's previous effectiveness. A damned good start. Or what would've been a damned good start if the Il Ronnians had left it alone. Lando sat up.

"Casualties?"

"Heavy, I'm afraid. Two hundred and fifty-nine in the most recent report. One hundred and eleven of those were KIA."

"Damage?"

"All the work accomplished so far has been destroyed."

"Damn. I'll meet you in the storeroom. Inform Cy and Dru-21."

Wexel-15 nodded heavily and withdrew. Lando knew how

the construct felt. They had taken a large number of casualties and had nothing to show for it. The situation was worse than bad. It had the makings of a full-fledged disaster.

The smuggler rolled over onto his elbow. Della was curled up into a fetal ball. She wore a shirt that would have fit a construct twice her size. It was bunched up around her waist. Della's face was calm, her red hair was tousled, and she looked like anything but a bounty hunter. He kissed her on the ear.

"Time to wake up."

She groaned and refused to open her eyes. "You're insatiable. Take a cold shower."

Lando smiled. "Sorry . . . different problem this time. The Il Ronnians attacked Village 241."

Della opened her eyes. "Bad?"

"Real bad."

"Damn."

"Yeah, that's what I said. Council of war, fifteen from now."

"That's a roger." Della rolled out of bed and headed for the shower. Lando followed.

What functioned as their bedroom had once served as a crew-sized dressing area, and the adjoining shower had been built to accommodate fifty heavies at once, so there was plenty of room.

Both of the humans stripped off their clothes, stepped under the shower heads, and shuddered as the cold water turned to hot. They were out of the shower and toweling themselves dry three minutes later.

Lando would have given almost anything for a cup of Terran coffee but knew that he'd have to settle for local tea instead.

The smuggler pulled on a rather ill-fitting assortment of local attire plus the custom-made, one-of-a-kind semiautomatic slug thrower that the constructs had made for him.

On his way to the storeroom/command and control center Lando stepped into the converted office that now served as Melissa's bedroom. She had kicked her covers off. He pulled them up around her neck. She looked sweet and vulnerable. The little girl said something unintelligible and went right back to sleep. Good. She needed the rest.

Wexel-15, Dru-21, Della, and Cy were already present when

Lando entered the storeroom. All eyes were on the jury-rigged comset. Their expressions were far from cheerful. One look told him why.

A light, one of the recently trained officer types, was on screen left narrating the action. He wore a bloodstained bandage around his head, a filthy makeshift uniform, and a combat harness.

Lando nodded approvingly. The lights were leading from the front. Good.

Behind the construct, and in the distance, a hilltop village could be seen. Blue-white flares drifted slowly downward, bathing the ruins in a ghastly glow, as helicopters and air cars hovered overhead. Spotlights and energy beams probed the rubble and tracers drew lines through the night. The construct spoke in hushed tones.

" . . . the last of our surface-to-air missiles. The wounded are being moved toward the rear. We will withdraw as soon as they are clear."

Cy held a mike up to his speaker grill. "Roger, that. Now get the hell out of there before they locate your position and blow your skinny ass right off the surface of the planet!"

Cy dropped the mike as the screen snapped to black. "Damn! It'll be a wonder if he survives the night."

"Yes, it will," Della replied soberly. "But it's not his fault. He's going up against some of the best troops in known space, with a week's worth of training, and no experience. This isn't war, it's murder."

Della was right, but saying so wouldn't help, so Lando changed the subject instead.

"Do we have any idea why they chose to attack Village 241?"

Dru-21 frowned. "Because we were making repairs?"

"Possibly," Lando agreed, helping himself to a cup of tea. "Although I thought there was a good chance that they would chalk it up to some sort of harmless eccentricity. At least for a while."

"Cap might have spilled his guts," Della said darkly.

"He probably did," Lando admitted, "but he didn't know about the size of God's circuits. He was captured after we figured things out. Remember?"

Della nodded mutely.

"So the Il Ronnians are mean bastards who attack anything that moves," Cy concluded.

"Well," Lando said, taking a sip of his tea, "if the shoe fits . . ."

Wexel-15 was pragmatic as usual. "So now what?"

The group was silent for a moment as everyone thought it over. Della was the first to speak.

"We could send crews all over the place, force them to attack everything in sight, and hide the real repairs."

"But God *is* all over the place," Lando objected. "The additional damage would make things worse instead of better."

The silence returned. This time Dru-21 was the first to break it. He seemed hesitant. "I have what you humans might refer to as a 'wild-assed' idea."

Cy laughed and did a quick 360. "Okay, Dru! You're coming along. Tell us about it."

The construct's skin seemed to glow slightly pinker. "The Il Ronnians want to find God, correct? Well, what if we told them where God is? They would have to stop the destruction or destroy the very thing they wish to steal."

Tell the Il Ronnians where God was? The idea seemed stupid at first. But as Lando searched for a polite way to say that the idea started to grow on him. Where was the harm anyway? The Il Ronnians didn't have enough troops to occupy the planet, they would have to send for more, and wasn't that the plan? Damned right it was!

Of course there were the repairs to consider. Repairs that were absolutely necessary in order to restore God's powers and retrieve the drifter. Repairs that would have to wait until they could force the aliens off the surface of the planet.

But that in no way lessened the value of Dru-21's suggestion.

The smuggler shook his head in amazement. "That is the most absolutely brilliant damned idea that anyone around here's had in a long, long time!"

Dru-21 flushed almost scarlet with pleasure.

"It *is* a good idea," Della agreed. "So what should we do? Send 'em a letter?"

A newly confident Dru-21 got to his feet. "I have a better idea. I'll be right back."

The rest of them looked at each other, shrugged, and resumed their discussion. Things had not progressed much beyond the "we could use a captured comset" stage when Dru-21 ushered a construct into the room.

"If I could have your attention please? I would like to introduce Rola-4. She was recently released from Holding Area Two. Rola-4, this is Wexel-15, Pik-Lando, Della Dee, and Cy Borg."

Wexel-15 heard himself say something polite but was almost dumbfounded by the beauty of Rola-4's lavender skin, the sparkle of her eyes, and the determined thrust of her jaw. He wondered if she was taken.

Rola-4 felt awkward in such elevated company. These were the leaders of the resistance, the almost legendary beings God had chosen for his work, and they were receiving her!

Rola-4 felt pride, fear, and a sense of wonder. One of the leaders was a heavy! A big, handsome brute with massive arms and an enormous chest. She could feel his strength clear across the room.

Guilt stabbed Rola-4's heart. How could she think such thoughts? With Neder-32 only recently dead? And with Neder-33 in such terrible danger? No, she must concentrate, and find a way to save her son. The light named Dru-21 was speaking.

"Rola-4 was taken early on, marched crosscountry, and imprisoned in Holding Area Two."

The construct turned her way. "You might be interested to know that Wexel-15 and Della Dee led the attack on Holding Area Two."

"We're sorry it failed," Della said.

"Yes," Wexel-15 added awkwardly, "we wanted to free you."

Rola-4 felt her heart soar. A heavy had led the attack! A heavy who had the respect of lights and humans alike. It was more glorious than anything she had ever imagined.

Dru-21 smiled. "I would like you to know that Rola-4 is something of a heroine. Because she had a disk on her person when captured, Rola-4 was able to communicate with God. He gave her messages for the other constructs and she passed them on."

"That took guts," Lando said admiringly.

"Good going," Cy added.

"Nice job," Della agreed.

"You deserve the respect of our people," Wexel-15 rumbled. "Thank you."

Rola-4 was so overwhelmed she barely heard what Dru-21 said next.

"Yes, Rola-4 deserves our thanks, and more. Unfortunately she was betrayed and the disk was taken away from her. Then came a period of solitary confinement that ended three days ago. It was then that the Il Ronnians summoned Rola-4, gave her instructions to find God, and took her son hostage. Our scouts saw her leave the compound and brought her here."

Della frowned. "She wasn't followed, I hope."

Dru-21 spread his hands. "No, the scouts were very careful."

Wexel-15 felt his emotions plummet. A son! She was taken then, and as unapproachable as the stars in the sky.

Dru-21 let the silence build, allowing the significance of his words to sink in.

Lando shook his head in amazement. "When you're hot, you're hot! We tell Rola-4 where God is located, she tells the Il Ronnians, and they free her son!"

Dru-21 nodded happily. "That is my plan."

"Devious," Della said approvingly, "very devious."

Rola-4 felt her head swim as she did her best to follow the conversation. The part about God made no sense at all. Everyone knew that God was everywhere and nowhere at all. But so what? They had a plan to free her son! Rola-4 forced herself to concentrate. She must understand this plan and do everything she could to make it work.

There was a lot of discussion after that. Meals were sent for, eaten, and the leftovers taken away. Reports arrived, were discussed, then acted upon. Ideas were put forth, debated, and occasionally accepted.

Finally, after the sun had risen and set again, the meeting broke up. One by one resistance leaders stood, stretched, and stumbled off to bed. The planning was over. Soon, within a matter of days, they would act.

Wexel-15 took the opportunity to escort Rola-4 to her room. Both wanted to talk but were afraid to do so. She due to his almost overwhelming presence, and Wexel-15 because of the tight feeling in his chest.

Finally, when they stood outside the door to her room, the

awkwardness closed in around them, and Wexel-15 cleared his throat.

"It was an honor to meet you, Rola-4. Your husband will be very proud."

Rola-4 looked up into his eyes. "The honor was mine, Wexel-15 . . . as for my husband . . . he is dead. The aliens killed him."

Wexel-15 felt his heart leap with joy. He knew it was wrong, knew he should feel otherwise, but couldn't help it. She was free! And with luck, with skill, could be his! He fought to keep the emotions from showing on his face.

"I did not know. I am terribly sorry. Perhaps I could help. Could I call on you?"

Rola-4 tried to resist, tried to say no, but was swept away by contrary emotions. Never mind the fact that both of them might be killed, that she had no home to call her own, that her husband was only recently dead. She wanted to laugh and cry at the same time.

"That would be nice, thank you."

"I will see you later then."

Wexel-15 gave a little bow, turned, and made his way down the corridor. It was only after he heard her door close that he jumped into the air, yelled "Yes!" and landed so heavily that an avalanche of dust fell from the light fixtures above.

22

It was raining as Rola-4 trudged up the long slope toward Holding Area Two's main gate. The steady downpour had soaked her to the skin. Il Ronnian ground vehicles plus the passage of hundreds of construct feet had churned dirt into mud. It was thick glutinous stuff that formed clumps around her feet and made it hard to walk. Her sandals were long gone, pulled off by the mud, and left behind.

The fence was off to her right, a heavy-duty affair made of heavy mesh, and patched where Wexel-15's attack had breached it.

Rola-4 felt a secret warmth seep into her heart at the thought of Wexel-15. He had been extremely worried about her safety and had wanted to come along. But while sympathetic, the other resistance leaders had reminded Wexel-15 of other even more pressing duties, and he had stayed behind.

Rola-4 was not without an escort however. Eyes watched even now, peering down from the surrounding hills, ready to intervene should something go wrong. It was a comfort, but a small one, since Rola-4 knew that whatever protection they could offer would end when she reached the gate. Once inside she would be on her own.

The road moved closer to the fence and Rola-4 peered through the mesh. There was the chance that she would see someone she knew, or better yet catch a glimpse of Tusy-35 and Neder-33. That was the hope anyway, but all she saw were dark ghostlike forms, shuffling through the rain, too discouraged to even look her way.

Though never especially good, the conditions inside Holding Area Two had grown even worse during her absence. All the more reason to deliver the photos, free Neder-33, and wait for the resistance to rescue them.

Rola-4 clutched the waterproof case to her breast and approached the checkpoint. It was a flimsy affair made from cast-off lumber, ragged tarps, and empty cargo modules.

There was nothing flimsy about the weapons emplacement however. It consisted of an armored personnel enclosure reinforced with sandbags. The only opening was a long narrow slit through which a bell-shaped muzzle protruded.

Rola-4 saw the gun barrel drift her way as a Sand Sept trooper stepped out into the rain. She had noticed that in spite of the Il Ronnian reverence for water they hated rain. This soldier was no exception. Had her errand been any less important his scowl would have sent her packing. He wore a rain poncho and kept his weapon pointed in her general direction.

"Say your piece, geek, and make it good."

"I am Rola-4. I have some information for your commanding officer."

The Il Ronnian saw the case and held out his hand. "Fine. Give it to me. I will see that he gets it."

Rola-4 took a step backward. "No! I mean thank you, but no. I have strict instructions to deliver the information into his hands."

This was not strictly true, but Rola-4 was determined to get inside, and doubted that anyone would question it.

The soldier made a jerky motion with his tail. "Stay where you are. I will check."

The Il Ronnian stepped into the shack.

So Rola-4 stood there, rain pouring down around her, feeling the mud ooze up through her toes. It felt comforting, like harvest time, when the crops came in and winter began.

The trooper emerged. His boots made sucking noises in the mud. He motioned her forward. "Stand in front of me."

Rola-4 did as she was told.

"Spread your legs and hold your arms straight out."

Rola-4 gritted her teeth as the alien touched her. Neder-33. She must remember Neder-33 and suffer through anything that would return him to her arms.

Satisfied that she was not armed, or loaded with explosives, the sentry gave a grunt of approval. He pointed toward the gate.

"You may enter. Go straight to the command post. Sixteenth Sept Commander Beed will see you there."

Rola-4 nodded her understanding and walked up the slight incline toward the main gate. Sixteenth Sept Commander Beed. So that was his name. He had never said and she had never thought to ask. Why? It was so stupid. What if she had needed to know? A human would have asked. A light would have asked. The Lords had given them a tremendous advantage. It wasn't fair.

Two soldiers guarded the main gate. They swung it open at her approach. Rola-4 waited for them to stop her but nothing happened. She walked on through.

Now she could see the prisoners more clearly. A vast mob of shuffling constructs, heads hung low, waiting for whatever fate held in store for them. Rola-4 thought of the resistance fighters and smiled grimly.

Just a little bit longer, she thought to herself. Things are about to change.

The brave thought melted away as she approached the command post. The resistance would win in the long run. She felt sure of that. But this was now and Sixteenth Sept Commander Beed held the power of life and death over Rola-4 and her son.

The sentry was expecting her and gestured toward the door. Rola-4 pulled it open and stepped inside.

The command post was just as before. A muddy floor but otherwise clean. Beed sat behind his makeshift desk. He was talking on a comset. Another alien was present as well. He was seated in one of the two guest chairs and was inspecting his right hoof. He barely looked up as Rola-4 entered.

The second guest chair was barely visible under a pile of body armor, helmets, and other military gear. Rola-4 was tired but knew better than to move the equipment and sit down.

Beed continued to ignore her as he finished his conversation, tapped something into a portable computer, and arranged the things on his desk. Finally, when everything was just so, he looked up.

"So, you came back."

"I have the information you requested."

Beed looked skeptical. "That is excellent if true. So where is the machine called 'God'?"

Rola-4 offered him the plastic envelope. Water dripped onto the surface of his desk.

Beed accepted the package but made no attempt to open it. "What is this? And where did you get it?"

Rola-4 had been expecting the questions and had rehearsed her answers. "They were waiting for me when I left here."

"For you?" Beed interrupted.

"For anyone who could provide them with information about the conditions here."

"Go on."

"So I told them what it was like and asked if I could help with the resistance."

"And?"

"And they took me to some sort of headquarters. They blindfolded me for the last part of the trip but the location was underground."

Beed made a steeple with his fingers. "Why do you say that?"

Rola-4 shrugged. "Because there were no windows and people talked about conditions on the surface."

The Il Ronnian made a gesture with his tail. "Continue."

"They put me to work cleaning offices and corridors. That is where I got the photographs."

"You stole them?"

"Yes, but they were copies, and will not be missed."

"Let us see what you have."

Beed lifted the envelope, found the seal, and pried it open. The photos made a swishing sound as they left the package. The Il Ronnian frowned, did some sorting, and lined them up on the surface of his desk. He looked up. His face was angry.

"This is garbage! Pictures taken from our own satellites. And worthless besides. Look! Do you see photos of one particular place? No, these shots cover hundreds of square units!"

Rola-4 steeled herself against the alien's anger. Beed was seconds away from throwing her out, from ruining the plan, from cutting her off from her son.

"What you say is true . . . but that is the secret. The resistance leaders discussed it as I mopped the floor. The streets, the buildings, even the statues are part of God. He is enormous and covers thousands of square miles."

Beed started to say something, frowned, and took a second look at the pictures. He sorted through them. Understanding started to dawn on his face.

"By all that is holy I think you are right! That explains why we could not find it! The blasted machine is everywhere!"

Rola-4 felt a tremendous sense of relief. Beed understood, her mission was accomplished, and Neder-33 would be freed.

"Could I please have my son back now?"

Beed reached for his comset. "Of course not. You are much too valuable to shuffle around in the rain. I will send you back and learn even more!"

The Il Ronnian fed the photos into a slot at the bottom of his comset and spoke into the handset at the same time. The alien had deactivated his translator so the construct couldn't understand what he said.

Rola-4 felt hopelessness settle over her like a blanket. The alien had lied. And he would continue to lie. He would never allow her to hold Neder-33 in her arms again.

Time seemed to slow. The construct moved sideways. She saw the chair heaped with armor and other gear. She grabbed the one thing she instinctively understood. A shovel-shaped entrenching tool. It caught on something. She sensed movement as the second Il Ronnian turned her way. The shovel came loose. The soldier opened his mouth and started to stand. Rola-4 swung with all her might. Blood sprayed as the edge of the tool caught the alien's unprotected throat. He clutched the wound, made a gurgling sound, and died.

Beed dropped the handset and scrabbled for his side arm. Had he been a little bit faster, or favored a less cumbersome holster, he might have made it. As it was the shovel hit him in the forehead just as the barrel cleared plastic. The second, third, and fourth blows were completely unnecessary.

Beed collapsed onto the top of his desk, slid backward, and slumped to the floor. A barely heard voice squawked from the receiver. Rola-4 replaced the handset. Silence filled the room. The construct had something in her hand. She looked down. It was a shovel. There was blood all over it. She laid it on the desk.

Now what?

The thought brought no answer.

• • •

Lando followed Wexel-15's broad back up the corridor. Della was right behind.

What light there was had a greenish quality and came from the walls themselves. Dust swirled through the air and made it hard to breathe. The floor was scratched and grooved where heavy equipment had been dragged the length of the hall. Equipment designed for mining, only this mine went from the bottom up, and would terminate on the surface.

The corridor emptied into a small chamber. Some scaffolding occupied the center of it. A pair of massive heavies stood atop the structure passing boxes of ammunition up through a hole in the ceiling. Something came loose and a small avalanche of rubble came tumbling down. Dust exploded into the air and Lando covered his eyes.

"How much longer?" Wexel-15's voice was strong and commanding.

"Not long," one of the heavies answered. "Ten laks at the most."

Wexel-15 gave a wave of acknowledgment. He turned to the humans. "Wait here while I check on the troops."

Lando nodded and took a look around. The walls were decorated with mosaic tile work that made his head swim. Wait a minute . . . he'd been here before!

The smuggler sidestepped some heavies and worked his way around the scaffolding. Sure enough, there was the door. A peek inside confirmed his suspicion. The room was dirty, and packed floor to ceiling with equipment and supplies, but the oval shape gave it away. This was the same room where he'd met with Dru-21, Dos-4, Zera-12, and Pak-7—the lights, who in their own way had shaped the future by opting for a policy of cooperation rather than domination.

Little had he known as he met with the lights that Il Ronnian Fire Base One was just overhead.

The aliens had landed, leveled a building called the Hall of Life, and built their base on top of the rubble. A more careful investigation might have revealed one of three different paths down into the hill's interior. But God had ordered work crews to seal the passageways off immediately after the first Il Ronnians had landed. Later, when the aliens destroyed the building, the entrances had been buried under tons of rubble, making them almost impossible to find.

Lando left the room to join Della in the antechamber. She was busy removing a layer of dust from her custom-made assault weapon. Chunks of masonry clattered to the floor as the heavies continued to pass supplies up through the hole. He kissed her ear.

Her voice was soldier-hard. "What did you do that for?"

"You're cute when you play with guns."

Her expression softened. "And you are weird. Very weird."

"Weird enough to marry when this is over?"

Her eyes found his. They searched for something and found it. "Yes, weird enough to marry you when this is over."

Lando nodded solemnly. "It's a deal then. Shake?"

Della laughed. "Shake." Her hand was small and firm in his.

"Good. Then be sure to survive."

"You too."

"I'm surprised that your father didn't have a saying for a moment like this."

Lando thought it over. The truth was that he'd been using his father's sayings less and less of late. What did that mean? Increasing independence? Old age? He smiled.

"As a matter of fact my father *did* have a saying for situations like this one. He said 'when you find something worth keeping grab it and never let go.' "

Della laughed. "You made that up."

Lando smiled. "Yeah, I guess I did. It's good advice though . . . so I think I'll follow it."

The smuggler was interrupted as a heavy said something unintelligible and a pile of debris crashed around his feet. Wexel-15 appeared.

"Are we ready?"

"Yes, sir."

"All right then. Get out of the way. We have a war to win."

The lighting in Ceeq's cabin was subdued by Il Ronnian standards. Teex held one of the photos under an overhead spot. Ceeq and Half Sand Sept Commander Heek were huddled together looking at the rest.

"Amazing, absolutely amazing," Ceeq said smugly. "The machine was all around you, literally under your tail, and you missed it."

"True," Teex said pointedly, "but these are *your* satellite photos, are they not? Hijacked without your knowledge? And analyzed by some rather primitive geeks?"

"And that is enough of that," Heek said sternly. The light came down across his forehead and made dark pools under his eyes. He looked like one of the old-time Ilwiks, as stern as the desert, and as hard as rock.

"There is more than enough blame to go around. While we have a common interest in minimizing the magnitude of this failure to our superiors . . . we must be honest with ourselves. To do otherwise would be to compound the errors already made. We have consistently underestimated the opposition, failed to interpret incoming data correctly, and have been slow to respond. We must act, and act now."

Teex and Ceeq looked at each other in surprise. This was a different Heek from the one who fell asleep during meetings. The crisis had removed ten cycles from his age.

"So, what would you suggest?" Ceeq asked meekly.

"First and foremost a change in tactics," Heek responded. "Now that we know the machine called God is built into the very infrastructure of the cities we must allow the repairs to proceed."

"But that's exactly what they want us to do," Teex objected. "It is logical to suppose that our attacks have damaged the machine's capabilities and the geeks are trying to restore them. The resistance will be strengthened if they manage to do so."

"True," Heek answered calmly, "but so what? The time has come to send for reinforcements. The computer, plus its unique design, provide more than adequate justification. Imagine! As the repairs are completed, the reinforcements arrive, and we take control of a fully operational machine. What could be better?"

The plan sounded good, but something was wrong, and Teex couldn't quite figure out what it was. He took one last shot.

"So, what do you suggest? Withdraw and wait for the reinforcements?"

"Of course not," Heek answered caustically. "We will continue to harass them. The human represents an opportunity. I suggest that we take advantage of it."

"Some sort of hostage deal?" Ceeq asked brightly. "Surrender or the human dies?"

"Exactly," Heek answered. "The geeks may or may not care about his safety . . . but we can assume that the humans do."

"An excellent plan," Ceeq said ingratiatingly. "I will dispatch a ship along with a request for reinforcements. Teex can handle the hostage situation."

Teex resented Ceeq's attempt to give him orders but decided to hold his tongue.

Heek signaled agreement with his tail.

Teex cleared his throat. "There is another matter as well. As we heard from intelligence officer Deez, the photos and the voice transmission that accompanied them came from Holding Area Two. Why was the transmission cut off? And why have all attempts to contact Holding Area Two met with failure?"

"Excellent questions," Heek rumbled. "Get some answers."

Rola-4 wanted to panic, wanted to do anything but stay in the command post and think, but forced herself to do so. Thinking took time and she must allow for it. She forced herself to ignore the bodies and the buzzing comset.

The question was how? How to escape and take Neder-33 with her? What would a light or a human do? Pick up a weapon? Call the sentry inside? Kill him? Then what? She couldn't kill them all.

No, there had to be a better way, something intelligent. Wait a lak, what about the first part of that idea? What about using the sentry instead of killing him? Yes, that was more like it!

Rola-4 checked to make sure that her clothing was free of II Ronnian blood, glanced around to make sure that the sentry wouldn't be able to see anything when she slipped out through the door, and took hold of the handle.

The door opened easily and closed behind her. The sentry was six or seven paces from the command post. He turned at the sound of the door. Rola-4 adopted her most servile persona.

"Excuse me, sir, but Sixteenth Sept Commander Beed asked that I give you a message."

"Well?" the sentry demanded. "Out with it? What does he want?"

Rola-4 cast her eyes down toward the sentry's muddy boots. "His Excellency Commander Beed asks that you locate the construct known as Tusy-35 and bring her here. And the child called Neder-33 as well."

The sentry gave a grunt of assent, turned his back on her, and trudged off into the rain. The position of his tail indicated what the trooper thought about officers who stayed warm and dry while he ran errands through the mud. But the gesture was wasted since the officer in question was dead and Rola-4 had no way to know what it meant.

The next twenty laks were the worst of Rola-4's life. Waiting inside the overly warm command post, with the scent of blood thick in the air, and the comset buzzing like some sort of insistent insect.

There was no way to know how long it would take Tusy-35 to arrive so she was forced into a constant state of readiness behind the door. She would have to kill the sentry, Rola-4 was certain of that, and the knowledge made her queasy.

She had chosen Beed's energy weapon over the other Il Ronnian's slug gun because it made less noise. The march, and the subsequent attack on Holding Area Two, had taught her which weapons did what.

Still, the buttons and levers were unfamiliar, so she had fired some test shots just to make sure. Steam rose from the holes in the floor.

Finally, after what seemed like an eternity, there was noise outside. The squishing of boots in the mud followed by the sentry's voice. "Get in there, geek, and take the brat with you."

Tusy-35 came through the door first as Rola-4 had assumed that she would. A lot of things happened all at once.

Tusy-35 caught sight of Beed's dead body and gave a gasp of surprise.

Neder-33 turned, caught sight of his mother, and said "Maa!"

The sentry realized something was wrong and pushed Tusy-35 aside.

Rola-4 waited for him to step forward, aimed at the side of his head, and pressed the firing stud. The bolt of bright blue energy burned its way through his head and hit the comset beyond. It stopped buzzing.

Rola-4 pushed the door shut as the sentry slumped to the floor.

Completely terrified, and afraid that she might be next, Tusy-35 offered Neder-33 to his mother. "Here . . . I took good care of him . . . see for yourself."

Rola-4 refused her son's urgings to pick him up and motioned toward the second guest chair with the still warm blaster.

"Shove the equipment on the floor. Place my son on top of the equipment. Sit on the chair."

Tusy-35 was really worried now. "Wha-what are you going to do?"

"Nothing half so bad as what you did to me," Rola-4 answered. "Now shut up."

It took a while to gather belts and equipment harnesses enough to tie Tusy-35 in place but Rola-4 got the job done. The other construct would eventually work her way free, but by the time she did, Rola-4 and Neder-33 would be long gone.

Tusy-35 snuffled piteously. "The aliens will blame me for this! They will kill me!"

"Really?" Rola-4 asked, slipping a gag into the other construct's open mouth. "That would be terrible. Good luck."

Neder-33 had crawled all over the floor by now, and was covered with mud, but Rola-4 hugged him anyway. And she was still hugging him when she opened the door, stepped outside, and made her way down toward the rest of the constructs. Her heart felt like it would beat its way out of her chest. It was evening, and the light had started to fade.

A section of fence separated the command post from the holding area with a gate to provide access between the two. No less than two sentries stood to either side of the gate, cursing the rain and wondering when it would stop.

One of them glanced at Rola-4, saw a female geek with child, and made an entry on his arm pad. Another waved her through. One and a half geeks came out, and one and a half geeks went back in. That's what they needed and that's what they had.

The other constructs paid scant attention at first. But a female from Rola-4's village saw her, remembered how she had been taken away, and called her name.

Rola-4 made no reply. She had an idea, the means to carry it out, and little time for idle chatter.

She'd been very, very lucky. Lucky that she had been able to retrieve Neder-33, lucky that no one had entered the command post, and lucky that the sentries had let her pass.

Now that luck would surely be running out, but before it did, she was determined to accomplish one last thing. Something that would free her and every other construct present.

The villagers followed along behind, excited by Rola-4's sudden appearance, and intrigued by her silence. She spoke with others, instructing them to tag along, and a crowd started to form.

In the meantime, on the far side of the compound, the sentries saw movement and realized that something was afoot. They radioed the command post for advice but received no answer.

The senior trooper, an assistant file leader named Geeb, signaled disgust with his tail and trudged up the slope. Officers were all the same. Stupid, and lazy to boot.

Rola-4 stopped in front of the fence. This was the most distant point from the command post and therefore the best. The other constructs watched in openmouthed amazement as she pulled a blaster out from under her clothes, aimed it at the fence, and pressed the firing stud.

Alarms shrieked as metal turned orange, red, and dripped downward. Rola-4 managed to make two vertical cuts in the fence before the power pak ran out. The crowd did the rest.

Assistant File Leader Geeb had just found the bodies, and was in the act of calling for help when the constructs pushed the fence outward and streamed to freedom.

Resistance fighters, the same ones who had been assigned to protect Rola-4, saw and took action.

Energy beams flashed, automatic weapons hammered, and Sand Sept troopers started to die.

Wexel-15 went first with Lando and Della right behind. The scaffold was easy to climb. The metal framework was cold to the touch and shook under their combined weight. Lando moved his hand off just in time to save it from an enormous boot. Della swore as an avalanche of grit fell from above.

Lando saw smiling faces look down, felt hands grab his combat harness, and was lifted through the hole. He landed on his knees and crawled forward to get out of the way. His assault weapon made a scraping sound as it dragged against the floor.

What light there was originated from portable work lights and was heavily filtered by the dust.

The smuggler tried to stand, felt cold concrete press down against his shoulders, and felt suddenly claustrophobic. He knew that there were uncountable tons of material pressing down from above just waiting to squash him flat.

"Over here." The voice belonged to Wexel-15. Lando checked to make sure that Della was okay, saw that she was, and duck-walked in the heavy's direction.

In the meantime a stream of heavily armed resistance fighters poured up through the hole, formed orderly rows, and waited for orders. Lando saw more than a few lights interspersed among the heavies.

Work lights back-lit them, threw gigantic shadows against the ceiling's uneven surface, and spread out to join the surrounding gloom. The crawl space was huge and seemed to extend endlessly in every direction.

Lando hit his head and swore softly. Wexel-15 nodded sympathetically. Given his greater bulk the confined space was even harder for him to maneuver in. His voice was little more than a whisper.

"We are very close. So close the aliens could hear us if they chose to listen. Follow me and be as quiet as you can."

Lando nodded, glanced at Della, and received a grim thumbs-up. She had smeared grease on her skin to darken it and wore a bandanna tied around her head. He noticed that a curl of bright red hair had escaped and dangled over her left ear. She looked fierce but very, very small.

The smuggler knew that she was a more experienced fighter than he was, knew that she had some of the fastest reflexes he'd ever seen, but still felt protective toward her.

And must have shown it in his expression because she winked at him and whispered: "I love you too."

Lando grinned and turned back toward Wexel-15. The heavy had turned his back and was in the process of crawling away. The smuggler held his assault rifle chest high, took the sling in his teeth to keep the weapon up off the floor, and crawled forward. It was easier on his leg muscles but hell on his knees.

The double row of lights reminded Lando of a runway. Wexel-15's bulk blocked them from time to time but they led arrow-straight off into the distance. Some flickered as their power paks wore down, and some were already dark, but they appeared and disappeared with monotonous regularity.

Time passed, and each minute brought more, and more pain. Pain in his knees, pain in his hands, and pain in his jaws where the unaccustomed weight of the assault weapon had started to take its toll.

Finally, just when Lando was almost sure that he couldn't take it anymore, he caught the faintest whiff of fresh night air. Mounds of rubble appeared to the left and right and the lights disappeared.

Lando imagined what it had been like, chipping away from below, breathing the ever-present dust, moving the debris one chunk at a time, waiting for the shock of sudden discovery. These were the true heroes, the constructs who had labored in secret, and opened a hole through which their comrades could pass.

Two of Wexel-15's heavies were waiting and both signaled silence by holding their hands palm downward over the ground. Lando needed no further warning. Stealth was everything.

The only chance for victory lay in putting a significant number of resistance fighters inside the enemy's perimeter right off the top.

If the Il Ronnians heard them, and found the opening right away, the entire plan would go up in smoke. Worse than that, the aliens would follow them downward, and find the arms factory hidden below. A serious if not fatal blow to the resistance.

There was a pause as the heavies whispered to each other. Wexel-15 nodded in response to a comment from one of the constructs, pointed toward the surface, and said, "Well, this is it. Time to—how do humans say it?—kick some serious posterior."

Lando chuckled. "That's how we say it all right."

"Good! Let the kicking begin."

The words were no more than out of Wexel-15's mouth than he was up and through the hole. Lando and Della came right behind.

The entry point was as good as they were likely to find. Away from the main bunkers, just north of the landing pad, and about a hundred yards inside the perimeter. A large pile of rubble had been dumped nearby and offered the resistance fighters an excellent place to hide while they prepared for the attack.

It took time to get two hundred–plus constructs through the hole and into Fire Base One. Time that Lando used to look around.

It was dark and a steady rain fell from the sky. Good. It would encourage anyone who was off-duty to stay inside. A section of fence gleamed in the distance. Pylons stood lonely vigil, their sensors and searchlights aimed outward, where there was nothing to see or sense.

A bit closer in lights appeared, then disappeared as doors were opened and closed. Snatches of conversation drifted through the night air. Shadows moved this way and that. Equipment clanked. A ground vehicle bounced toward the fence. Alien music wailed and was abruptly cut off. A voice complained. They were normal sights and normal sounds and all of them were about to change.

Lando felt a huge hand close around his arm. "Are you ready?"

The smuggler's throat felt suddenly dry. He swallowed to lubricate it. "Ready as I'll ever be."

Wexel-15's eyes gleamed with reflected light. "Myself as well. I want to thank you."

"For what?"

"For what you are doing, for what you have done."

Lando shrugged. "By helping you we help ourselves."

The construct smiled. "I know that, and Dru-21 reminds me of it from time to time. Still, you fight at our sides, and that speaks louder than words."

Lando smiled in return. "That's what friends do."

Wexel-15 nodded, looked right and left, and brought a toy whistle to his lips. There was nothing further to wait for. The whistle made a high-pitched warbling sound.

Loud though the whistle was, it was not that noticeable against the other background sounds, and provided the Il Ronnians with little warning.

The constructs covered the intervening ground with surprising speed, waiting until their targets were clear before they pulled the trigger, transforming the night into a hell of death and destruction.

The first five minutes of the battle would forever be burned into Lando's memory. He would never forget the heat and the smell of alien food as they burst into the underground mess hall. Nor would he forget the awful hammering of the automatic weapons, the screams of the dying Il Ronnians, and the sight of their bullet-ridden bodies.

Most of the troopers were off-duty, and had left their weapons in their bunkers, so there was very little in the way of resistance. Some tried to surrender and were immediately shot down. Others, like the noncom who charged Lando with nothing more than a two-pronged fork, died fighting as best they could.

It was slaughter pure and simple but the constructs had little choice. The Il Ronnians who were on duty would be heavily armed. In seconds, minutes at the most, they would figure out what was happening and launch a counterattack.

An attack that would move from the perimeter inward giving the constructs very little time in which to secure the bunkers and take up defensive positions. There would be no time, space, or personnel available to deal with prisoners.

The killing spread outward from the mess hall to the surrounding bunkers. What had been relatively easy became suddenly hard. Warned by the sounds of battle, the Il Ronnians still in the bunkers were able to arm themselves and fought valiantly. These were crack troops, hardened in previous battles, and fighting for their very lives.

Scores of relatively inexperienced constructs died making the mistakes that newbies always make, but a constant stream of reinforcements continued to pour up out of the ground, and rushed to replace them.

But that couldn't last forever. As both luck and circumstance would have it, File Leader Reeg was the one who led the Il Ronnian counterattack. He had been on a tour of the perimeter when the attack occurred.

It took some time to confirm that the attack had come from below, rather than from outside the fence, or from above, but once that fact had been established Reeg organized an immediate response.

An attack from below meant one or more points of entry. The first task was to seal the tunnel or tunnels off and prevent the geeks from reinforcing their initial assault team. That plus the timely arrival of some reinforcements should carry the day.

Reeg found a portable radio, selected the emergency frequency, and gave a long string of orders. Troops gathered, were assigned to ad hoc files, and led in toward the center of the compound.

They found the hole, discovered that it was heavily defended, and placed troops all around it.

Reeg decided that the reinforcements could deal with the hole later, mustered his remaining troops, and attacked the bunkers.

The insurgents had control of the bunker complex by now, but it was a tenuous control at best, and there were some rather stubborn holdouts to deal with. Still, the bunkers had been designed and equipped for a last-stand defense, and that worked in the constructs' favor.

The Il Ronnians came in a series of short advances, some providing suppressive fire, while others ran forward and threw themselves down.

Lando was hunkered down in one of the trenches that connected the bunkers together. He squeezed the trigger on his assault weapon, felt it jerk in his hands, and winced as it ran out of ammo.

It was routine by now: hit the magazine release, ram a new one home, and resume firing. Della and some others joined him but it did little good. The Il Ronnians were experienced, brave, and really pissed off. They kept right on coming.

Cap's eyelids felt as though they weighed a thousand pounds apiece. The wonderful, wonderful alcohol had taken him into deepest darkness where there were no problems, no emotions, and no failures.

He tried to open his eyes, tried to see what the aliens were up to, but couldn't quite summon the energy. Still, he could hear them well enough, and wore a translator. Like the hands that pushed and pulled at his body the words were rough and empty of all compassion.

"Look at this creature. Have you ever seen anything more disgusting? So inebriated that he cannot move. No wonder the humans have failed to expand their empire any farther. They lack the moral fiber necessary to do so."

There was a reply, but it was beyond the range of the translator, so Cap was unable to understand it.

He understood one thing however, and that was the fact that they had placed him on a stretcher of some sort, and were moving him to another location.

Another cell? Another ship? Down to the surface? His heart leapt with alarm and Cap felt his stomach muscles tighten preliminary to sitting up. He could do it now, he knew that, but should he? As long as the Il Ronnians thought he was unconscious, they might say or do something that would provide him with valuable information. He ordered his muscles to relax and spied on the Il Ronnians through slitted lids.

He saw the back of one Il Ronnian's uniform and assumed that another followed just behind.

The auto cart, or whatever conveyance he was on, moved smoothly, and tilted right or left as it negotiated the curves.

The bulkheads had the same tunnellike appearance that he'd observed before and were occasionally marked with alien script.

Then things changed, as the three of them entered what was unmistakably an air lock, and paused while it cycled them through.

And just as the air lock gave itself away through the way it functioned, so did the landing bay, with its vaulted overhead, briskly moving maintenance bots, and space-cold air. They were taking him somewhere. The only question was where.

Sorenson saw utility craft, aerospace fighters, and shuttles pass to the right and left. Interesting. The bay would remain open to space under normal conditions, facilitating the arrival and departure of smaller ships, and forcing the crew to wear space armor. Someone, either he or someone else, was deemed important enough to pressurize the bay.

Cap felt the cart slow. He opened his eyes a little bit wider and saw a smallish shuttle with an Il Ronnian officer standing next to it. One of the same officers that he'd met before. The one the others called "Teex." Sorenson closed his eyes as the Il Ronnian approached. His translator made the conversation intelligible.

"The human remains unconscious?"

"Yes, sir."

"Load him in the rear and be quick about it."

"Aye, aye, sir."

Cap felt himself sway back and forth as the surface under his back was lifted free of its undercarriage and handed in through the shuttle's rear door.

Then someone, a crew member perhaps, said something terse, and Sorenson was dropped into place. The impact made his head hurt. He considered sitting up and asking for something to drink but felt sure they wouldn't give it to him.

He felt them put the straps in place. One across his chest, the other over his legs.

He heard them move away and opened his eyes a tiny bit. The shuttle was very small. Two, maybe three rows of seats had been removed to make way for the stretcher, and Teex occupied one of the four positions that remained. The control compartment was forward and invisible behind a sliding curtain.

There was a lengthy wait while the bay was depressurized. Then Cap felt the shuttle vibrate, lift, and move forward. The artificial gravity disappeared a few moments later, letting the human know they were free of the larger ship and on their way.

The shuttle had been under way for little more than a minute or two when the message came in. The pilot piped it over the intercom. There was a speaker nearby. Cap's translator allowed him to listen in.

"I have Quarter Sept Commander Ceeq on freq five, sir."

"Put him through."

There was a pause, followed by a burst of static, followed by another voice. "Teex?"

"Affirmative."

"We have a condition six at Fire Base One."

"How bad is it?"

"Bad, very bad. The geeks found a way to come up through the ground. They took the main bunker complex. The mess hall was full. They slaughtered everyone in sight. Most of your officers are dead. File Leader Reeg launched a counterattack, but that met with strong resistance, and he has not been able to retake the bunkers."

Anger, sorrow, and frustration took turns trying to dominate Teex's emotions. He pushed them back. "Anything more?"

"Yes," Ceeq replied, "we have reports that the geeks are moving up the hillsides. The automatic weapons systems have engaged them but are insufficient by themselves."

Teex thought it over. The new assault could be a feint, designed to draw Reeg away from the bunkers, or it could be the real thing. The unmanned perimeter would make a tempting target. He came to a decision.

"Order Reeg to withdraw to a more defensible position. What about reinforcements?"

"They are loading now."

"Order them to hold. I will return and assume personal command."

"Affirmative. Ceeq out."

"Affirmative. Teex out."

Sorenson felt momentary G forces as the shuttle made a turn and headed back toward the larger ship.

His mind raced a mile a minute as he absorbed the news. A major attack! Lando and Della would be in the thick of it, with Cy and Melissa not too far away, and indirectly at risk. Teex, plus the reinforcements, meant almost certain disaster.

Cap felt the pressure close in around him like an ocean, weighing him down, suffocating him with its thick unbreathable mass. A drink! He needed a drink.

But there was no drink, only the knowledge of what he needed to do, and the desire to do it.

He pulled his hands out from under the strap with surprising ease. The buckle was a simple thing and came loose without difficulty. Weightlessness pulled him upward but the remaining strap held him in place. It came free as well. He floated away. The translator bumped him in the chin. He shoved it down under his shirt.

Then, with the stealth made possible by the complete lack of gravity, Cap gathered both ends of the second strap into one hand. Now came the moment he had been dreading, the moment of conflict, the moment when thought became action.

Teex remained where he was, facing forward, completely unaware of the human's actions. His entire being was engrossed in the problem at hand, plotting strategy, devising tactics, and repairing the damage.

That's why it took him a moment longer than it should have to understand the synthi-leather strap that passed in front of his eyes, to sense the presence behind him, and to bring his arms up.

By then it was too late. By then Cap had placed both of his feet on the Il Ronnian's shoulders, had pulled both ends of the strap in opposite directions, and was braced for the struggle that followed.

Teex did not die easily. He was a warrior, and had been all of his life, so he fought and fought hard. His side arm was in his overnight bag, and out of reach, but nature had given his kind long, sharp talons. They raked down along the lower part of Cap's legs. Blood spurted and fogged the air.

But the effort was wasted, having as it did no effect on the strap around the Il Ronnian's neck. He called for help but nothing came out. It was hard to breathe. Very hard to breathe. And hard to think. Very hard to think. He was doing something wrong. What was it? The harness! Yes! It was the harness that held him in place and gave the human such excellent leverage.

Darkness worked its way inward from the edges of the Il Ronnian's mind, crowding his thoughts, blocking all ambition. His fingers sought the release button, found it, but lacked the strength to make it work. Teex felt the final darkness pull him under.

Sensing the cessation of movement Cap loosened the strap. Nothing. Good. Tiny globules of blood floated past his head as Cap pulled himself down in front of the Il Ronnian's body.

Gun, gun, where was the bastard's gun? He was an officer, wasn't he? That meant a handgun of some sort. A blaster would be best, but a slug gun would do. Nothing. Dammit anyway.

Then Cap saw it, a small duffel bag, stuffed into the netting on the starboard bulkhead. His fingers felt like sausages as he pulled the netting outward and grabbed the bag. He opened it. Yes! A blaster! He kept the weapon and let the bag drift free.

After that it was a simple matter to pull the curtain aside, grab a handhold, and pull himself into the control compartment.

The pilot and co-pilot never knew what hit them. He shot each of them in the back of the head, hit the release on the pilot's harness, and dragged him out of the way. A gentle shove was sufficient to send him through the short passageway and into the compartment beyond.

The pilot's seat felt strange, the controls were different from anything he'd ever seen, but the basics were fairly easy to figure out. Some gentle experimentation confirmed which controls did what. The cruiser loomed large in his heads-up display. A voice flooded the cabin.

"Shuttle two-niner-one. I have you vector four, priority one."

Cap glanced around. The comset was obvious as was the seldom-used hand mike. He held it in front of the translator rather than his mouth. "This is shuttle two-niner-one. Affirmative that. Vector four and priority one."

There was a moment of silence, indicating that Cap had violated procedure somehow, and that the individual on the other end wondered why. But the moment passed, and whatever the gaffe was, it would die with everyone aboard.

"Shuttle two-niner-one is cleared for landing."

Cap smiled grimly and added power. Thoughts flashed through his mind. Visions of his long-dead wife, moments with Melissa, the disappointments of a life never quite realized.

Well, this would put it right, would put some sort of meaning into the whole thing, and provide an escape better than alcohol.

The shuttle entered the cruiser's bay at thousands of miles an hour, exploded, and took the *Wrath of Imantha* with it.

In a fraction of a second the fleet's most powerful ship was destroyed, the three most senior officers were killed, and the reinforcements for Fire Base One were lost.

Time would pass, and still more lives would be lost, but the war was effectively over.

Epilog

Lando stepped out onto the veranda and took a long, slow look around. The sixteen-room villa, the swimming pool, the terraces, the gardens, and the surrounding fields had been the property of some long-dead lord. Now they belonged to him. Well, to *them*, since Della and he were married now, and had adopted Melissa.

He dropped into one of the human-style chairs that Della had brought back from Pylax, leaned back, and enjoyed the breeze that swept across the hill. It brought no smoke, no stench of ozone, no smell of rotting flesh. Just the odor of wildflowers from the hillsides below.

Children shouted with excitement as they played hide and seek through the gardens. Melissa appeared from behind some shrubbery, waved, and disappeared again.

Lando smiled and waved back.

More than six standard months had passed since Cap had crashed the shuttle into the cruiser's launch bay. An act of heroism that had been patched together through logical supposition and eyewitness accounts from other ships.

The official version was different of course. The Il Ronnians maintained that the crash was the result of an equipment failure, and human officials had decided to agree, since to do otherwise would be to admit that one of their citizens had attacked an Il Ronnian warship. A provocation that might tip the scales in favor of war.

Things weren't quite so rosy right after Cap's death however. The loss of three senior officers, plus the *Wrath of Imantha*, plus the reinforcements marshaled in her launch bay had been a major blow. But the Il Ronnians were tough. Lesser officers took command. Help was on the way. It would arrive soon. They must hold until it did. The fighting went on.

But the tides of war had shifted. First at Fire Base One, where the much-needed reinforcements never arrived, and then at lesser fire bases across the land, and Holding Areas One through Five.

One by bloody one, the battles were fought, and the Il Ronnians were defeated.

Meanwhile, and with increasing speed, repairs were made. Repairs the Il Ronnians wanted to destroy but couldn't because it would mean the destruction of the very thing that they wanted to steal: God.

And God healed quickly, so quickly that he was soon able to direct his own repairs, and to summon the drifter. For he agreed with the strategy that the bio bods had devised and was eager to implement it.

And so it was that the ancient spaceship flashed out of hyperspace, inflicted even more damage on what remained of the Il Ronnian fleet, and plucked Lando, Della, Melissa, Cy, Wexel-15, and Dru-21 off the surface of the planet.

The Il Ronnians had a big head start, and should have won the ensuing race, but didn't. Unfortunately for them, the courier had departed *before* the *Wrath of Imantha* was destroyed, so its crew was unaware of the way that things had changed.

Because of that, and the fact that Il Ronnians typically make decisions by consensus, valuable time was lost.

Which is not to say, Lando reflected, that things had gone smoothly at their end. Not at first anyway.

The trouble started the moment they dropped hyper near Pylax. The inquiries had been routine at first, "Pylax Control to unidentified ship, please provide name, registry, and world of origin," but quickly escalated to "halt or be fired on."

This in spite of the fact that all of them wanted to "halt" and none of them wanted to be "fired on."

The problem was that Cy's control of the drifter was tenuous at best and it had an awkward tendency to do whatever it wanted to do. Still, in response to Cy's urgings and whatever influence God had from afar, the ship did settle into an orbit around Pylax.

Some tense moments followed as a pair of destroyer escorts came alongside, were quickly englobed, and brought aboard even as they tried to fire every weapon that they had.

Only the combination of Della's calm logic, and the drifter's ability to suppress all of their electronic systems, caused the naval officers to listen to reason.

But that was nothing compared to what ensued. Lando was thrown into prison, Melissa was placed in an orphanage, and Della, Cy, Wexel-15, and Dru-21 were interrogated. First by a long secession of underlings, then by the Imperial consul himself. And that was when the table started to turn.

True to the strategy agreed on in advance, Dru-21 represented himself as president pro tem of the newly formed construct government, and Wexel-15 as his second in command.

Confronted by a heretofore unknown race of sentients, and faced with the power of the spaceship they had arrived in, the consul had little choice but to go along with their claims. For the moment at least.

The result was a tremendous amount of bowing, scraping, and ass kissing, an activity which annoyed Wexel-15, but came more naturally to Dru-21. He made fun of the humans in private, and thought the whole thing was absurd, but could hobnob with the best of them.

And once it became clear that a still functioning artifact world was at stake, a world blessed with a rather unusual computer, and who knew what other kinds of technological goodies, Dru-21 found himself in an increasingly powerful position.

A position so powerful that he was able to name Lando as his ambassador to the human empire, a position invested with diplomatic immunity, and therefore exempt from human law.

And since Lando wasted little time marrying Della and adopting Melissa, his newfound status extended to them as well. Protecting both from the charges that piled up in the wake of their escape from Pylax.

This particular stratagem made the consul very angry, but was considered rather trivial by his superiors, and written off to political necessity. And given the fact that conversations with Lando had revealed him to be loyal if not patriotic, a human ambassador could be considered something of a coup.

And so it was that a small but rather powerful fleet had been assembled and "loaned" to Dru-21. The "loan" being a thinly veiled strategy by which the human empire could avoid direct conflict with Il Ronnian warships.

But when the fleet arrived, and found only remnants of the original Il Ronnian task force opposing them, the possibility of war was considerably reduced.

The Il Ronnian reinforcements did come, but only after all of their ground forces had been forced to "redeploy" aboard what remained of their ships, and the ships had been "assigned" to orbits a few hundred thousand miles out.

It took weeks of careful negotiations before the Il Ronnian fleet finally departed, and far from empty-handed too, since they were allowed to keep many of the artifacts looted from the planet.

A compromise that drove Lando crazy, but was of little importance to the Imperial consul, who was primarily interested in the drifter and the machine called God.

More than that, the consul was interested in something that had escaped Lando during the excitement, something far more valuable than either one of the artifacts.

He was interested in the fact that God could communicate with the drifter from millions of light-years away, and could do so *instantaneously*, something that had escaped sentients up until now.

After all, a faster-than-light means of communications could bind the empire together, could make billions of credits, could win wars, could change the course of history.

Lando chuckled. Assuming God would share the secret, that is . . . something he hadn't agreed to do. Not yet anyway.

Like the Il Ronnians before him the Imperial consul wanted to dismantle God and perform an electronic autopsy on his corpse.

But the newly confirmed government, headed by Dru-21, had forbidden any such action. More than that, they had proclaimed God a citizen, with all the rights attendant thereto. Which, Dru-21 had been quick to point out, included only one vote, just like everyone else.

So, while hundreds of scientists spent their days and nights playing mind games with God, sensible people, and Lando included himself in that category, spent their time enjoying life.

And what was not to enjoy? Both the constructs and the human courts agreed that the drifter belonged to those who had found her, and thanks to the claim filed by Captain Edna shortly after their unexpected departure from Pylax, that made Lando, Della, Melissa, and Cy the ship's legal owners.

Nine hundred million credits can go a long way, even when split among four people, five counting Edna and her ten percent, so all of them were fixed for life. All except Cy that is, who was gambling again, and down to a measly five million or so. Or had been the last time they'd seen him back on Pylax.

Yes, Lando reflected, life was good, or would be if he weren't so damned rich. The problem with having money was that he didn't need to get it. And since the process of getting money had occupied all of his adult life up till this point, he had nothing left to do. Confusing . . . but true.

Lando heard someone approach and didn't even consider reaching for his slug gun. It was hanging in his closet for one thing, and completely unnecessary for another. He had nothing left to fear. No competitors, no bounty hunters, no homicidal aliens.

Della gave his ponytail a playful tug, kissed him on the ear, and dropped into the chair beside him.

"Where's Mel?"

Lando pointed down the hill. "Down there. Playing with the other kids."

Della nodded approvingly. "Good. Wexel-15 and Rola-4 are coming for dinner. We'll serve as chaperones."

Lando smiled. "What's holding them up? A shortage of preachers or something?"

Della laughed and shook her head. "No, the constructs don't have a religion as such . . . but there are customs to observe. Neder-32 has only been dead for six months or so."

Lando shrugged. "Whatever. As long as they're happy."

Della nodded approvingly. "Exactly. Which brings us to you."

Lando looked surprised. "To me? What do you mean?"

"You're bored."

Lando shrugged. "Yeah . . . so what? I'll get used to it."

"*Junk* is sitting up there in orbit . . . just waiting for something to do."

Lando raised an eyebrow. "Like what?"

"Like carrying some cargo to Pylax. Dru-21 wants to open a consulate. Establish some trade. Use some of those factories the Lords left lying around."

Lando thought about it. Not just *Junk*, but other vessels as well, a regular shipping line. The same business that he'd been in, only legal this time, with legitimate cargoes and semihonest customers. The Lando Line. The name had a ring to it.

He took Della's hand. She smiled. Yes, the whole idea sounded like fun.